# Murder in the Crescent City

## By

## Mickey L. Strain

ISBN: 1-4033-7897-5 (Paperback)
ISBN: 1-4033-7896-7 (e-book)

Library of Congress Control Number: 2002094662

This book is printed on acid free paper.

Printed in the United States of America
Bloomington, IN

1stBooks – rev. 11/21/02

# Chapter 1

I couldn't believe it! Just moments ago everything had been going according to plan. Terry was reading in his easy chair and I was in the workshop creating another item, of what I think is art.

Yesterday, at work, plans had been made for a quiet evening at home while everyone else we know had plans for going out. We had decided we were tired of the Saturday night outings and just wanted an evening together.

John Kingsly, an employee, called around 6 PM to see if we were really staying home. I told him, "Yes, my workshop misses me and Terry wanted to veg tonight." It was my evening to cook. I had planned the meal to be good but quick. Our favorite wine was already chilled. The New Orleans BarBQ Shrimp was quickly put together, served, and cleaned up. After dinner, I headed for the workshop with great anticipation. Terry took a hot shower and headed for his chair.

It was great being out in the workshop. My little playground that was just for me. As I looked around, I saw the remnants of my last artistic attempt. Lets see now, where did I put that can of odorless mineral spirits? Of course, next to the clean paint brushes.

I was reaching for the container of brushes when Terry burst into the workshop, screaming, "I'm shot. I'm shot." As he said "shot" the second time he was on his way down to the floor. There was blood all over his robe. At first I couldn't see where he had been hit. Then I saw his hair was wet with blood and his right

1

arm didn't look right. I screamed, running to him. Just as I reached him, a man burst through the door. A mean looking .357 Magnum, pointed at Terry, until he saw me. Now the gun shifted in slow motion, aiming at me. He fired. All I remember is a flash and a loud boom like a cannon echoing off the walls of the workshop.

As I began to come around, there was blood all over the floor. A siren wailed in the distance but I couldn't associate it with what was around me. Looking up, I saw Terry. He wasn't breathing and the way he was laying was odd. For some reason, I couldn't comprehend what had happened. Everything seemed like it was in slow motion and very distant. As if I really wasn't a part of it.

The police were at the door, with guns drawn. The guns scanned from side to side, again in slow motion. Some one yelled, "Clear", and more cops ran in. The paramedics took one look at Terry and came to me.

"No! No! Help him! Stop! Help him!" was all I could yell! No one would listen to me. I couldn't move. They kept holding me down. I was screaming but no one would listen to me.

The next thing I remembered was a hospital room. It was cold, sterile and no one else was there. I looked around trying to figure out where I was and what was going on. All of a sudden, I remembered, Terry! Fear gripped me. Fear for Terry, "No, No! This can't be true," I tried to scream but couldn't. Something was wrong; I couldn't open my mouth. It was taped shut with a tube going down my throat. I tried to move my hands but they were tied down. Each muscle I tried to move screamed in pain. I couldn't tell exactly where I was hurt, but it felt like everywhere. Just then a monitor started beeping. A nurse rushed in and looked at the monitor then at me.

She told me, "Be still and try not to move. I'm your day nurse and my name is Linda Blank." She had one of those voices that put you at ease but you don't know why or how. "Ms. Tucker, you've been shot in the right side of the chest and right thigh. The tube in your throat will be removed tomorrow, so try not to talk or move around to much."

Everything was in a haze. My mind wasn't working right. I thought of Terry and all I could do was let the tears roll down the side of my head. Where was he? Wherever it was, he was alone. I needed to be with him. Somewhere in all those thoughts I went to sleep.

I woke up again when a doctor came in. "Hello, I'm Dr. Johnson. I'll remove the tube in your throat in just a moment," Had a day passed? He started to remove the tape. He said, "Take a deep breathe." and pulled the tube out. "Don't try to talk right now. It will take a few minutes for your throat to adjust." "Now let me look at the bandages." I tried to move and the pain shot through my chest. "No! No! Don't try to move. It will be a few days before you should try. You can tilt the bed if you want but nothing else." Dr. Johnson untied my arms and put the covers up over my chest. "Now don't try to get out of bed and call the nurse if you need anything. I'll have some food sent in and you need to drink as much as you can."

I tried my voice "Thank You! How am I really doing? How long will I be here? Do you know anything about Terry Williams? He was with me."

3

Dr. Johnson quickly looked away then back at me. "Ms. Tucker, I'm sorry Mr. Williams died at the scene." I closed my eyes and started to cry. Dr. Johnson, moved to take my pulse and said "Ms. Tucker, I'll get you something to help you sleep."

I gave him a look that could kill and said with a voice that was very raspy, "I don't want to sleep. I want to know what happened. Who did this? I want to know why? I want to kill one son of a bitch that killed Terry. I want to know how long I'm going to be here. Has anyone called his parents or my parents? I've got to call the office. I've got to make arrangements." As I was ranting a nurse put something in my IV and I went out.

"Nurse, keep an eye on her, she should sleep for about four hours. Let's keep her sedated. The police are outside but they'll just have to wait. Oh, and don't bother with a food tray now. When she wakes up, get her some food." Dr. Johnson updated the chart and left.

It was Monday. I knew because the morning news was on the TV. How could I have slept two days? I tried to move a little and my body screamed at me. After the first attempt it went a little better. At least the pain was relatively isolated to the wounds. I could move my arms, left leg and head. So I elevated the bed and there was a man sitting in the chair at the end to the bed. Fear struck me. I guess it showed because he quietly started talking.

"Ms. Tucker, I'm Lt. Hanson. I'm a homicide detective and working on your case."

I looked at him and was a little confused. He didn't look like any homicide detective I'd ever seen on TV. He was about 6 feet tall, blond, a little over weight

4

.

with a smile that was really friendly. If I had to guess I'd say he was around 55 years old.

"Ms. Tucker, tell me what happened the other night at your house. What do you remember about the incident? Take your time but try to keep the events in sequence." His voice was very calm and even. Almost like a soft feeling than words.

I was trying to think but the only thing that came to mind was, "Sequence, What sequence?"

"Let see if I can help you. What time did you get home from work Saturday evening?" His voice was easy and didn't seem pressing.

I thought for a moment, "We got home at 5:15 PM."

"What did you do when you first got home?" Looking at him, he seemed very interested. I felt like I wanted to answer his questions.

"I started dinner. No, I changed clothes first." My mind was fuzzy and not working right. It was hard to think and I had to concentrate on what was being said.

"Did you see anything that was out of the ordinary?"

I had to think for awhile again. "No, everything was as we left it that morning."

"What did you do next?" His words were beginning to irritate me.

"Why do you keep asking about me and not about Terry? We lived together for 5 years and did everything together. When are you going to ask me about him?" I was getting upset with the questions. He should be concentrating on Terry.

"I'm getting to him. I just thought if we started out with what you did that it would be easier for you. I'm

5

sorry you felt I wasn't interested in Mr. Williams. I'm very interested but let's keep this nice and slow. I don't want to hear things out of sequence."

"Sequence, what do you mean, sequence? Nothing was out of the ordinary until Terry came into the workshop and had already been shot." I started crying and couldn't stop. It just seemed to hit me. I wanted Lt. Hanson to go away. I just wanted to be left alone.

"I'm sorry Ms. Tucker. I'm just trying to figure out what happened and when. Why don't we take a break until later today? I do have one more question. Do you know of anyone that would want to hurt either of you?"

"No. There's no one. Please leave me alone now. I can't answer anymore questions." I couldn't think. All I could do was cry.

"OK, I'll come by this afternoon. Try to get some sleep."

The nurse came in again with another shot. "I don't want that if it's going to put me to sleep."

"It's for pain and sleep. Sleep is the best healer. This will allow you to get the rest you need." The nurse started for the IV tube.

"I don't want it. Talk to Dr. Johnson and tell him I want something for pain only. I know I'm crying all the time but I have a damn good reason to. I just lost everything in my life that counted. Now please, leave me alone."

# Chapter 2

The pain shot was working. I was just lying there thinking. Terry and I met 5 years ago in Washington D. C. while attending a Small Business Association Seminar. Some how we ended up sitting at the same table. At first we didn't speak to each other. Actually, no one at the table talked. I guess we all thought we should be listening to the speaker. The speaker finished and we all got up to go to the buffet. For once, the buffet looked good. Back at the table, we all introduced ourselves.

Terry said, "Hi, I'm Terry Williams from New Orleans, LA. I have a small tourist business in the French Quarter." I guess he saw my mouth drop because he looked at me and asked, "And you are?"

"My name is Toni Tucker and I'm from New Orleans. I have a small tourist business in the French Quarter. I can't believe we haven't met before." It seemed like the other people at the table didn't exist. All I could see was Terry and that face that glowed when he smiled. I don't know when we became the only people at the table but it seemed so natural. Terry's business was on Decatur Street, just off Jackson Square. It was a small T-shirt and souvenir shop called the New Orleans Express. My shop is on Jackson Square, just around the corner from Terry's.

We ended up on the same plane back to New Orleans. I'm sure the seminar had some good ideas and points but I didn't remember a single one of them.

Terry and I just hit it off. We both loved New Orleans and all that entails. We started dating the day we met. Six months later we moved in together. At first, we moved into my French Quarter shotgun house. It's called a shotgun house because you can open the front and back door and shoot a shotgun through and not hit a thing. It was as old as every thing else is in the French Quarter, and we loved it. I had set up my hobby shop in the back shed and Terry set up a library in the living room. After another six months, we consolidated our shops into one on Jackson Square. Business was good and having a larger shop didn't make the work any harder. On the contrary, with one shop instead of two it made life very sweet. We had four employees who tended the store. Terry and I did the books and kept up with the other businesses in the French Quarter.

Life couldn't have been better. After two years we bought a big house on Conti Street. There were three bedrooms, a study, a modern kitchen, and a workshop in the back with an old tack room attached. It was two and a half stories high. The attic was the half story and great for storage. We had spent several months restoring the house. We did put in two more bathrooms. One went upstairs by the two bedrooms and one out in the workshop. The one downstairs had to be modernized. Terry and I designed the kitchen and it came out perfect. There is plenty of counter space and all the modern appliances you could ask for. We loved the high ceilings and the floor to ceiling front windows. The porch was the best feature. It was 30 feet long and 7 feet deep. The house set back about 15 feet from the sidewalk, giving a nice courtyard to enjoy. There was a stone wall instead of a fence, making the courtyard private. Like all houses in the

French Quarter, the house was very long, making the rooms large and airy. The most important item was central air conditioning and heat. Air conditioning is a must for the New Orleans hot humid summers. We never opened the windows on the sides of the house because the houses on both sides were two feet away. Just enough room to walk between the houses. We didn't have a car. No one in the French Quarter has one, since parking is at a premium. There isn't even a way to get a car back there. When we needed a car, there were friends who would loan us one or we would rent one. That may have happened once a month.

Terry was as good of a cook as I am. We both took cooking classes at various shops in the French Quarter. We knew all the chefs that were real chefs in the area. There are such a variety of restaurants in the French Quarter that you could eat out every day for a year and not eat at the same restaurant. The food in New Orleans is a pleasure and we took full advantage of the experiences. Terry and I were lucky, we could eat just about anything, and as much as we wanted and not gain weight. Terry exercised everyday, I watched him do it.

Our social life included the people that worked for us and those people with other shops around ours. We had standing outings every Saturday night with a variety of people and a variety of places to go to.

I had met Terry's parents about three years ago. Bill and Jenny came in for a weekend a couple of years ago. Bill worked in catalog sales as an independent. Actually, he's like a middleman between manufactures and retail stores. It was such a quick weekend. I never really got much information about his business. Bill gave us a 1-800 number to call anytime we wanted to. Jenny was light hearted and the consummate housewife. She had her house, clubs, gardens, and Bill to take care of. She did have an extensive knowledge of world events but only contributed to discussions when directly asked.

We did the whirlwind tour of New Orleans. Bill and Jenny are young 60's and ran us ragged. We walked the French Quarter and pointed out every little nook and cranny that most tourists never see. Of course, the cemetery tours are always a must. We rented a car and drove to several cemeteries and walked through 5 or 6 of them. Each has their own personality. I was quite surprised with their knowledge of New Orleans without ever visiting before. Several times we were on St. Charles Ave. and Bill told us the history of one house then another. He said he had browsed the Internet before coming. I never thought of it again, but enjoyed learning something about my city. We tried to get them to come in the same time my parents planned to visit but couldn't work it out.

My relationship with them was very good. I fell in love with them and they with me. It seemed we all got along very well. Even though Terry and I had never really discussed marriage I knew it would make them happy.

When my parents visited, Terry couldn't do enough for them. Mother likes regular coffee instead of the chicory coffee we drink. He went out and bought another coffeepot so all of us could have what we liked. Each morning Terry went jogging and came back with bagels, biscuits, or beignets. Mom and Dad were getting spoiled in just the few days they were here. Mom wanted to cook for us and Dad wanted to work around the house but there just wasn't enough time for it. While Terry and I worked, they would stroll the French Quarter, visit the Aquarium or just watch the Mississippi River roll by. Jackson Brewery has some wonderful little eateries where you can watch the river. Mom and Dad couldn't get over being able to walk down the street with an alcoholic drink in their hands. They loved Pat O'Briens piano bar and sang with everyone else. They knew just about every song that was played. Of course the Hurricanes helped loosen up their voices. They each had two Hurricanes. Each Hurricane has 4 oz. of rum and tastes like fruit punch. I'm just glad we didn't have far to walk to get home. Terry and I would meet them at a local restaurant for lunch or dinner.

Terry's relationship with his parents was like mine with my parents. Close while far away. Months would go by before one of us would think of calling our parents or them calling us. My parents loved Terry. They kept asking when we were going to get married. We were happy just the way we were. Children were not a part of our future by joint agreement. So we didn't feel getting married was something we needed to do. We used to joke saying, "If were still together in 40 years, we'll get married".

We're both 33 years old. It seemed like there wasn't a past for either of us. There was never a reason to talk about the past when the present was so perfect. I had gone to Texas University and Terry had gone to Tulane University. We both had a degree in Marketing and enjoyed working in the French Quarter. Every day was another experience of joy and happiness.

11

*Mickey L. Strain*

We had season tickets to the Le Petit Theater on St. Peter Street. Only three block from the house. Every month a new play opened. We knew all the actors and every cast put together on every play. Many times when we got together, they tried to get us to take parts in their plays. Terry and I couldn't act at all so we skipped the offers. The threats about one of us taking the stage from them were our biggest jokes. We also had season tickets to the Saenger Theater and the New Orleans Symphony. All the in places young business entrepreneurs of New Orleans were seen on a weekly bases. There is always Pat O'Brien's for the younger set. Of course, you never go to Pat O'Brien's on Friday or Saturday night because that's the tourist times. Pat O'Brien's still makes the best drinks for the money. The Garden Bar was the place to be with all the in people. Year round you'll find the regulars in the Garden Bar.

We loved to watch old movies on TV and rented at least one movie a week. TV was also good for what we thought was our intellect. Public TV, Discovery and A&E were our favorite channels. We knew everything there was about Alaska's bears, whales, birds, volcanoes, and all of natures work that TV had to offer. We loved all the educational programming. We did learn about MS Office Word software, which really came in handy at work.

Terry and I had the same approach to retail work. It always sounded easy but it really isn't. Find out what the customer trends were and be ready before they are. Of course, there is the normal range of tourist items that will always be around. The trick to those items was finding the most consistent, cheapest and best suppliers available.

How could all of this have changed in a matter of seconds?

# **Chapter 3**

Lt. Hanson walked into my hospital room with the same warm smile. "Well, I'm glad to see you're doing better. They say sleep is the best medicine and you've had a large dose of it."

"Hello, Lieutenant, what have you found out?" I asked the question but really didn't want to know the answer. I wanted him to tell me Terry was out in the hall and that a car had hit me.

"I've been waiting to ask you more questions before I ventured into any answers. Do you feel up to answering some questions for me?"

"I guess so. But I don't know anything that would help you." The only real thing I knew was that my heart is broken. If you're lucky, you only find one soul mate in your life and I had lost mine.

"Well, let me be the judge of that. I think we had better start where we left off last Saturday night. Just so I can get things in sequence again."

That word again, sequence. What made him think there was any sequence to what happened? I was beginning to hate that word, sequence. "Where did we leave off last time, I don't remember much of our conversation."

"Let's start with what time you got home and what you did after that."

"I think we got home about 5:15 PM. It was our night to stay home and we were looking forward to it. I changed clothes and started dinner. Lt., I'm not sure I can do this. This all seems so unreal."

"Please try to continue. Take a deep breath and start again."

I tried to take a deep breath but the pain shot through my chest. It made me catch my breath. It was just enough shock to stop my dwelling on Terry so I could go on. "It only takes about 30 minutes to fix the Bar BQ Shrimp and pasta. While I was cooking, Terry took a shower. We ate, cleaned up the kitchen and went our separate ways. Terry had a book he wanted to read and I wanted to work in my workshop. Terry went to his easy chair and I went to my workshop."

"How long were you in your shop before Terry came through the door?"

"Less than 5 minutes, if that long."

How long was Terry in your shop before the gunman came in?"

"Seconds" Those seconds flashed through my mind. Not it slow motion but in a whirl. Flashing over and over. The Lieutenant's voice stoped it.

"What do you mean seconds. Did Terry say anything to you? Or write down anything?"

"I mean seconds. Terry hit the door, and said he was shot. He fell to the floor just a few feet inside the door. As I was running to him when the gunman came in."

"Can you repeat what Terry said?"

"I'm shot. I'm shot. That's all he said." I was starting to get hysterical.

"Are you sure that's all he said? There was nothing else said?"

"I'm sure, that's all he said, it was just a few seconds. That's all I remember." I'll always remember Terry's last words. They were burned into my mind and heart. The look on his face was as if he were asking for help. Help I couldn't give him. I couldn't save him. Crying was a way of life for me now. I needed Terry. Can't the Lt. understand that and leave me alone?

Lt. Hanson sat there being quiet for about 10 minutes. Letting me cry, then very gently said, "What did the gunman look like?"

His voice startled me. "I don't know. All I saw was the gun."

"You said before it was a .357 Magnum. How do you know that it was that kind of gun?"

"That's what we have at the shop for protection. At least, it looked the same. It could have been something else. I don't know. It was a big gun. It made a big noise and as you can see, it made some big holes in me. What kind of gun was it? I don't know enough about guns to really be sure."

The Lt. listened to me then said. "It was a .357 Magnum."

I was getting hostile with these questions. With the addition of pain in my chest and thigh, I wasn't in good humor. "Then why are you asking me these questions. You think I shot Terry then myself and ate the gun?"

"I'm sorry Ms. Tucker, I have to ask these questions. It's just the way an investigation is done. I don't mean to accuse you, but I do have to ask these questions. Were you and Terry getting along?" My anger flared.

"We were more than getting alone. Everything was great. We didn't argue at all. We discussed differences of opinions and those usually only applied to work. We

16

never brought work home because we didn't need to."
I was getting more hostile and my voice was raising
with each word. "I can't remember a time that even a
difference of opinion created a raised voice. I know
what you're trying to get at and you can just change
that thought. We were perfect together. As anyone we
know will tell you."

"I'm sure they will. Now, what was your business
arrangement with Terry?"

"We owned the shop together, 50 - 50. We both did
the books, ordering, hiring, firing and anything else
that had to be done. We didn't need to check with each
other before making a decision, we just did it. We used
a computer software package to handle the books and
inventory, so we always did it the same way."

The door swung open and it was Mom and Dad.
Mom burst into tears when she saw me. Dad was
trying not to cry. Seeing them just made me fall apart.
We hugged and cried. I couldn't think, all I could do
was feel the pain of losing Terry. Mom and Dad will
help me deal with the pain by just being there.

"Mom, Dad this is Lt. Hanson. He's investigating
the shooting. We were just going over what happened
Saturday night."

"Lt. Hanson, it's good to meet you. I hope you can
find out who did this and put them behind bars," Dad
said, as he shook his hand. "Do you have any leads?
What kind of person does something like this? We
Thank God that Toni will be all right."

"I'll never be all right Dad. Not without Terry."
Tears were streaming again.

Dad tapped Lt. Hanson on the shoulder,
"Lieutenant, why don't you and I get a cup of coffee.

17

These ladies need a little time together. I also have some questions that I think you can answer." Dad opened the door and held it for Lt. Hanson.

Mom was trying to be strong for me. It didn't help. What helped was to have someone to cry with me who could understand what I was going through. Terry and I had been inseparable. We spent 24 hours a day together. Everything I did involved him, grocery shopping, cooking, house keeping, and work, just everything. Why did this happen? Mom held my hand and cried with me. "Honey, if there is anything your Dad and I can do for you? I just can't believe this has happened. Do the police have any idea as to why someone would do this?"

"No. Lt. Hanson has been here all morning asking questions. Mom, what am I going to do? I can't go back to the house. The police have been all over the house. I can't imagine what it looks like now. Right now there's no way I can go back there."

"Honey, your Dad and I will take care of it for you. Don't worry, these things take time. We'll be right here to help you with everything. I'd like to see your doctor. How are you feeling? I just can't believe my baby has been shot."

"I'm doing well. The bullet went through my chest but didn't hit anything vital. It chipped a rib and grazed the lung but it's really not that bad. It does hurt like hell. My leg is worse but only because of muscle damage. The doctor said I'd be out of here in an about a week to 10 days. They want to watch for infection. I've never known such pain. Mom, I don't know what to do. Will you call Terry's parents? I've been so doped up, I couldn't think of calling them. I guess the police called them but I haven't heard from them. I don't know what to do. If I can't reach them should I make the funeral arrangements? Terry and I never talked about this. I haven't a clue of what his wishes would be. I need to talk to his parents. Please try and get them for me."

Dad and Lt. Hanson returned. "Ms. Tucker, I still have a few questions I need to ask. Do you feel up to finishing?"

"Yes. Anything I can do to find out who did this."

"Mr. and Mrs. Tucker, I need to talk privately with your daughter."

"Honey, your mother and I will come back later. Were staying at the Fairmont Hotel for now. We need to get settled in. You get some rest and we'll be back around 5 PM."

Lt. Hanson didn't give them time to leave the room before he resumed questioning me. "What about your employees? How long have they been with you? Did you have any problems with any of them? Did Terry have any special problems with them?"

"No! Terry got along with everyone. Our employees worked at both our shops before we merged. John Kingsly has been with me for 8 years. John manages the shop for us. There's, Ben Dryer, he's been with me as long as John has. Ben and John are lovers and have been together for 25 years. You couldn't ask for better people or employees. They have lived in the French Quarter all their lives. Joey Clark and Mary Robichaux worked for Terry before we merged. They are both highly valued employees. Joey is 25 and very much into the French Quarter way of life. He's single, but has several women he sees

19

regularly. Mary lives down in the Parish (St Bernard Parish), but has worked in the French Quarter all her life. She's a widow and doesn't work for the money, but to keep busy. Mary has worked at dozens of shops and is a great customer person." No sooner had the words been out of my mouth than Mary walked into the room.

Her face was brave but her lower lip quivered, "Hello dear, how are you feeling?"

I turned to smile, "I'm better. Mary, this is Lt. Hanson, with the homicide division of NOPD."

Mary looked at him, then to me, "I hope you find out who did this. We are all just beside ourselves. We can't think of any reason why anyone would do this. Toni, was anything taken?"

"I don't know Mary. I haven't been home and no one has told me." I was trying to think of something worth killing for in the house.

"Toni, we are keeping everything at the shop going. John has taken control and everything is fine. Don't worry about a thing." Mary was close to tears, but held them back. "I'll go now. John and Ben will be by later today. Joey says he can't come. He just doesn't know what to say. Rest child, we'll take care of everything." She backed out the door, like she was afraid to touch anything.

Lt. Hanson looked at me. "She seems very nice. How long has she worked for you?"

"She worked for Terry first then for us. I think she was with Terry about a year before we merged. So I guess that totals up to about 6 years."

"Ms. Tucker, are there any employees that have been fired in the last year?"

"No. The four we have today have been with us for many years. We do hire temporary help from time to time but not often."

"I'd like to go over the sequence of events on Saturday again. This time let's start when you left work."

That word again, sequence. I can't stand that word. Nothing has a sequence for me any more. "Terry and I finished the weekly books at 4:30 PM. We chatted with John and Ben for a little while then started walking home."

"Did you notice anything different on your walk home?"

"No. We walked down Chartre's Street until we got to Conti Street. We turned right, walked half a block then into the courtyard. There was nothing out of the ordinary."

"What did you do first when you got home?"

"Lt. I can't go over this again now. Please leave me alone. I'm so tired and the pain is getting intense again."

"I'm sorry, Ms. Tucker. I'll come again tomorrow. Maybe we can come up with something that will help solve this case."

As he left, all I could think of was how is it that I survived and Terry didn't. It just didn't seem fair. We didn't have anything anyone would want. Even if we did, they could have had it without hurting anyone.

The pain was getting very intense. I rang the nurse's button. As I waited for someone to come, I thought of the sequence of events. That word again. How I was beginning to hate it. There was nothing different from the time we left until we got home. Even at home nothing was strange. Besides repeating everything for Lt. Hanson, I had gone over it in my mind every waking moment. There was nothing I could think of that made me think of anything that made any sense.

The nurse came in and gave me a pain shot. After checking all the equipment, she came to my bed. "Ms. Tucker, would you like something to eat? You haven't had anything solid for several days."

Once she mentioned food, I decided I was really hungry and thirsty. "Yes I would. What can I have?"

"You can have anything on the menu. Let's see how about some gumbo and baked fish? We won an award for the best hospital food in the city. You must remember, it is still hospital food."

"That sounds good. I'd also like some coffee, but real chicory coffee."

"I'll call for a tray as soon as I get back to the nurses station. It will take about 15 minutes. Now try to rest and don't move around too much. So far everything is looking good. Maybe tomorrow Dr. Johnson will let you start moving around more. I'll be back as soon as your tray comes up."

The pain was easing up and my mind kept running through the sequence of events. That damn word again. I forgot to tell Lt. Hanson that John had called. He just wanted to confirm Terry and I were staying home. John and Ben usually got to where ever we were going on Saturday night first and got us tables and chairs. John could get a table for 10 at the Superbowl without a reservation. John just needed to know how many chairs to get at Papa John's for the evening and it was done. I'll tell Lt. Hanson tomorrow.

The food tray arrived. I started with the gumbo and it was great. It deserved a culinary award. I finished everything on the tray. Even the bland mashed potatoes were good. I was having great luck; there were two cups of delicious chicory coffee. After I ate, I went to sleep.

I woke up screaming. A nurse came running in. "Ms. Tucker, are you OK? We heard you screaming. Let me check everything." My heart was pounding and fear ran through me. It was a dream. The nurse checked everything and announced I was fine. "Would you like something for sleep so you don't dream?"

"No. It's the first dream I've had since I've been here. Maybe it won't happen again. I usually don't dream"

I was just settling down when there was a tapping at the door. John and Ben came in with flowers and balloons. There was not a pretense of being up beat. They came in quietly and gave me hugs and kisses. We just cried quietly for about 20 minutes. It seemed that's what we needed. After that we tried to do some small talk. That didn't work, we were too good of friends to not say how we really felt. Ben started talking about what fun we used to have on our regular Saturday nights out. We talked of the different places we had gone together and how we all loved Terry. Ben and John are more like family. They stayed for about an hour. When they left around 4 PM, I felt some of the guilt of my still being alive leave me. I was starting to heal more than just my body.

Mom and Dad came by at 5 PM. This time we didn't cry. They had tried to get Terry's parents but no one answered the phone. "Maybe they are on their way

23

here. I guess the police reached them. We can ask Lt. Hanson about it tomorrow. We're only going to stay a minute. You need to rest and you can't if we're here. We'll see you in the morning." We kissed goodbye. I guess I looked like I needed to rest. I was glad they didn't stay. I needed some time alone.

The night passed without dreams to disturb me. I awoke feeling better. I was still very sore but I could move around a little. I was ready to get out of bed. That bedpan didn't suit me very well. Besides, it hurt like hell getting on and off it.

I rang for the nurse and asked to have some help getting to the bathroom. About 15 minutes later, an aid came in to help me. It was a slow and painful trip and I was glad to be back in bed. But I had the feeling I had accomplished something. I decided right then that I wasn't going to stay in bed. It was time to start moving to get what happened identified and to punish those responsible. I was starting to get angry. I'm told that's another phase of grief management.

Mom and Dad came to the hospital every day. They stayed at the Fairmont Hotel for six days before the police would let them into the house. Dad had cleaned the workshop. Mom couldn't go out there. The police had gone through everything in the house. It took Mom three days to get everything back to normal. Dad took care of the yard by getting a service company to come and do it. He said I didn't need to be worrying about the yard for a while.

John, Ben and Mary came by everyday. They staggered their visiting times to make sure the shop was covered. John and Ben were taking care of everything. Once in a while John would bring something for me to sign or approve. Joey just couldn't bring himself to come. He had been 17 years old when he went to work for Terry, about three years before I meet him. It's the only job Joey had ever had. Terry had taught him the business. They had been almost like father and son. John said Joey was taking this very hard. He had missed some work but not enough to worry about.

# **Chapter 4**

I'd been in the hospital for 10 days. Everyday, Lt. Hanson came by and asked for the same sequence of events to be described. I have now come to despise the word sequence. I'd had physical therapy and could take care of myself. I was feeling pretty good.

When I knew it was about time for me to leave the hospital, I told Mom and Dad, I wanted them to go home. At first, they resisted. I explained to them, it's my grief and I've got to work through it myself. I asked them just to help me get home and to have some food in the house so I wouldn't have to go out.

Mom went and talked to John and Ben. After that she felt she could leave. Of course, John and Ben had a list of things to do for me and phone numbers to call if they thought I needed them.

Dad had made up the guestroom downstairs for me. I knew I wouldn't be able to sleep upstairs without Terry. Beside, going up and down stairs wasn't good for my leg and wouldn't be for a while.

We left the hospital at 10 AM. It was great being out of there. Mom and Dad went around checking everything, then tearfully left.

The first few moments alone were very hard. I just couldn't believe that 10 days ago my life changed so dramatically. I could see Terry in every thing around me. There had been so much joy in this house. I wasn't going to let it be destroyed. Terry loved this house and I was going to continue loving it.

Around 6PM, John and Ben came by with dinner. They had stopped at Brennan's for Blackened Trout,

Stuffed Eggplant, Dirty Rice and Bread Pudding. It was good to be home with friends and to have some great food to enjoy. What made it really good was having enough food for the three of us. Ben set the table. John had a great wine chilled in a plastic bag of ice. I hobbled to the table and ate everything they brought. The wine helped me to relax. Ben cleaned everything up and they left around 7:30 PM. I was ready for bed. The day had taken alot out of me. I just wanted to sleep. I was so glad I didn't have to climb the stairs. With the covers just barely pulled up over me, I was asleep.

I woke with a start. Listening for what I thought I had heard. The clock said 2 AM. What was that sound? Was there really a sound or was it a dream. Listening and hearing nothing out of the ordinary, I made myself calm down. It was no use trying to go back to sleep. My mind was going to fast.

Terry kept coming to mind. All of a sudden I realized I hadn't talked to his parents. They hadn't called me in the hospital. In five years I thought we had a good relationship. Of course, it was a hit and miss affair. But the time we had spent together had been happy and fun. I couldn't call them at 2 AM but I would call them first thing in the morning. I just couldn't imagine why Bill and Jenny hadn't called me. I know the first few days in the hospital would have been a problem but surely I should have heard from them by now.

What about Terry's funeral? No one has said anything about it. Maybe the coroner hadn't released the body yet. Now my mind was really going crazy. Has Terry been buried? If so, where and when? If not, why not? How was I going to find out? Then Lt. Hanson came to mind. He would know. But he hasn't mentioned it either. Because Terry and I were not married, no one had to wait for me. I wish they would have but then again, maybe not. This wasn't making any sense. As I mulled all this over in my mind, I fell asleep.

Morning came at 9 AM. I can't believe I slept this long. Usually, as the sun rises, so do I. Coffee was really going to taste good this morning. I slowly made my way around the kitchen and started the coffee. As it was brewing, I decided I am going to get dressed. It's been 11 days since I'd had real clothes on and I was looking forward to it. Shorts and an over sized T-shirt were the order of the day. It was a bright sunny day outside and I planned to spend most of my time on the porch.

With coffee and newspaper in hand, I found the best place on the porch to sit. Terry and I had bought a hammock and hung it across the end of the porch for the morning sun.

I must have fallen asleep. The noise of the gate closing woke me. There was a man walking up to the porch. He hadn't seen me yet and I didn't know who he was. At first, I got scared, but no one in a three-piece suit is going to do any harm. I cleared my throat so he would know I was on the porch. He jumped and almost fell down the steps. "Excuse Me! I didn't see you there. Are you Ms. Toni Tucker?"

"Yes. Who are you?"

"My name is Jeffery Breaux and I'm with Breaux, Bailey and Demas. My company carries life insurance, property insurance and retirement plans."

"I'm sorry, Mr. Breaux, I'm not interested in insurance and I have a retirement plan."

"Ms. Tucker, I'm not here to sell you anything. On the contrary, I'm here because you are the beneficiary on Mr. Terry Williams's policy. We thought we would give you enough time to get out of the hospital before we came to see you. I do hope you are feeling better."

"Terry and I have insurance with Metropolitan Life to cover our business and the house. I don't recall ever hearing about Breaux, Bailey and Demas."

"This policy has been in effect for about 12 years. Mr. Williams made you the beneficiary about 4 years ago. I have some papers for you to review and sign. The payment will be deposited into your bank account, unless you would prefer something else."

"Mr. Breaux, what is the amount of the policy?"

He opened his brief case and shuffled some papers. Finding what he wanted he flipped through several pages. "Ms. Tucker, the total amount comes to $16.4 Million. I'll be more than happy to assist you in any way I can." About that time he looked up at me and stopped moving. "Ms. Tucker, are you all right? Can I get you anything? Is there any thing I can do for you?"

My mouth had dropped and all I could do was stare. "You must be kidding. There is no way Terry could have had a policy for that much. You better read that again." It took me a second to gain my composure, then I had to chuckle a little. This guy must be crazy.

Mr. Breaux reviewed the documents again. He looked up at me. "Ms. Tucker, that is the correct amount."

All I could do was sit there. This was not sinking in at all. How could this be? I had to think fast. How could I get Mr. Breaux to go over those papers again? They must be for someone else. What about his parents? They should have this money not me. "Mr. Breaux, I still can't believe this. What about Terry's parents. Shouldn't they get this?"

"I'm sorry, Ms. Tucker, you're the beneficiary. Beside, Mr. Williams's parents have been dead for over 15 years. My firm handled the entire family's estate."

"You have the wrong person. I've met Terry's parents, several times. They were here in this house last year. They stayed a week. Bill and Jenny Williams of Grand Ile, Michigan. They're both retired and travel a great deal. Mr. Breaux, I wish that money was mine but I'm sorry, you have the wrong person."

"I was told at the firm this morning that you would be hard to convince. I assure you, you are the right person and this money does belong to you. I can't explain the people you met or who you thought they were but Mr. Williams's parents died in a plane crash 15 years ago. I was their account manager then and knew them quite well. Their bodies were recovered from the crash site and identified without a doubt."

"I need a drink. Mr. Breaux, would you care for some tea, coffee or bourbon? I've got to go in and sit down on something more stable than this hammock. Please come with me. I still can't believe this is happening."

Mr. Breaux came into the kitchen and sat at the table. I got us some coffee while he started getting papers out of his briefcase. It took him as long to get all the papers out as it did for me to get the coffee together.

I sat down and we started going through the papers. He showed me where the policy total was and he was right. We went through everything. The money was going into an account that I could access, as I needed, and the firm would handle investing for me.

Mr. Breaux put away all the insurance papers. We both had more coffee. I thought everything was done and he was just being friendly.

"Ms. Tucker, Terry's will has to go through probate. My firm is the executor of the will. The reading is to be held tomorrow at my office. Now I know you aren't well, so I thought we could do it here if you don't mind. We'll have to have a couple of witnesses. I think you should have a witness of your choice and we'll have the necessary people available to get everything done. Would 10 AM be all right with you? My office will have brunch catered and take care of everything. I believe we can have everything finished tomorrow. I hope you know Breaux, Bailey and Demas will do everything necessary to do this quickly and quietly. We'd like to represent you, but if you would like someone else, we will still do everything possible for you we can."

"Mr. Breaux, I didn't know Terry had a will. We had set up the business to go to each other in case something happened but that was all. What can you tell me about the will? I can't imagine Terry having one. Of course, I would never of thought of an insurance policy for 16.4 million either."

"Ms. Tucker, until the will is read I can't tell you anything. It's the law. After tomorrow I'll answer any questions you have. Until then you can rest assured everything will be handled correctly. I'm sorry I can't

31

say any more but the law is very strict." Mr. Breaux gathered up his briefcase and stood to leave. "Please rest. If you don't feel up to doing this tomorrow, here's my card. Call any time, day or night. I'll be here at 10 AM tomorrow, unless you call. I'll see myself out. Thank you for the coffee." With that he left. I must have sat there for an hour. This just didn't seem real.

John and Ben came by at 6 PM with dinner. This time they stopped at Brennen's for Pane'ed Pork Chops, Oyster Dressing, Creamed Sweet Potatoes and Salad. Ben set the table up for us and John opened a bottle of wine. We chatted about the shop during dinner. Everything was going well and they didn't need me to interfere.

"John, Ben can you two come here tomorrow at 10 AM? It seems that Terry had a will and it's going to be read here tomorrow morning. The firm Terry had taking care of the will said I should have a witness of my own for the reading. I didn't even know Terry had a will. I don't have one, so I guess I had better get one done."

"I'll be happy too. I'll bring some pastry and come early to make the coffee."

"You don't need to do that. This firm is catering this tomorrow."

"Wow, this must be some firm to cater a will reading. I've never heard of that before."

"Believe me. There are a few other things you haven't heard of before. Terry had an insurance policy and I'm the beneficiary of it. Mr. Breaux of Breaux, Bailey and Demas was here this morning to execute the policy."

.

# **Chapter 5**

The sun was just coming into the room. It was just about 6 AM. I had slept well through the night. I didn't have to get up and check the doors and windows during the night. The smell of coffee wafted through the house. Alarm clocks for coffeepots were a great invention.

The first moves in the morning are stiff and sore. Slowly I headed for the coffee. By the time I got to the kitchen I was moving better. I have to go back to the doctor next week to get the stitches out but other than that, I'm doing pretty well. I'll be glad when the bandages can come off. Changing the bandages is not fun. Thank God for John. I think he can do just about anything. He changed the bandages last night and will do it again today.

That first cup of coffee just seems to get my day going. There's nothing like New Orleans chicory coffee. Getting dressed this morning I decided I had better wear something better that shorts and a T-shirt. Finding something that was loose and nice looking took longer than I thought. Just as I was putting a loose shift over my head the doorbell rang. John and Ben were right on time.

John started out by saying. "I've never been to a will reading before. Does anyone know the rules of the game? Am I dressed well enough for it"

Ben said, "He has been like a crazy person all morning. He got me up at 6 AM and has tried on every stitch of clothing he has. I finally had to throw a fit to make him stop. He also had me at the shop at 8:30

AM. After we got there all he did was pace back and forth. Mary got there at 8:45 AM. I made John walk around Jackson Square twice before we started over here."

"Well darlings, I don't know the rules and I've been up since 6 AM. I'm with John; I haven't a clue of what to expect. TV always shows the lawyers and the greedy family members sitting around. I hope y'all didn't eat. I hope the caterer is good. I'm getting very hungry." Just then the doorbell rang. As I answered the door, a middle-aged man addressed me.

"Ms. Tucker?"

"Yes, may I help you?"

"I'm Jon Lafarge, your caterer. If you're ready I'll have things brought in."

"Yes, of course. Where would you like to set up? The kitchen is quite large and so is the dining room."

"Mr. Breaux would like to use the dining room for business. If I may see the kitchen, I'll figure out what I want brought in first. You see I have a complete kitchen just outside your gate in that truck." He came in and was very pleased with the kitchen. I introduced him to John and Ben, then he started to work. I would have never thought that many people could fit in that truck. There were china and crystal settings. A waiter set up six place settings. John, Ben and I just stepped back and watched. It only took them about 15 minutes to have the dinning room completely set up.

At precisely 10 AM, Mr. Breaux rang the doorbell. As I open the door, I saw two other men. All were about the same age, of around 60. Mr. Breaux started out by saying. "Ms. Tucker, this is Mr. Bailey and this is Mr. Demas. I hope everything is ready. Are you feeling up to this? If not, we'll be happy to reschedule."

"Thank you. I'm doing fine. Mr. Breaux, this is Mr. John Kingsly and Mr. Ben Hebert. You said I might want a witness so I decided John and Ben are whom I wanted. John and Ben have been my friends for many years. Mr. Lafarge has the dining room set up. Would you like to come and sit down? He does make great coffee."

"Yes. I would like to get started. I reviewed the will yesterday and it will take a while to go through it completely. I think you'll enjoy what Mr. LaFarge has in store for us." We made our way into the dining room. Mr. LaFarge had name cards made and placed where he wanted us to sit. We all took our places. Everything was very impressive. A waiter came in with a small plate for each of us with miniature bagels, chive cream cheese and locks. The arrangement was beautiful. As we ate, Mr. Breaux started pulling out various folders of papers. Mr. LaFarge set up a folding table next to Mr. Breaux for all the folders. Mr. Bailey and Mr. Demas started doing the same thing. Again, Mr. LaFarge set up folding tables next to them. It was amazing how Mr. LaFarge just appeared and had in hand just what was needed.

John and Ben kept looking over at me. Both had that twinkle in their eyes. None of us had ever had anything like this before. Of course there was no way we were going to say that. The three of us could have won an Oscar with our acting.

The small plates were cleared away. The next plate had Eggs Benedict with a small garnish of black caviar. After that there was a small bowl of fresh

35

prepared fruit. There was a light cream sauce on the fruit that was out of this world. Coffee was served at the end. I don't know what blend it was, but I have never had coffee taste that good. A waiter cleared all the dishes. Then each of us had our own carafe of coffee.

Mr. Breaux cleared his throat, like a signal to get started. "Ms. Tucker, I'd like to start the reading of the will if you're ready."

"I am."

"The first part of this will is the standard language stating that Mr. Terry Williams was of sound mind and acting on his own free will. I don't think we have to read all that unless you'd like for me to."

"No, that's fine Mr. Breaux. I trust your judgment."

"All right. Section II, reads as follows: "All possessions I hold under my names, Terry Williams, Joseph Casio and Jules Le Breton are to be given to Ms. Toni Tucker upon my demise. If anyone questions my decisions of this will, 3% of all my cash assets will be set aside to handle the legal processes to maintain my wishes. I'm sure that Mr. Breaux can handle any possible problems that might arise. Now, Misters Breaux, Bailey and Demas, please hand over everything to Ms. Toni Tucker. Please explain all assets and provide all assistance to Ms. Tucker that may be necessary."

"Toni, I know you don't understand all of this. Just know that I loved you as I have never loved anyone. You made my life. It was wonderful being with you and living so happily."

"Ms. Tucker, that is the extent of the personal message in the will. The rest describes all assets. We will be happy to go over them with you. I'd like to start with the cash assets. There are twelve different bank accounts. The total cash value is $345 million."

"What! You've got to be kidding. Terry and I had maybe $8,000 in the bank. You're telling me he had $345 million in cash?"

"Yes. Various banks hold the accounts from New York to Hong Kong. He felt no matter where he was in the world that it was better to spread it around for easy access."

"Mr. Breaux, I can't believe this. I can't even grasp the concept of that much money. We were together for 5 years. We didn't travel. We were rather conservative. I just can't comprehend any of this."

"Ms. Tucker, I don't know why Mr. Williams did what he did. We were his legal advisors and have been for over 15 years. We served his parents before that. Mr. Williams was born into wealth, but he more than tripled it. When he met you, he decided to live like most people. He wasn't raised that way but he loved it. You made him very happy. He knew that you loved him for him, and not for his money."

"I think it is time to go over the various properties. Mr. Williams has 22 different houses and businesses in the French Quarter. There are condos in Hong Kong, Paris, Honolulu, New York, Dallas, London, Key West, Berlin and Sydney. Each has caretakers and staffs. Mr. Williams had each with duplicate items so he didn't have to pack when he traveled. We'll be more than happy to clear those things out for you."

"The next items are stocks and bonds. The total assets of the stocks and bonds are approximately $500 million. All are Blue Chip stocks or Bearer bonds. Our firm has maintained these for Mr. Williams. Every year Mr. Williams came by the office for a review of his holdings. Even though Mr. Williams didn't seem to keep up with all of his holdings, he always knew what was what. He knew every account, property, condo, stock and bond he owned. He always amazed us with the amount of detail he knew, though he only came by once a year."

"Mr. Breaux, I'm totally in shock. Please, tell me there's no more to tell me. I'm not sure I can handle all this."

"There's only a few more items and I'll be finished. There are land holdings in just about every state in the union and 1/3 of the countries of the world. The total value of these assets are approximately another $400 million. Let's see we've been working for about two hours, I think it's time to take time for brunch. Mr. LaFarge has prepared a wonderful brunch. We hope you'll enjoy it with us."

Just as though on clue, Mr. LaFarge came into the dining room. The three lawyers put all their papers aside. Several waiters came in a set the table. There were several wines to chose from. Mr. LaFarge recommended a Merlot to start with. Our first course was a French Onion Soup. It was very good. I was sorry the bowl was so small. The bowls vanished and were replaced with a shredded fresh vegetable medley with freshly made vinaigrette. After the salad plates were removed, Mr. LaFarge refreshed our wine.

All of a sudden I realize John and Ben hadn't said a word for the past three hours. Looking at them, they looked lost. They didn't know what to say, so they said nothing. "John, Ben, are you two OK?" They just shook their heads yes. "Come on guys, I need you here with me. You can't be in any more shock than I am."

John took a sip of his wine. "Toni, I don't know what to say. Terry didn't seem that private about himself. Neither Ben nor I would ever have guessed any of this. I must say this is the first time Ben has been truly speechless. Mr. LaFarge, I'm very impressed with you're food and wines. I can't wait for what is next."

"Thank You, Mr. Kingsly. Your next course is a medallion of beef, marinated in Merlot with sautéed mushrooms. Along with roasted seasoned potatoes and a light spinach soufflé. I hope you enjoy it." Just then a waiter came in with plates just as Mr. LaFarge said. The presentation of the meal was very simple and elegant. It didn't take any of us a second to dive in. Mr. LaFarge had outdone himself. The beef melted in your mouth and could be cut with a fork. We couldn't decide what was the best. We decided it was what ever was in your mouth at the moment.

There really wasn't much talking during the meal. For the three of us it was a blissful experience. For the three lawyers, they seemed to act like it was a normal brunch. I don't know how anyone could think any of this was normal.

The last fork was laid down, when a chilled bowl of fruit was placed in front of us. It was topped with a lightly sweetened cream sauce. I didn't have enough nerve to ask for the recipe. John and Ben would have been mortified if I had asked. But I knew they wanted it too.

To finish the meal, more coffee was delivered for each of us. Again that was Mr. Breaux's cue to start work again. "Ms. Tucker, our firm will handle all the property changes to your name. Unless you have someone else you would rather work with."

"No. I believe you know everything there is to know about what Terry had. I guess I'll need a report itemizing everything. I can't remember half of what has been said. After I receive an inventory, I'll need time to go over it. Is there any thing I need to do right away?"

"Yes. We need your signature on these papers. This will give us the authority to have all the property and accounts transferred to your name. With the international properties and accounts it may take several months to compete it all. However, you'll have access to everything immediately. I have papers here for you, which will force anyone to allow you access to anything you would like. And like all legal documents, every thing is in triplicate. We need to have a picture of you taken so we may send it to the various caretakers of the properties and accounts. We have a photographer outside. If you wouldn't mind doing it today. If you would rather do it at another time, we'll make arrangements for you."

"Well, I must say I don't look like picture material but we might as well get it done. Would you like me to call him in?"

Mr. Breaux went to the front door and asked the photographer to come in. "Ms. Tucker, this is Mr. Nigel Clive, our photographer. He has worked for the firm for many years. He has never taken a bad picture, so I'm sure you'll be happy with the results."

"Thank You, Mr. Breaux. Ms. Tucker, if you'll sit over here, I'll set up the lighting and my camera. This will only take a few minutes. The pictures will be ready this afternoon for your review. Would 5 PM be all right to bring the proofs by?"

"Certainly, I'll be here. I take it you do your own developing? I can't think of a photo processing service around here that could get this done that fast." As I talked he was busy getting all of his equipment set up. It seemed to only take minutes for him to be ready.

"Yes, I do. That way I know what is going to come out. Now, if you'll raise you chin just a little and look directly into the camera, we'll be finished." I did what he asked. The camera was shooting very rapidly. It must have take 20 shots in just a few seconds. "Thank You, Ms. Tucker. I'm finished. I'll be back by at 5 PM. I hope you'll be happy with the finished product." He turned to Mr. Breaux. "Goodbye Mr. Breaux. If Ms. Tucker accepts the pictures, I'll have 30 copies in your office, first thing in the morning." With that he picked up all of his equipment and was gone.

Back at the dining room table, I started signing my name. Each sheet of paper was explained before I signed it. The signing took two hours. It was now 4 PM and I was very tired. Mr. Breaux must have sensed it, because he started hurrying a little. By 4:30 PM everything was signed. It took another 20 minutes for Mr. Breaux to close the meeting. Mr. Bailey and Mr. Demas thanked me for my time with assurances that all legal matters would be handled. Mr. Demas seemed to be very business like, very cool. Mr. Bailey was friendly and warm.

As the lawyers were just out the door, Mr. Clive arrived with the proofs. While still on the porch, we all looked at his work. I chose one that everyone agreed with. With that, it was a blessing to go back into the house with just John and Ben. They were as tired as I was. We were relaxing in the living room when the doorbell rang. I just groaned. Ben got up and answered the door. It was Mr. LaFarge with six waiters behind him. "Ms. Tucker, I know you must be very tired. I've prepared a medium to light dinner for you. We will set up the table and put out the food. It is all in warming dishes and will be ready for you when you are. One of my service people will come by tomorrow morning and pick up every thing. Please, just leave the table when you're finished. I have a linen cover that can be thrown over the table so you won't see the mess. Unless you would prefer us to stay and clear tonight?"

I was in shock. It was 6 PM and we were getting hungry. Ben was just saying he would go and bring us dinner. "Please. Mr. LaFarge, the dining room is yours. And tomorrow would be fine to pick up everything" In 10 minutes the table was complete with candles and the waiters excused themselves. Mr. LaFarge kissed my hand and was out the door.

John, Ben and I couldn't wait to see what he had prepared. We felt like children, sneaking a peek. The chafing dishes were elegant. You would never have guessed they were functional. There was a bowl of Oyster Artichoke Soup for each of us. Ben poured the wine, a light Bordeaux with an excellent aroma. The crystal was different from what was used at brunch. It's a wonder what was in that truck of Mr. LaFarge's.

After the soup, Ben started uncovering the dishes. There was Chicken Rochambeau. Next was seasoned rice pelar, and steamed asparagus. I'm glad he said medium to light dinner. We took full advantage of the meal. The portions were perfect. Again there were those coffee carafes full of that excellent coffee. John noticed another dish at the end of the table that was covered with lace. He lifted the lid and found hot spiced Apples with Double Cream. It had all been pure heaven. John used the linen cover and covered the table. We went into the living room and sprawled on the furniture, too full to move.

John moved around a little and said. "Toni, I'll never forget today. I'm still in such shock I don't know what to say. I don't know where to start with a question."

"That's good because I couldn't answer it. I'm in just as much shock. I can't believe I'm rich. Not just rich but wealth beyond my wildest dreams. I can't even think about it in any type of perspective. I guess I can pay off the mortgage on the house and the shop and have some left over." John and Ben started laughing and I joined in. I guess the day had gotten to us because we laughed until we cried.

Ben was trying to catch his breath. "Well, boss. Do you think we can have a 10% raise?" John started laughing all over again.

"I think I can manage that and for Joey and Mary too. Maybe we can redecorate the shop if it doesn't cost too much." We laughed more.

43

We began to settle down. John said, "I think it's time to call it a night. We'll come by tomorrow and see how you're doing."

"OK, but don't tell Joey or Mary about today's events. I think I should keep it quiet for a while. I've got to get used to it myself before others know about it. Just tell them I needed you with me today. I don't know how I'm going to handle any of this. It's still going to take me a couple of weeks before I'll be ready to go back to the shop. Maybe by then I'll have a clue of what I'm going to do."

"Don't worry, we'll keep it quiet. Besides I'm not sure I would know where to begin. I don't think anyone would believe me anyway." Ben looked at John and he nodded in agreement. Both kissed me good night and left.

Now that I was alone, I began to think of what had transpired. Terry was the sweetest person I've ever known. I thought we had an open relationship but today's surprises were a little much. After I changed into by PJ's, I sat on the side of the bed and cried. I don't know why I was crying. I missed Terry something awful but the shock of today made me a little angry. How could he have not told me? We were together for 5 years and I knew nothing. My feeling were so mixed up. I was exhausted. I laid there thinking how much I loved Terry and ashamed of being angry with him. Some time through the thoughts and tears I fell asleep.

# Chapter 6

I slept until 9 AM. The coffeepot had come on and turned itself off already. I haven't slept that late in years. I love the mornings out on the porch before the city got really ready to stir. There's something about the French Quarter in the mornings. Listening to the horses and carriages, clip clopping along the quiet streets getting ready for the day. Usually, there's not any traffic accept for delivery trucks. In the early morning the smell of fresh baked bread wafts through the streets. Living only six blocks away from the famous restaurant Café duMonde the aroma of the coffee and beignets smelled like home. The only way to make a typical morning better is to have had rain before you went out. Rain that has cleansed the streets of the nights before revelry.

Today was my first day as an almost billionaire. It still didn't seem real to me. I began by trying to think of what I was going to do. There really wasn't a place to start. No matter what I thought, I kept coming back to Terry and all of his secrets. I guess a person with wealth couldn't trust many people. Maybe that was why Terry never said anything. But why the rouse with his parents? He could have simply said his parents were dead. I wouldn't have thought anything about it. How did he meet Bill and Jenny and get them to go along with the story? Why go to such lengths to keep the story going.

I guess I really didn't know Terry at all. How was I going to find out about him? I could call Mr. Breaux and ask him what he knows. If he wouldn't answer, I'd

45

have to get an investigator to find out. Through out my life, I have always had a plan of action. My mind was running along its normal problem solving process. First, I'd call Mr. Breaux. Second, I'd hire an investigator. What kind of investigator? There was nothing I knew about investigators. Third, I had no clue. Maybe I'll think of something by the time I finish #1.

Not being someone to waste time, I started with Mr. Breaux. "Mr. Breaux, is there any way I could see you? After yesterday, I have millions of questions. I think getting to know more about Terry is a good place to start. What would be better for you? To come to my house or for me to come to your office?"

"Ms. Tucker, I'm completely at you're disposal. Where ever and when ever you would like is fine with me. I'm not sure I can answer all of your questions but I'll do my best."

"I'm still a little tired from yesterday. I'm not as recovered as I thought. Could you come to my house tomorrow at 10 AM?

"Of course, would you like Mr. LaFarge to cater the meeting? I hope you were pleased with his work."

"If it's not too much trouble and he's available. That would be great. I need to think about having John and Ben here with me. I haven't decided on that yet. What would you advise?"

"There are some things you may not want Mr. Kingsly or Mr. Hebert to hear. I don't mean to alarm you but there are some private things. I worked for Mr. Williams or his family for over 30 years. I believe I can provide you with what you're looking for."

46

"How soon do I need to let you know if John and Ben will be here?"

"You don't, Ms. Tucker. I'll have Mr. LaFarge prepare for four. He will be prepared for whatever you decide, at the time."

"Thank You, I'll see you tomorrow at 10 AM."

After I hung up, I starting thinking of what questions I really had. I should make a list. Be prepared has always been my motto. There was the entire day to think of the questions. I'll turn on the computer and start the list there.

I had to decide about John and Ben. Mr. Breaux said there are some things that are very private. How private can it be? He's dead. What could possibly be said that I should keep to myself? Now I was getting nervous. Did I want to know? John and Ben have been a part of my life for so many years. They have gone through everything with me. Breaking up with boyfriends, opening the shop, and helping me when my brother died several years ago. They know about my new finances and as managers of the shop, my prior finances. Maybe I should listen to Mr. Breaux first then decide if I should tell John and Ben about what I learned. That was it. That is what I'll do, listen first.

At the computer, I tried to think up some questions. I guess Terry's parents should be the first question. Why the rouse of Bill and Jenny? Second, why didn't he tell me about his money? Even though I think I understand that a little. No one I know would know how to act around that kind of wealth. So I guess I'll not ask that unless Mr. Breaux brings it up. That also lets me know I shouldn't say anything to anyone about

47

the will either. John and Ben won't say anything. They have always kept my secrets.

The doorbell rang. I guess I'm more afraid than I thought because I peeked through the curtains before I went to the door. Mr. LaFarge was there with three helpers. I opened the door for him. "Ms. Tucker, I come to clean the dining room. Is this a good time or would you like us to come back later?"

"No, this is fine. I had forgotten there was a mess. The cover you had for the table is very effective. Please, come in."

The helpers went to work on the table. It took them just minutes to have everything back the way it was. Mr. LaFarge supervised the helpers, watching every move they made. They didn't speak, but nodded when told to do something. One of the helpers had gone to Mr. LaFarge's truck and returned with a large carafe. "Ms. Tucker, I brought you a pot of the coffee you liked. I hope you enjoy it. Keep the carafe, you may use it again some time."

"Oh, thank you. I did really enjoy the blend you've made. I will enjoy this today. Thank you also for the carafe. I'll be seeing you again tomorrow. Have you talked to Mr. Breaux?"

"Yes, he called this morning. Do you have something in mind you'd like to have for lunch tomorrow?"

"I trust your judgment and I'm sure I will enjoy anything you prepare. Oh, I almost forgot. It will only be Mr. Breaux and myself."

"Thank you. I'll have something very nice for you. I'll be here at 11 AM and do everything like we did yesterday. Thank You Ms. Tucker, until tomorrow then, have a good day." With that, he was out the door, across the porch and was gone.

With the carafe in hand, I went looking for a cup. I don't know what he puts into this blend but it is wonderful. There's a hint of chicory, but just a hint. Other than the chicory I had no idea what was in it. I took my cup and headed back to the computer.

There had to be more questions. Thinking about the upper class of New Orleans society, I couldn't remember the name Williams being included. That's not a French name. I always read the society pages of the New Orleans Times Picayune newspaper and I don't recall ever seeing the name. I hope Mr. Breaux can tell me why I haven't. It does seem strange but I guess it's possible.

I looked at my watch and it was 12:30 PM. No wonder I was hungry. I slid my chair back and headed for the kitchen. As I got close to the front door the doorbell rang. I jumped a mile. Again my heart was pounding and I peeked out the curtains. It was John and Ben, with Styrofoam containers. I opened the door. "Here we are again bearing gifts. Hope you're hungry. We would have been here earlier but we got busy and forgot about eating. You haven't eaten yet have you?"

"I was just heading to the kitchen for something to eat. It smells good, what have you got?"

Ben smiles, "How would you like some Crawfish Bisque from my house? I made it last night after I got home. I wasn't tired and I couldn't sleep so I got up and started cooking. That's when I do my best work."

"If you think I'm going to turn it down, you're crazy. That looks just about enough for me. What are y'all going to eat? I can fix you some toast." I laughed.

49

"Yeah, right! Of course we have enough for all of us. I'll set the table up. John why don't you get some glasses with ice? I brought some Sun Tea. Mable over at Papa John's gave us several gallons a few days ago." Ben transferred the bisque to a glass bowl for the microwave. John poured the tea and I just sat there and let them do it.

We savored the bisque. Ben should have been a chef. I think he would have if he could do it at 2 AM for 20 people at a time and they all eat the same thing. Of course, it would have to be a place that Ben could open on the days he wanted to cook. I don't think his restaurant would last with the hours Ben likes.

"Toni, how are you feeling? You look better today. Last night, you looked like you were whipped."

"I slept late this morning. I was whipped when I went to bed last night. It took me a while to fall asleep but I slept very well. I feel a lot better today. I'm just about ready to go out today for a walk. My leg is still sore but it works OK." I got to thinking, I was feeling a lot better and I did want to get out of the house. I needed some fresh air and some different surroundings for a little while.

John looked at me saying. "Be careful. Don't over do it. You have to go back to the doctor soon. You don't want him yelling at you for pushing too hard."

"I know. I really do feel much better. I think, I'll walk over to the Moonwalk and watch the good old Mississippi roll by. That's only three blocks away and I'll rest there for awhile. I'll be careful."

We finished eating the bisque. "Ben, you've done it again. You've created another culinary wonder. I

50

think you should leave John and move in with me. Besides, I know I'm cuter than he is."

"Yes you are but there are other assets that you just can't come up with." John and I laughed at that. Ben always has an answer that's cute.

"Ben, we've got to get going. We do have work to do. Today is inventory and there must be a thousand things to count. Mary and Joey are probably looking for us. Lets get this mess cleaned up and head off."

"That's OK, I'll clean up. I appreciate the food and company. It's the least I can do for my keepers. Besides, washing three forks, three plates and three glasses is not going to over extend me. Y'all go ahead, I don't mind slaving over the sink." They gave me a hug and headed out the door. It only took a few minutes to clean up everything. I even dried the dishes and put them away. Usually, I just let them drain dry. But this time I wanted everything in its place.

It was a good idea to go for a walk. The Moonwalk has steps going down to the water and a few benches. I locked the door and started off. It took about a block for my leg to loosen up. The weather was great, a slight breeze, low humidity and about 77 degrees. It was beautiful. There are always tourists in the French Quarter. There were a lot of people on the streets. It was a great day to be out for a walk. As I made my way to the Moonwalk, I saw an empty bench and headed for it. The sun was nice and warm. I watched the Canal Street ferry go back and forth across the river. The ferry carries cars and pedestrians from Canal Street to Algiers Point. The West Bank of New Orleans is almost as old as the French Quarter. People live over there and work down town. The ferry has to give way for ships so they'll leave the dock and float around until the ship passes. Sometimes the trip across the river would take 15 minutes, other times it would take 30 minutes. You can't be in a hurry and take a ferry.

The ships that pass all have foreign flags. Terry and I use to have contest trying to identify what country the flag was from. Oh God, Terry! I miss you so much. Why did this happen? With that thought I started back to the house. It just wasn't fun out there without Terry.

By the time I made it back to the house, I was feeling much better. The exercise helped a lot. I opened the gate and was surprised to see Lt. Hanson sitting on the porch. It made me jump at first.

"Good Afternoon, Ms. Tucker. I'm glad to see you up and about. It's such a beautiful day." He always has that warm smile. He seems so friendly but it does make you wonder what he is really thinking.

"I was wondering when you would be coming by. I hope you have something to tell me that will solve this. Do you have a suspect yet?"

"I'm sorry to say no. We went through this house from top to bottom. We didn't find any fingerprints that couldn't be identified and disregarded. I do have a few more questions for you."

"OK, let's go inside." I decided I wasn't going to tell him anything that he didn't already know unless he brought it up. I unlocked the door and set my keys on the entry table. "Why don't you go into the dining room. I'll be there in a moment."

I went into the kitchen and filled two glasses with ice and Sun Tea. Taking them into the dining room I asked "Would you like some sugar or lemon for your tea?"

"No, this is fine, thank you." He fished a small notebook out of his coat pocket and flipped through several pages. "Ms Tucker, have you thought of anything that you hadn't told me about before?"

"No, I've gone through that evening over and over. There's nothing that I can add. I can't think of a reason for any of it. There's just not anything that could possibly have caused this. Could they have gotten the wrong house? I know there are only three permanent residents on this block of Conti. Mr. Visko is to the right of us and is 86 years old, so I'm sure it wasn't for him. Then there is Mr. and Mrs. Ollivett on the left. They have lived there for 50 years. He use to be a dentist and has been out of practice for 15 years. I doubt if one of his patients is coming after him after all this time. The rest of the buildings on this side of the block are businesses that have been there forever. I don't know a thing about them really. We go to the stores and bars on the block occasionally. Excuse me, we went to them. I can't think in the past tense yet. We were friendly with the clerks but I couldn't tell you their names. Of course, the Wildlife and Fishery Building takes the entire block across the street. So, where does that leave us?"

"I understand, we have investigated the same areas and have come up with nothing. I know you were in the hospital and couldn't make arrangements for Mr. Williams, can you tell me who did?"

"Yes. Terry had a will with the firm of Breaux, Bailey and Demas here in New Orleans. I have a card for them if you need it. The law firm handled everything. He was cremated the day the body was released from the Coroners office."

"What about his parents? We have tried repeatedly to call the number you gave us but no one answers. The police in Grand Ile, Mi. say the address you gave us is a mail drop. Anything received at the mail drop was forwarded to a P.O. Box here in New Orleans. What can you tell me about this?"

"Until a few days ago, I couldn't have told you anything. Since I've been out of the hospital I've learned a lot. I don't understand any of it but I'm learning slowly that I really didn't know Terry." I noticed a spark of renewed interest on his face. "The people I thought were Terry's parents, were not. I don't know why Terry set that all up but he did. His real parents were killed over 15 years ago. All three lawyers were here. Mr. Breaux is the gentleman I've dealt with the most. He says his firm has represented the Williams family for over 30 years. That's all I know about that."

"Mr. Breaux didn't give you a reason why Mr. Williams set up fake parents?"

"No, he really didn't seem to know. That was something Terry did on his own and they really didn't know anything about it."

"What else have you learned about Mr. Williams since I saw you last?"

"I've learned a few things but I'm not sure if any of it would help you. In some ways I don't believe it's any of your business."

"Ms. Tucker, I want to solve this murder but I can't do it without your help."

"I understand what you're saying but what I've learned is history and that has nothing to do with what I've known about Terry for the past five years. Mr. Breaux 's firm knows more than I do. Maybe you should talk to them. All I can tell you is that there is nothing that I know about Terry that would cause someone to kill him or me." I could see the frustration on Lt. Hanson's face. He wasn't angry but he wasn't happy either.

"You said Mr. Williams had a will. Tell me what was in it. Was there money to be distributed, and if so to whom?"

"There was some money and everything came to me. There doesn't seem to be any relatives alive. My name was the only one in the will."

"OK, how much did he will to you?"

"I'm not sure that's any of your business. I understand why you're asking but I don't think I'm obligated to answer it. Let's just say it's more than I had thought it would be. Of course, I didn't know he had a will. I was very surprised."

"You know I can find out. A will has to go through probate and that will be public record."

"I guess that's how you'll have to find out then. I'm not going to say anything about it. Mr. Breaux is my attorney now. I'll talk to him. If he says to tell you, I will."

"I can see I'm not going to get anywhere today. I'm sorry you feel this way. I hope Mr. Breaux will explain to you the process of probate and public records. I've got to go anyway. I'll be back to see you in a few days. I'm really glad you're feeling better.

Thank you for the tea, it was very good. I'll see myself out." With that he got up and walked out the door.

It was so quick. I was left sitting there just staring after him. I do need to talk to Mr. Breaux. I hope he will be my attorney after he's taken care of all the will stuff.

I headed back to the computer. Lt. Hanson will ask Mr. Breaux about everything. I wonder if he'll do it today? Maybe I should call him and let him know what Lt. Hanson asked me and what I told him. Looking at my watch, it was 4 PM. I don't think Mr. Breaux would talk to him at this time of day. I'll tell him tomorrow during our meeting.

I couldn't think anymore about questions, so I closed the file and shut the computer down. I flipped the TV on and Oprah was on. Her topic was "Secrets of Loved Ones" I wasn't ready for that. Turning off the TV, I turned on the stereo for some nice soft jazz.

Tonight I'll order in a pizza and read a book. It was a busy day and I'm tired of thinking for one day. I'll hit the sack early so I can enjoy the early morning on the porch.

# Chapter 7

It was 2 AM and I had been sleeping very soundly. Something woke me but I couldn't figure out what it was. It felt like instinct but what instinct? For some reason I became frozen with fear. I was barely breathing trying to listen to the sounds in the house. The air conditioner was on, so that muffled other sounds. I was straining my ears to determine if there was any sound that shouldn't be there. Afraid to move and afraid not to at the same time. There was a gun in the nightstand. Dad had put it there, just in case. I moved as slowly as I could toward the night stand. The sound of the sheets sliding over my arm sounded too loud. I slid the draw open and found the gun. I lifted it out and took the safety off. Pulling the gun under the sheets, I moved back into a normal sleeping position. My heart was pounding. I still couldn't figure out what was scaring me but it was really doing the job.

There, a floorboard squeaked. Where was it? It sounded like the dining room. That's the next room. Do they know I'm sleeping downstairs? If they didn't, that would give me more time to prepare. Is it one or two? For some reason I started calming down. My brain was completely clear. It was like I had practiced something like this and was ready. Slowly I got out of bed. Thank God for the streetlights around the Wildlife and Fishery Building across the street. There was just enough light to make out where everything was in the room. With the gun in one hand, I made the bed with the other. It looked like it hadn't been slept in. I didn't make a sound. Moving over to the closet, I opened the door very slowly. Again, not a sound. I stepped into the closet and closed the door. The door had louvers so a small amount of light got in. As slowly and I could and careful not to make a sound, I moved behind the hanging clothes. There was Terry's trench coat in the corner. It was long enough to hide my legs. I inched my way into the corner behind Terry's coat. I peeked just over the shoulder of the coat. There was nothing to see. Every sense I had was on high alert.

I heard very soft steps on the stairs. Then I heard the floorboard squeak in the dining room again. It was more than one person. Were there more than two? Someone stepped into the room. I heard them before I saw a silhouette through the door. He had a gun and he was dressed in black from head to toe. He made a quick sweep of the room. I was barely breathing. Very slowly he opened the closet door. Just as slowly he closed it. Terry's coat saved me. The man quietly left the room, heading for the living room. Just as he got there the other man came down the stairs. This time he wasn't being quiet. The man in the living room spun around with his gun raised. "What are you doing?" said the man in the living room.

"Hey man, there's no one here. I checked everything, even the attic. Where could she be? I saw her leave the house today but I know she was here this evening. I watched the lights go out around 9 PM."

"Well, none of the beds have been slept in. So how do you explain that? How did she get by you?"

"I don't know, man. I didn't take my eyes off this house."

"Let's go. When we tell the man about this he isn't going to be happy. Make sure nothing is out of place.

We'll have to come back in a few days. Next time we better not miss her."

With that they opened the front door and left. I started to shake all over. I couldn't stand up. Sliding down the wall in the closet until I was on the floor. Now I was breathing like I hadn't had a breath the entire time they were there. I couldn't have walked if I'd wanted to. I sat there for 30 minutes, afraid to get out of the closet. When I could move I left the closet but there was no way I was going to turn a light on. I kept the gun with me. I crept into the kitchen and switched on the coffeepot. I sat on the floor in the corner of the cabinets until the coffee was brewed. I got up and got a cup from the cabinet and filled it. Back into the corner and on the floor. The clock on the coffeepot said 3:15 AM. An hour. They were in my house for an hour. Terry would never believe I could be still for an hour. Damn him!

I sat in that corner drinking coffee and waiting for time to pass. At 6 AM I crawled to the phone and called John and Ben. Ben answered the phone, "This better be good at this hour. Who is it?"

"Ben, its Toni. Two men broke into the house this morning. I hid and they didn't find me but they were talking to each other and said they'd be back to get me. They thought I had left the house and missed my leaving. Can you two come over? I need to be with someone."

"We'll be there in five minutes."

"Ben, use your key. If they are watching, they'll think I'm still gone."

"Toni, should we call the police?"

"No. I need to think about this first. Just please get over here." With that Ben hung up. I could picture him trying to explain to John what was happening and why they were coming to my house. It took them five minutes to get here.

They unlocked the door and switched on some lights. The sun was up but it was still dim in the house. "Toni, where are you?"

"I'm in the kitchen". As they walked I stood up, but away from the window. John saw the gun in my hand and stopped still. Ben saw it at the same time. He came over to me and took it out of my hand. He put the safety on it and laid it on the counter.

"Girl, this is some kind of serious. How did they not find you?

"Something woke me up, I don't know what. Then I heard a sound and at first I couldn't figure out what it was. When I did, I got the gun out, made the bed and got into the closet. I hid behind one of Terry's trench coats, afraid to breathe. One of them opened the closet door but didn't see me."

"You mean there was more than one? What did they want? Did they take anything? John said and started shaking.

"They wanted me. I don't know why. I listened to them but they didn't say anything as to why. I couldn't tell if they wanted to just kill me or take me somewhere. They said something about The Man wasn't going to be happy about this. I have no clue who The Man is. I'm so scared, that after they left I couldn't stop shaking for half an hour."

John said, "That sounds to me like they will be back. What are we going to do? Should we call the police?

"No. They thought I wasn't here. According to what they said they had been watching the house all day. They couldn't figure out how I had left the house without them seeing me." Now was the time to ask Ben for a bit of deception. "Ben, I want you to take some of my clothes and go back to your house. Once you're there, change into them and try to look like me. Then come back. That's the only way I can see how I'm going to get out of this house. You need to bring your clothes back with you so you can change again. At least that way they'll think I'm just returning to the house. Then the three of us can leave together. What do you think?"

Ben and I went to the bedroom to select some clothes. Ben was having a good time matching colors. He loved to cross dress and he had the figure for it. Once in a while Ben would go in drag to the gay bars with John. We put all the stuff in a grocery bag. Ben left carrying the bag.

John and I sat in the dining room. At first in silence, then we started talking about what I was going to do. We would wait for Ben to come back, and then the three of us would leave. I'd call Mr. Breaux from their house and change the meeting to his office. I'd take a cab instead of walking. We had three hours before the meeting. Mr. Breaux would have to reach Mr. LaFarge and change lunch to his office.

Ben was back in 30 minutes. He really did look like me from a distance. He crossed the street, opened the gate and came to the door. Ben used his key to open the door and came in. "Now, you know I look better in this than you do." We laughed. John swung him around saying, "Well good looking, would you like to come to my house?"

"I'd love to, but I've got to get these hose off." Laughing he headed for the bedroom to change clothes. After Ben came out of the bedroom and I went in bedroom and put those same clothes on. I was hoping we could fool the men watching the house. I got a handbag out and put some papers, money and a few cosmetics in it. I went up stairs to the bedroom and found my passport.

The three of us left the house. We were laughing and talking so no one would think we knew the house had been broken into. We arrived at John and Ben's apartment on Decatur St. in just 5 minutes. Once we were inside, we all peeked out the windows to see if anyone was watching the apartment. We didn't see anyone but did we know what to really look for? I doubt it.

At 9 AM I called Mr. Breaux's office. He wasn't there but his secretary said she would contact him and Mr. LaFarge and change the meeting to the office. She assured me there was no problem that they could accommodate any change I desired.

John, Ben and I walked over to Cafe duMonde for coffee and beignets. We were trying to pass time so I could catch a cab to Mr. Breaux's office. We thought it would be hard to follow me from there. Decatur Street has lots of cabs and is a very busy street. The morning traffic was heavy so we figured if some one was trying to follow me, the cab would get lost in the traffic.

At 9:45 AM I hailed a cab. I gave the driver the address on Canal Street and off we went. It took 10 minutes to get there. I couldn't tell if I had been followed or not. If I was, what could I do about it, anyway?

# **Chapter 8**

The entire office building belonged to the law firm. The lobby was elegant, with oak-paneled walls and a security guard. A receptionist was right in the middle of the lobby. I started walking over to her to ask directions to Mr. Breaux's office. As soon as she saw me, she came around the desk. "Good morning Ms. Tucker. Mr. Breaux's office is right this way. May I get you some coffee or tea?"

"No thank you." I followed her to a set of large double doors. She just opened the door for me and stepped aside.

"Good Morning Ms. Tucker. You are looking well. How are you really feeling? Mr. LaFarge has everything set up in the conference room. Won't you join me?" As he talked he was walking over to another door in his office. He opened it and indicated that was the direction I should go. I went through the door. It was the largest conference rooms I'd ever seen. There was carved wood walls with a matching conference table covered with an immense sheet of beveled glass. The one window in the room was stained glass of the most beautiful swamp scene I had ever seen. There wasn't an item in the room that didn't cost more than my house.

Mr. LaFarge was standing at the end of the table. There was a brunch that was beyond belief. It was Eggs Sardou. You would never think poached eggs would taste so wonderful while sitting on artichoke hearts and anchovy fillets. Cover that with Hollandaise sauce and truffles. It's a culinary delight. Along side of that was fresh biscuits, apricot marmalade and that fresh fruit and sauce I enjoyed so much before. Of course, there was that wonderful coffee blend Mr. LaFarge creates.

Mr. Breaux directed me to a chair and pulled it out for me. As I sat down I couldn't take my eyes off the table. The presentation was something out of a movie. I've been to some very elegant restaurants before but nothing like this. I guess this is normal for Mr. Breaux. I was trying not to stare like a country hick.

"Ms. Tucker, why don't we start eating and we'll talk over coffee. Mr. LaFarge was very happy to be cooking here. You see he has a complete kitchen in the next room. He uses his truck very well but he likes his kitchen better."

We started eating and I felt like I was in Paris somewhere. Brunch is done slowly when you have food like this. I'm not sure I could get use to this but I know I would love to try.

The table was cleared of everything except the coffee. Mr. Breaux looked like he was ready to start. "My partners don't need to be here. I managed most of the Williams accounts and things. I knew the family well and I've been like a stepfather to Terry from time to time. I know you have a lot of questions. I can understand that there would be. I thought about this all day yesterday. I thought I'd ask you if it would be all right to tell you of the family first then about Terry since his parents died. Then if I haven't answered the questions you have, I'll do so.

"That would be fine. I do have many questions, but what I do want is to know everything you can tell me."

"The Williams came from money. They lived in New Orleans but a short time after their marriage. It seems New Orleans wasn't where they wanted to live. That is one reason why there are so many condos. Mr. Elmer Williams got into oil during the boom and made more money than his father had in cotton. Ester Williams wanted her child to be born in New Orleans. So they came back when Ester was six months pregnant. After Terry was born, they left again. Mr. Williams and I kept in contact on business frequently. The three of them traveled the world until Terry got to be about 15 years old. They moved to Hong Kong and stayed there until their deaths. Terry was 18 when his parents died. Elmer and Ester were flying from Hong Kong to Paris on business. Terry had been left in Hong Kong. For some reason the plane went down in France. The investigation indicated equipment error and pilot error."

"Terry stayed in Hong Kong until he started college. He came to New Orleans and attended Tulane University. He majored in Marketing. As soon as he graduated he left. Initially he went back to Hong Kong but stayed there only about a year. While in Hong Kong he invested in Japanese electronics. Terry tripled the wealth his father had left him. He had also invested in various weapons systems in various countries. With the world always in conflict somewhere, he made more money."

"He lived in Paris for about two years. By that time he was 26 years old. After that he seemed to travel extensively. He didn't seem to have any place he wanted to be. Then all of a sudden he came back to

New Orleans. When he did he quit traveling completely. He never said why and I didn't ask."

"Right after he arrived here he went to Tulane Medical Center and had some plastic surgery done. He had his ears bobbed, the eye shape changed and his chin filled with an implant. I don't know why he had it done, but it changed his appearance dramatically. He never said anything about it. Shortly after that he opened the T-shirt shop. Then he met you and you know the rest."

"I wish I did know the rest. You don't have any idea where he was traveling or any reason for plastic surgery? I wonder what he looked like before the surgery.

"No, he never alluded to it and I had learned a long time ago not to ask. I always wondered why he got into weapons but he did so well I forgot about it."

"Was that what you thought should be kept a secret?"

"I thought that should be for you only. Not knowing why he did it, I just thought it shouldn't be public knowledge."

"Could he have been involved in anything illegal or with the government?"

"I have no idea. Why do you ask?"

"Last night my house was broken into again. I was there but I hid and they didn't find me. They didn't take anything from the house. I listened to them talking and they wanted me. There is nothing I could tell anyone. I don't know why they want me. One thing that scared me to death is that I couldn't tell if they wanted me dead or taken somewhere." Just thinking about it made me start to shake again.

"Ms. Tucker, did you call the police? Do you know what they look like? What can we do to help you?" Mr. Breaux looked like he was near panic.

"I didn't call the police. I wanted to talk to you first. I was hoping you might tell me something about Terry that could explain why these people are after me. So far you've told me nothing that can explain it. You do raise more questions as to what Terry was doing during his extensive traveling." More questions kept jumping out at me. So many I couldn't get them into any sort of order to ask about.

"Mr. Breaux, please ask your secretary to call Lt. Hanson at NOPD, here's his number. I think I need to tell him what happened but I'd rather do it here than at the house. I'm a little afraid to go back there."

"Of course, just a moment and Mrs. Carter will have him on his way." He got up and took the number to Ms. Carter and returned.

I told Mr. Breaux about the break in and how I got out of the house. He was amazed with it all. Plus what I went through to get to his office. He understood why I didn't call the police to the house. The people watching would have known they missed me in the house.

Lt. Hanson arrived about 15 minutes after he was called. I explained everything that had happened. He too was amazed. He did agree with why I didn't call him to the house.

"If you'd like Ms. Tucker I can put some men to watch the house for a few days. I'm not sure these men wouldn't spot my men and disappear. And I can't guarantee those men won't come back when my men have to leave. You said they had gloves on so looking for fingerprints would be a waste. If we could figure out a way for them to think you're in the house when you're not. We could set up some men in the house or cameras. Maybe a motion detector that would notify us when they came in. We need to set up a plan to catch these guys."

"You can figure out anything you want but you can leave me out of it. I was so scared last night it took me an hour to stop shaking. When I told Mr. Breaux about it and then you, it made me shake all over again. I'm too afraid to go back to the house. I packed a few things and I want to leave town as soon as possible. I just don't know where to go or how to get there." I really didn't know what I was going to do. I thought by the time I saw Mr. Breaux I would have thought of something, but I haven't.

Lt. Hanson was trying to think of something. "Ms. Tucker, I'll make sure you're safe. Is there a way into your house other than the front door?"

"The houses and buildings butt up against each other in the back. There is a 2-foot easement between the two houses on each side of my house. Oh, there's an opening on the roof. You can get to and from the building behind mine. The house is about 6 feet higher that the building behind it. I can go in and then open up the roof door for you. But how long are you going to do that before you have to stop?"

"I'll do it until we catch them or we know for sure you're out of danger. Does that answer your question?"

"I'll try it for a while. The first minute I don't feel safe, I'm gone." I turned to Mr. Breaux and asked; "Can I speak to you a moment after Lt. Hanson leaves?"

*Mickey L. Strain*

"Of course, Ms. Tucker anything you need."

"Lt. Hanson, I'll be home in about an hour. As soon as I get there, I'll go up to the roof and open the door. Can you be there by then?"

"Yes, If I have to scale the building myself. I'll leave now and get things together. See you in an hour." Lt. Hanson almost ran out the door. I guess it was going to be close to getting everything done in an hour.

"Mr. Breaux, I need a few things. I hope you can help me. First, I want to hire a private detective, one of the best with international connections. Next I want a jet plane, purchased, fueled and with a pilot on stand-by. I need a bodyguard service for 24-hour protection. I want someone from the protection agency to be here to get me home and stay with me. Can you do what I ask?"

"By all means, just give me a few minutes and I'll get things going." He rang a buzzer under the table and Mrs. Carter came in. "Mrs. Carter, ask the other partners to come in please. I also need you to get Mr. Livingston on the phone."

"Yes Sir." She darted out of the room.

One minute later, both partners we're in the conference room. As if on cue Mr. LaFarge came in with more coffee cups and coffee. Then he was gone. Mr. Breaux started giving directions. "Mr. Demas, call Aeroline and purchase a luxury jet. I want it in a hanger, maintenance crew, fueled and a 24-hour stand by flight crew. Build housing in the hanger if necessary. Buy the hanger while you're at it. I want the Botner Security Group to establish the security. The extreme top of the line security. Mr. Bailey, I have a call into Mr. Livingston. I want you to set up a

70

bodyguard for Ms. Tucker. It will be 24 hours a day. Minimum of two people on each shift. One with her and one watching, under cover. Each will have to have a Top Security clearance and be experienced in martial arts and various weapons. I want them now. At least two of them here in 30 minutes. Any questions?" The partners looked at each other, nodded and were off to do their assignments.

"Ms. Tucker, I have one more call to make and then we'll be ready." He dialed the phone. "Hello, may I speak to Lafitte Roux? Mr. Roux, this is Mr. Breaux of Breaux, Bailey and Demas; I have a client who needs your services immediately and exclusively. Can you come to my office right now?" He listened for a moment. "Thank You, we'll we waiting." He hung up the phone.

"I think we have everything covered. Mr. Roux will be here in 15 minutes. He's the best private investigator in the city, with international connections. He's a little abrasive but he is the best. His fee is the best also. Do you have a problem with that?

"Not at all. I'll spend it all if I have to. I want to live and make this all stop." I had forgotten about the money. I guess I don't have to worry about that part any way.

Mr. Bailey and Mr. Demas came in together. Each taking their previous seats. Mr. Demas started first. "The jet and hanger have been purchased. Maintenance and flight crews are standing by. Botner will have the security completely set up by 6 PM." It seems that his report was cut and dry. He just didn't seem friendly at all. There was nothing you could put your finger on, it was just a feeling.

Mr. Bailey started his report right on cue. "Mr. Livingston says he'll have two people here in 30 minutes. He verifies they are bonded and with the security clearances you asked for. All will have the experience asked for and a complete rotation of people will be on hand this evening. He has the best people in the city. He is also setting up a supervisor with additional roving patrols at various intervals so that the area can be mapped. Every spot on the street will be identified and will be monitored. They are aware of the men watching the house, and will be on the look out for them. Ms. Tucker, Mr. Livingston has never had any of his people on a stakeout identified. They are very good." He seems to be concerned and reassuring.

I sat there in total shock. I was finding out that money talks and with a very loud voice. In a total of 30 minutes, I had a private investigator, jet plane, hanger, crews for the plane, and bodyguards. Two weeks ago I couldn't have gotten cable in my house that fast.

Mrs. Carter came in. "Mr. Roux is here."

"Please send him in." Mr. Breaux got up and headed for the door. Mr. Roux was around 45 years old and very distinguished looking. He had salt and pepper hair and beard. Slender with an athletic build.

"Mr. Roux, it's good to see you again. May I introduce your client, Ms. Tucker." We shook hands and said nice to meet you. "Mr. Roux please sit down. Would you like some coffee?"

"Yes, thank you. You said it was an emergency and that you needed me right now. What's up?"

"Ms. Tucker's life is in danger. We don't know why or where it's coming from. We have bodyguards, surveillance, and police protection. We don't know much of anything. I think what we'd done so far will keep her safe maybe and even catch the guys trying to hurt her. Ms. Tucker was living with one of our clients and he was killed two weeks ago. It was a hit, not a robbery or any thing like that. They had lived together for five years. There was nothing to indicate this was going to happen. We want you to investigate Terry Williams. He's the man who was killed and we need to know everything about him that could possibly connect his murder and the attempts on Ms. Tucker. Are you willing to take the case?"

"Yes, I'll take it. I'll need every thing you've got on Mr. Terry Williams. I've got a few things to finish up tonight. Mr. Breaux can you meet me here at your office around 9 PM? I need to find out what I can from you. Ms. Tucker, I need to come by your house tomorrow so we can go over everything you know about Mr. Williams. Do you have a problem with that?"

"No, please come by. I'm a little concerned about you coming to the house. There are men watching the house. They might know who you are and get scared off. I want to know why some one wants to kill me."

"OK. I'll change my appearance before I come. I'll knock on the door and introduce myself as Mr. James Howard with Metropolitan Life Insurance. You can tell your bodyguards and the police to expect me. It will be around 10 AM."

"Thank you. I'll expect you tomorrow." Mr. Roux shook my hand and left the room.

"Ms. Tucker, let me introduce your body guards and get you back home. Each of the bodyguards should have ID, identifying them as working for Mr.

Livingston. The bodyguards should check the next two coming on. You should only see one of them, the other will be under cover and you shouldn't see him. Mrs. Carter has checked the two you're going to meet." Mr. Breaux went to the door and asked the men to come in. The first one looked about my size. He didn't look like he could protect anyone. Mr. Breaux was reading from a card that Mrs. Carter had given him. "Ms. Tucker this is Jack Armond, he has worked for Mr. Livingston for 10 years. He has a black belt in Judo and is a master of a variety of weapons." He shook my hand and stepped aside for the other man. "This is Mr. Castro. His speciality is undercover work and he was a Green Beret for 5 years in the Army." Mr. Jose Castro shook my hand and stepped aside. He looked like his name. A scraggly beard, dark eyes and clothes of a street person. "Gentleman, please see that Ms. Tucker gets home safely." The three of us left the conference room. When we entered the lobby, the men stopped me.

Mr. Castro started by saying, "Please let me leave first. I want to have a look around for a moment. Then I'll head to your house and find a position I like."

Mr. Armond directed me to a chair in the lobby. As we sat down, Mr. Armond started talking, "Ms. Tucker, we need to use our first names. Otherwise someone might hear us talking and not understand why I'm going into your house. My name is Jack. The man that will come and relieve me will use the roof door but I'll go out the front door. Do you have any questions?"

"I don't know what to ask. I've never been in a situation like this. I think we'd better stop by a grocery store. There's not enough food in the house for everyone that will be there."

"You don't have to feed us. We'll do just fine. Besides, we'll have food delivered for you. Just make out a list and we'll have it at your door in no time."

"I don't want to be a prisoner in my own house. But at the same time I do want to be safe. I have a few friends and employees that will be coming by from time to time. Is that going to be a problem?"

"No, just tell us who they are before you let them in the house. Are these people aware of what has been going on?"

"Two of them do but no one else. What am I going to tell them, why there are so many people in the house?"

"We'll be sure to handle that for you. The police will disappear into a back room or up stairs. I'll go to another part of the house. But rest assured we will only be a few feet away and will hear everything going on." The look on my face must have given my thoughts away. "Yes, we are going to bug the house, every room, even the bathroom. I'll show you where that one is so you can turn it off when you want."

"I'm glad of that. I never knew they had on and off switches." This was getting crazy. The more I thought about it the more I began to understand why these things were being done.

We had sat there for 20 minutes. I didn't realize the time had passed so quickly. Jack stood up and indicated it was time to leave. I got up and we went out the door. Jack hailed a cab and back to the French Quarter we went. When we got to the house, we walked up to the porch and unlocked the door. Once we got through the door he pushed me a little to one side while he quickly searched the house. He came back in just a moment. "Everything is fine. OK, where would you like me to disappear to and leave you alone?"

"You don't have to disappear. Make yourself comfortable and I'll get us something to drink." I headed for the kitchen to get us some tea. Jack seemed to be going over the house with a lot more care. He checked every window and door. When he came back, he announced, "All the bugs are planted."

"They're all planted? Where did you get them?

"I brought them with me. They are very small. I had 15 of them in my shirt pocket. Right now there is a truck somewhere within 2 blocks listening to us. I also placed a few motion detectors. One by each door and window. Even on the roof and the roof door. It doesn't take long to set up for electronic surveillance."

"Can you tell me if there were any bugs here before you put those here."

. "Mr. Livingston had the house scanned right after he was first called. There were none found. They didn't place the bugs when they were here before because they wanted me to plant them. They're job was to scan."

We were standing in the kitchen and we heard a noise upstairs. Jack looked at his watch and said, "That will be the police. They never could be quiet. Just to be on the safe side, why don't you sit here on the floor and I'll go check it out." He was up the stairs in two steps and to the attic door in one step. He waited until the door was opening and grabbed the door. Pulling it with great force. The police officer behind it fell on his face. Jack was stepping on the man and pointing his gun on the next man in line. They didn't know what was happening. Lt. Hanson was behind the second man.

"Jack! Are you having fun or what? You know what time we were going to be here. What are you trying to do?" Lt. Hanson was not happy at all. The two men with him were down right mad.

"Well Lt., surprise is a key element to a strong offense. I'm just doing my job. What if it hadn't been you? The donut shop could have been busy."

"Very funny. Now how do you have things set up? And get your foot off my man, jerk."

Jack chuckled and moved his foot. "OK, gentleman there are four large windows down stairs. Which mean you three have to stay up here. Who ever is watching this house saw me come in with Ms. Tucker. Meaning I'm the only one expected to be down stairs with her. Now were going to have some tea and watch some TV. See you later."

"Jack, ask Ms. Tucker to come up stairs in a few minutes. We want to set up some things but we need her to turn on some lights for us. Tell her that I'm here."

When Jack got down stairs he told me Lt. Hanson was upstairs. He told me about the lights they wanted on. But he chuckled and said, "Let them wait a few minutes. They have to stay up stairs anyway, they should get to know it in the dark."

I waited about 10 minutes and climbed the stairs. The first light I put on was the hall light. There were four men, including Lt. Hanson. "What room would you like to set up in? The master bedroom only has one window that faces the Ollivett house. There are drapes in there so there won't be any shadows."

Lt. Hanson said, "That would be great. Leave the hall light on too." After I got the lights on in the master bedroom, all four men started moving equipment in. "Ms. Tucker, we've brought some dim lighting we'll use after 10 PM. Can you come up stairs then and turn off the other lights. That way it will seem you just forgot the lights earlier."

"Sure I can do that. There is a TV and telephone in here you can use. Is there anything I can get for you?"

"No. We have everything we need. But thank you. We'll be fine."

On my way down the stairs the doorbell rang. I jumped a mile. Jack was by the door in two steps. He motioned to me to peek through the curtains to see who it was. I did and it was John and Ben. I told Jack it was OK. He put his gun away. I opened the door.

"Hi, guys. Come on in. It's a little different visit than this morning, isn't it?"

John started talking before I could finish my statement. "Toni, why didn't you call? We have been going crazy all day. Ben ran over here twice today and you weren't here. Are you trying to drive us nuts? And who is this guy?"

"Calm down you two. You know I went to the lawyers' office. I talked to them and they arranged some security for me. This is Jack and he's my bodyguard."

Ben took a good look at Jack and said, "If she doesn't need you honey I do."

"Ben, behave. Jack is doing his job and he doesn't need any harassment from you." I shook my finger at him. He is always saying something he shouldn't."

John shook his finger at Ben, "Boy, you better behave. Toni, we didn't know if you were going to be here or not. So we didn't bring any food. What would you like, we'll go and get it."

"Actually, I just want a ham sandwich. I've had so much rich food the last few days I want something simple. I've got some pistolettes, ham, and Swiss cheese. There are also plenty of chips and pickles. Would you be interested in joining me?"

"I don't think so. We never get too much rich food so I think we'll head over to Brennan's. Since you are in such capable hands." Ben just gave Jack a look. Luckily Jack has a good sense of humor. "Would you like us to come back after we eat?"

"I don't think so. I'm really tired. I could go to bed now at 6 PM but I'd be awake at 3 AM. Beside, Jack will only be here until 10 PM then someone else will be here. I think I will really sleep tonight. I get the stitches out tomorrow so I'm not really ready to do any more running around than I've already done. You two go and have a good time. John, why don't you come by in the morning with the books. I haven't seen them for a while and I think I need to have something to do."

"OK love. I'll be over around 9:30 AM. I think you'll be pleased. I've been keeping them up and I've kept Ben out of them." We laughed at that. Ben was trying to look hurt but just couldn't bring it off and had to laugh too.

John and Ben left with a kiss on the cheek. As I closed the door, Jack said, "I'm glad Mr. Livingston had told me about those two. I could have been offended if I hadn't known already they are gay. You've got to realize a guy my size anywhere in the French Quarter is asking for a come on of some kind. I don't get as offended as I use to."

"I'm glad you weren't offended. They have worked for me for years. I don't know what I would do without them. Especially now. John and Ben can run the shop completely. I just want the books so I'll have something to do. When you work six days a week, it is hard to do nothing." It's been three days since I left the hospital and two weeks since I looked at anything about the shop. "I don't even take vacations over three days long, so two weeks away is really a long time for me."

"Why don't you fix that sandwich and I'll go in the living room and turn on the TV. What do you normally watch on a Friday night?"

"Not much of anything. Terry and I usually did something else. I would usually go out to my workshop. But I'll be more than happy to watch TV. I can't go out to the workshop. Too many memories. You decide what you'd like to watch and I'll be there in a moment. Would you like a sandwich?"

"No thanks. I've got a dinner date after I get off and that's only a few hours away. Thank you any way."

"It is amazing that restaurants are open for dinner at that time of night. The French Quarter never sleeps and is always ready for anything. Where are you going to go at 10 PM?

Jack followed me into the kitchen. "There are several places on Decatur and some on Dauphine

Street that are good. To night it's a little place on Royal Street call Jack Dempsey's. It's a little neighborhood place that follows the standard New Orleans fare."

"I've been there, that's across the street from a place called The Port. The U. S. Navy has a base there. During WWII it was a booming place. Now it is called the F. Edward Hebert Complex. The food is good there. I guess on a Friday night it will be hopping."

I had made my sandwich while we were talking. Jack poured two glasses of Sun Tea and we headed for the living room. There was a TV tray in the corner by the sofa. I sat everything down and was ready to eat. I just noticed I hadn't heard anything up stairs for a long time. I decided to go up stairs before I ate. "Jack, I'm going up stairs, I'll be back in a minute." I went to the kitchen and fixed up a large jar of tea with some sugar and lemon on the side. Everything fit into a bag with some cups of ice and I took it up stairs.

"Lt. Hanson! I have some tea for you and your men." I didn't get a response. "Lt. Hanson?" I had raised my voice a little. I was about to say it again when Jack was by my side, motioning me to say it again. "Lt. Hanson?" Jack stepped around me and pushed me toward the stairs. He pointed for me to go down the stairs and put his finger to his lips indicating to go quietly. Jack pulled a gun from some where as I started down the stairs.

All of a sudden, Jack yelled. "Get out the front door. NOW!"

# Chapter 9

I dropped the bag of tea and cups and opened the front door. I started running and kept running until I got to Brennan's restaurant. Knowing everyone that works there I ran in. Stopping at the door, looking around until I saw the maitre'd. He was by the kitchen door since no one was waiting at the door. I ran over to him, pushing him into the kitchen. I scared him as much as I was already scared. "Toni, what's wrong? Are you OK?"

"No, call the police. Get them to my house now. Tell them Lt. Hanson is suppose to be there but he doesn't answer. Call them, call them now."

Arthur grabbed the phone and dialed 911. When some one answered he handed me the phone. "This is Toni Tucker at 703 Conti, Lt. Hanson is at my house. But he wouldn't answer when I called for him. My bodyguard told me to run, so I ran. Get someone over there now. I don't know what's happening but there were four policemen there and they didn't answer. Get some one there. Hurry!"

"Ms. Tucker, please calm down. What was Lt. Hanson doing there?"

"He was under cover with three other officers. There was a murder at my house two weeks ago and it was broken into last night. Hurry!"

"I have already dispatched two cars there. Where are you?"

"I'm at Brennan's restaurant, in the kitchen. When I ran, I left the door open. My bodyguard is there too. His name is Jack Armond."

"What does he look like?"

"He's about 5' 6", 170 pounds, brown hair, blue jeans and a gray T-shirt that has and eagle on it. He does have a gun. There's another bodyguard outside some where. His name is Castro and he looks like a young Castro but is dressed like a street person. I don't know where he is. He may be in the house."

"Ms. Tucker, stay where you are. I'll send a car to the restaurant. Do not leave. Do not go back to your house. Stay in the kitchen and two officers will come and get you. They will be uniformed officers. Ask the management there to direct them to you. Do you need any medical attention?"

"No, I'm just shaking like crazy. Just get over there."

"There are officers there now. Try to calm down, the officers will be there in just a moment." With that she hung up.

The maitre'd brought me a cup of coffee. I had to hold it with both hands. "Toni, what's going on? Are you all right?"

"Yes, I'm OK. Just shaken up. Please go look out the door and see if the police are at my house."

He left and was back in seconds, "Yes, they're there. They are all over the place. There are three ambulances and six cop cars. The lights are on and they are searching every where." Just at that time two uniform officers came into the kitchen.

"Are you Toni Tucker?" The first officer asked me.

"Yes. Is Lt. Hanson OK? What about the other officers and my body guard? What's going on? Can I go over there?"

"Yes Ma'am. We'll go there now if you're ready?"

"OK, can you tell me anything about Lt. Hanson and the other officers? They just wouldn't answer when I called to them."

Both officers walked me over to the house. They wouldn't let me in. I could only go as far as the porch. They directed me to sit down. Then no one would talk to me. It felt like a long time that I sat there but it was only a few minutes. The screen door opened and there stood Jack. I jumped up and ran over to him. "What happened? Is everyone all right? Where is Lt. Hanson and the other men?"

Jack put his hand on my shoulder and directed back to the chair. "They will be fine but they will have a very bad headache. Some one came through the roof door and set off a gas canister. It knocked them out in seconds. They didn't have a chance to warn us. When you started up stairs and was calling them and they didn't answer, I got suspicious. That's why I came up the stairs behind you. When I got to the landing I smelled something I had smelled before and knew what it was. Most of the gas was in the bedroom and not in the hall. That's why it didn't effect me. I yelled at you, then held my breath and went to the bedroom."

"Did you see anyone? Was he still up there?"

"Yes, I saw someone. They were going out the attic door. I got one shot off. I think I hit them. If I did it wasn't a fatal wound. I thing it just grazed his upper arm and then not very much."

"You mean I almost walked into them? Boy, I'm shaking all over again. I'm glad I'm sitting down. What did he look like?"

"That I couldn't tell you, all I saw was a shoulder, arm and one leg going through the door. They didn't seem to be too large of a person but I really can't say for sure. I've given all the information I could to the police. Who knows about the roof and attic door?"

"I don't know. We had a house warming party when we bought the house but that was years ago. Terry and I never used any of the attic. We didn't need to. Neither of us are pack rats. The closets aren't even packed with stuff."

"Try and think if you've shown the doors to anyone. Have you had any work done on the house that the workman used either door?"

"No, wait! We had the roof repaired last year. But the company has been in the city for eons. Most of the men on the job have worked on most of the houses in the French Quarter. All of them were bonded."

"Well, think about it. Maybe you'll come up with some one. The police are going to ask these same questions."

"I haven't seen Mr. Castro. You would think he would be here with everything going on."

"You won't see him. Remember he's under cover and doesn't want to give himself away. I did call him and let him know everything was OK. He's still out there looking around. With all the police here he can take some time to look at the different people standing around. I told him I clipped the guy so he'll be looking for that too."

Lt. Hanson walked out the door, holding his head. He saw Jack and I sitting at the end of the porch and walked over. "Thanks Jack. That was a little to close for comfort. If you hadn't opened the window and turned on the ceiling fan, we would have been dead. Man, my head hurts. We've got to go to the hospital to get this stuff out of our systems. Ms. Tucker, I'm glad you're OK. I don't know how this happened. I'm sorry. You can bet this house will be the safest place to be tonight. There are men on the roof, behind your house, on your house. One on each side and two in front. We don't want anyone to mess up anything the man might have left behind. I'm sorry, I've got to get to the hospital. This head is making me sick to my stomach. I'll see you tomorrow." One of the ambulance attendants came and got him and put him in the ambulance. The other officers came out holding their heads and were directed to other ambulances and taken away.

"Ms. Tucker, I'm Capt. LaSalle. I'm sorry to meet you like this. We are grateful to Jack. We talked to Jack and we think we've got the whole story. Lt. Hanson will see you sometime tomorrow and go over everything with you. Please don't go up stairs, we have it taped off for forensics tomorrow. I think you'll be safe here tonight. I've got eight men to make sure the house is secure. Again, I'm sorry and thank you for calling so quickly."

Capt. LaSalle shook my hand and left. The other officers were stationed around the house. Jack and I went back inside. My sandwich was still there but I didn't want it any more. Now it was 9:30 PM and I was spent.

I sat on the sofa and tried to gather up my thoughts. What is happening? In 14 days my life has been turned upside down. There is no reason for it. No one knew about Terry's money. That's the only reason I can think of that could cause all this stuff. Why would some one want to kill me? I don't have a will and according Louisiana law, everything I have would go to my parents. Who is after me? With the events of the evening and my mental questions, I just couldn't think straight.

Jack brought me a cup of coffee and sat across from me. "Ms. Tucker, I'm going to stay tonight too. My relief will be here in a few minutes. I warned the police he would be coming over the roof. But I think you would feel better with some one you know a little better than my relief."

"Thank You, I would feel better with you here. I know I just met you but with the gas and that man in my house and what you did, I would feel better. I am so tired. Since you're going to be here I don't have to stay up and meet your relief. I'm going to bed; I'm done in. Help your self to anything in the kitchen. Good night."

"Good night. Sleep well." Jack turned off most of the lights and put the TV on low. I didn't hear his relief come in. Exhaustion had taken its toll and I slept.

I was awakened by noise in the living room. I put slacks and a T-shirt on and went out of the bedroom. It was 9 AM and people everywhere. Jack saw me and handed me a cup of coffee. "I'm sorry, I tried to keep every one quiet but I guess not quiet enough."

"No, you did very well. I usually don't sleep this late. I was exhausted. Thanks for the coffee."

"Lt. Hanson is here. He's up stairs. Let me let him know you're up." He went to the stairs and yelled. "Lt. Hanson, Ms. Tucker is up. Come have some coffee with us."

Lt. Hanson came down the stairs. "Good morning, how are you feeling?"

"Actually I feel pretty good. Jack has the coffee ready. The question is how are you feeling? Last night you looked like your head was going to pop."

"It was. The gas would have killed us if Jack hadn't gotten to us in time. I'm really glad you thought of us and were bringing us some tea. I guess you did more to save our lives than Jack did. Thank you both."

The forensic people were every where up stairs and the roof. So far they hadn't much to go on. He had worn gloves so no fingerprints. No hairs were found. There was a very small amount of blood by the attic door. The bullet was imbedded in a rafter and attached to it was a tiny piece of leather.

Lt. Hanson took his cup of coffee and we went to the dining room table. There he took out his notebook. "Ms Tucker, I don't have any idea of what is going on. Do you have any idea why some one would want to kill you?"

"Not one. It seems that who ever murdered Terry and almost got me is the one we need to find. I've haven't even gotten a parking ticket before." The doorbell rang. I went to the door and it was Mr. Roux.

"I guess with all the police here I don't have to use the name James Howard. What's going on?"

"Join me in the dining room with Lt. Hanson and my body guard Jack and we'll bring you up to date. There was another break in last night. This time I had lots of protection but the protection all most became the victims. I don't have a clue of what or why this is happening." We explained everything that had happened in the past 18 hours. Mr. Roux was as amazed as the rest of us.

Mr. Roux said we should call Mr. Breaux and let him know what has happened. "I think Mr. Breaux may have some suggestions of what to do. I also want to put in a call to Mr. Livingston for more security here at the house. Does anyone have a problem with that?" Everyone agreed to the suggestions and the calls were made.

# Chapter 10

Mr. Breaux arrived in 10 minutes. Not being a spring chicken I wouldn't have thought he would be here that fast. He brought Mr. Bailey and Mr. Demas with him. Like a commanding general he took charge. His presence alone is enough to make you listen to him. Now we had Jack, Lt. Hanson, Mr. Roux, the three lawyers and myself at the dining room table. If I had been looking in from the outside it would have looked like a war strategy meeting. It all seemed so strange to me. My life had been quite normal until two weeks ago.

Mr. Breaux called his office for Mr. LaFarge to set up lunch for everyone and for some presentation supplies. Everything he asked for was there in minutes. An easel with a large pad of paper was set up at the end of the table next to Mr. Breaux. With that he started to identify what we already knew.

"We need to establish a chain of events and see what we can come up with. I don't think we are all seeing the same picture. Ms. Tucker, may I call you Toni?" I nodded. "I thought we would write down the sequence of events and go from there." That word again sequence. I never want to hear it again.

Mr. Breaux started out like a professor; "The first thing was the murder of Terry Williams and the wounding of Ms. Toni Tucker. Nothing happened until after Toni came home from the hospital. The next item that occurred was Terry's insurance and will. Leaving everything to Ms. Tucker. Next, another break in with two men looking for Toni. She out foxed them. Then with four policeman and two bodyguards one person breaks in, and gases the police with a chemical that almost killed them. Toni had started up the stairs with some tea for the officers and was calling for Lt. Hanson. When there wasn't an answer, Jack stepped in and told her to run. Jack got one shot off and hit the intruder but not hard enough to stop them. Jack saved the officers by venting the room of the gas. Does that seem to be every thing?" Every one around the table agreed. Mr. Breaux continued being the commanding general.

"Mr. Roux, I know you've only been on this for less than 24 hours but have you come up with anything we should know?"

"Not a thing. I have some calls in but so far I haven't gotten anything. I've got six men working on this right now. Three in Europe, one in Hong Kong, one in Iran and one in Washington D. C. As soon as I get something I'll let you know." Mr. Roux didn't seem happy with his part of the puzzle. He felt he should have had more information but he didn't.

"Lt. Hanson, what have the police come up with?"

"Not much more than you have. The gun used to kill Terry Williams was a .357 Magnum with hollow point bullets and regular bullets. The hollow points hit Terry Williams and the regular bullets hit Ms. Tucker. We've never seen anything like that before. There were no fingerprints found from any of the three break-ins. There has been nothing to indicate a reason for any of this. The chemical used on us last night is only found in the military in the United States. It is easier to get in the Middle East. The canister we found is being traced. Right now we don't know the origin of it. We should know some thing today. I'll let you know when I know."

Mr. Breaux made notes on the pad of paper. "Jack, did you notice anything that could help."

"No. The person I got a glimpse of last night was around 5 feet 6 inches tall. As I said before not a large person. All I saw was a shoulder, arm and part of a leg. I'm surprised I hit him. I can't figure out how they got over the roof and through the roof door and the attic door without being heard. Lt., I know you weren't expecting anyone from that direction except for my relief but that person was two hours early for my relief."

Lt. Hanson said, "We didn't hear a thing. The first thing we heard was the canister rolling across the floor. The gas worked instantaneously. All of us went down together." The look on the Lt.'s face was of stress and exhaustion.

Mr. Breaux looked at me. "Toni, have you thought of leaving town? I mean, it seems who ever it is knows this house and you."

"No, I'm not leaving. I know where I am in this city. If I left, first I wouldn't know where to go. Then wherever it might be I wouldn't know the area. I'll stay here. Believe me, I'm very scared but I feel better at home than some place strange."

"OK, I'll call Mr. Livingston and set up more security. We'll have this house covered day and night. I doubt anyone will try anything when they see all the security. Toni, I'd also like someone on the inside too. How do you feel about that?"

"That's OK with me but the more I think of this the more I'm beginning to worry about my parents. I want security for them. I'll call them and let them know what has been going on. They are the only people anyone could harm that could get to me. Please, ask Mr. Livingston to set up security for them."

Mr. Breaux turned to Mr. Bailey, "Bill take care of that right now. I'm sure we can have your parents under protection within the hour." Mr. Bailey almost jumped out of his chair. Pulled a pocket telephone out and started dialing as he headed for the living room.

Mr. Breaux turned to Mr. Demas. "Harry, contact Mr. LaFarge and order groceries for the house. Make sure there is bottled water and everything that will be needed for 10 to 15 people for two weeks. Ask Mr. LaFarge to acquire any thing he thinks he will need." With that Mr. Demas was out of his chair and on his remote telephone.

"Mr. Roux, I think you may need to put more people on this case," Mr. Breaux said with firm direction. "Just tell me what you need and I'll get it for you. Since we don't have a clue as to whom or why all this is happening. We need your people working fast."

With a nod of his head Mr. Roux was out the door and gone. Mr. Breaux hasn't let the police get a word in. But Lt. Hanson didn't seem to want to interrupt. Mr. Bailey came back to the table. "Jeffery, security is started on all points. Mr. Livingston will set up a command center in his office on Rampart Street. He will have everything established by the morning. He has an office in Lake Charles that will handle security of Mr. and Mrs. Tucker. He said they are driving to their house now"

Mr. Demas came back into the dining room, "Jeffery, Mr. LaFarge is on his way. He has people

93

doing the shopping now. He asked if Ms. Tucker would mind a couple of extra appliances in a back room." Mr. Demas turned to me, "Ms. Tucker, I told him to do what ever he needs to do. Is that acceptable?"

"Yes Mr. Demas. Whatever it takes." "Mr. Breaux, I don't want this place looking like a fortress. We are in the French Quarter and every thing is noticed. I bet my neighbors are going crazy. I need to go and talk to them."

"Toni, I think you're right. Mr. Livingston will handle it correctly. I think when you talk to your neighbors that you should let them know we will be providing security for them also. We wouldn't want them used. Someone could use their houses to get into this one. If they would like, we can have someone on the inside of their homes at all times."

"I think I'll go see Mr. Visko now. Who wants to go with me?"

"I'll go." Lt. Hanson got up and started for the front door. "They may feel better with a policeman than a security company."

When we got out side, I took a look around. There were still too many police cars and uniform officers around. Lt. Hanson must have read my mind. "Don't worry they'll all be gone in an hour or so. Then every thing will look like it usually does."

I rang Mr. Visko's doorbell. He doesn't move to well so it took him a while to get to the door. "Toni, It's so good to see you. How have you been? I've been meaning to get over to see you but you know how hard it is for me to get around. I'm sorry about Terry. I really miss him. Who's this man?"

"Mr. Visko, this is Lt. Hanson with the NOPD. He's trying to find out who killed Terry and almost got me."

"Come in and sit down. I can't stand by the door all day." He turned and made it to his recliner and sat down. "Now tell me what is going on dear. I've been seeing a lot of people over at your place, day and night."

"Mr. Visko, the people that murdered Terry are still trying to kill me. I don't know why but they are. Lt. Hanson is providing some security and I've hired a security company to have more. Mr. Visko, who ever this person is, he won't stop at anything to get to me. Because I'm in danger, it puts you in danger."

"Honey, don't worry about me. I've got my shotgun and I'll use it too. Just let that pole cat come over here and I'll teach him."

"I'm sure you could, but I'd like to handle the security myself. Would it be all right with you to have some one in the house with you for a few weeks?"

"Toni, two weeks! The city isn't going to pay for that. They are so cheap, they don't buy the officers bullet proof vest."

"I know Mr. Visko. I'm paying for it. Actually Terry is. He left me some money and I know he would want it used to keep his friends safe. There will also be a couple of people in the front yard and side alleys."

Mr. Visko looked straight at me. I couldn't tell if the look was because he was afraid or excited. He had this little smile on his face. "Toni, I'll do anything I can. Will I be able to leave the house?"

"Of course, we would like to have some one with you when you leave. It's for your safety. Mr. Visko, if you would rather go on a long vacation, I'd be more than happy to pay for it. Would you like to go some where?"

"There isn't any place I'd like to go. I would rather stay here. I don't get around like I use to so I'd better stay home. You can have people in my house if you need too."

"Thank You Mr. Visko, we'll try and get these people caught as soon as possible. Lt. Hanson will bring the first security officer over. Each security officer will call prior to their arrival and be checked before entering your house. Mr. Visko, if there is anything we can do for you, just let me know."

We showed ourselves out and started over to the Ollivett house. "Lt. I think Mr. Visko is going to enjoy all this. The most excitement he's had in years are the Mardi Gras parades." We knocked on the door. We waited a few minutes then we heard Mrs. Ollivett make it to the door and open it.

"Toni, darling how are you doing? We're so sorry about Terry. We wanted to send flowers but we didn't know where to send them. Come in dear."

"Mrs. Ollivett, this is Lt. Hanson with the NOPD, he's heading the investigation into Terry's murder. We need to talk to you and your husband if we may. There have been some other things happen you need to know about."

"Hold on, I'll go get Jacob. He's in the study reading. I tell you, if we have one book we have a thousand and he's read them all." Mrs. Ollivett started down the hall, "Jacob! Jacob! Come out here, Toni is here with the police. Jacob! Come on out here."

Mr. Ollivett met his wife in the hall. "Sarah, I'm not deaf. Quit yelling. What's going on? Toni! How are you doing? Should you be up and around?"

"I'm fine Mr. Ollivett. I do have a problem I need to talk to you both about. May we sit down?"

"Of course. Would you like some tea or coffee? Sarah get some tea." Mr. Ollivett sat on the sofa.

"Mrs. Ollivett, we don't want anything. Please come sit down. I need to talk to both of you." They both sat down and we told them the whole story. They were shocked they hadn't heard anything that had happened at my house.

"Mr. and Mrs. Ollivett, I want to provide protection for you. I'm actually being selfish. Protecting you is protecting me. There are two ways of doing it. The first is that you two stay here and allow security officers in your house 24 hours a day, but I don't know for how long. The second is what I'd really like but it's up to you. I'd like for you to go on a vacation at my expense. Terry left me a lot of money and I can't think of a better way of using it. There is an Alaskan Cruise that leaves tomorrow. I don't want to frighten you but I think leaving is the best course of action. If you were here I would worry about you. Lt. Hanson has enough to think about without having to worry about your security. There isn't much time to think about this. So, what do you say?"

Mr. and Mrs. Ollivett looked at each other then to me. "When would you like us to leave? We've always wanted to take that cruise but you don't have to pay for it."

"Yes, I do. Please let me. When everything is sorted out we'll have a good dinner and you can tell

97

me about your trip. Well, how long will it take you to pack?"

"Sarah, get this Lt. to get the suit cases down. We'll be ready in a couple of hours. Sarah, don't just sit there, get moving."

"Jacob, pack your own clothes. I've got a couple of other things to do.' Mrs. Ollivett was up and moving. Lt. Hanson got the suitcases down for them and we left.

Lt. Hanson was chuckling as we closed their door. "Ms. Tucker, those two are a card. They're pretty spry for their age. I'm glad they are leaving."

Breaux was still in the dining room when we got back. "Mr. Breaux, would you please arrange for a limo to pick up Mr. and Mrs. Ollivett in two hours? I also need the plane made ready for them. They are going on an Alaskan Cruise if we can find one that leaves tomorrow. We need to make arrangements in San Franciso for them to stay tonight, then get them on a cruise ship. I want the best accommodations available. I don't want them to pay for a thing. I'm grateful they're leaving."

The phone was on its way to his ear as he said, "It will be done in a few moments. What about Mr. Visko?"

"He's not leaving. I think he is too excited. It is hard for him to get around but he never was one to travel. He did say we could keep security people in his house all the time for as long as we need to. Just remember who you put in his house will have to listen to him. He'll talk their ear off. This really wasn't the way I wanted to add spice to his life."

Mr. LaFarge made his entrance with four helpers toting food in different stages of preparation. There were four men moving in two refrigerators, a small freezer and cabinet to store food in. Behind them were boxes of food coming in and put into the kitchen. Mr. LaFarge took over the kitchen. He opened every cabinet and drawer like he was taking inventory. The utility room was filled along with an upstairs bedroom. The one item Mr. LaFarge liked the best was a large coffee urn. He could make cappuccino, coffee Au Lait, and regular coffee. Being a city that lives on coffee, everyone was happy to see the urn.

Mr. Livingston arrived with a group of security people. Everyone had a badge on. Mr. Breaux introduced him to me. "Ms. Tucker, I'd like to introduce Mr. Andrew Livingston. He is our security specialist."

"Hello, Mr. Livingston. I'm glad you're here. Mr. Breaux speaks highly of you. I hope we won't need your services to long. I'm not well versed in security so I'll depend on what ever you say."

"It's nice to meet you. We to hope this won't last long. You safety is our only concern. The badges you see are identifications that everyone will have on, or they don't come in without your say so. There is a badge reader on the porch that will scan each person for a badge. If one isn't there, the system will notify us of a security risk. You don't have to swipe the badge through a machine so no one knows about the security badges. I have a necklace for you to wear. It has an electronic chip in it that we can know where you are at any given moment. I mean worldwide. It is set up with a satellite. The necklace is just for now. We usually put one of these tiny things under the skin. I know that doesn't sound pleasant but the alternative is much less pleasant. Dr. V. Talmage will be here soon to insert the device if you agree."

"I would never have thought of any of this. I guess it would be OK. I have to trust you; I don't have a choice. Are you working with Mr. Roux?"

"Yes. I've worked with him before and we do well together. We'll find out what is going on, why someone wants to kill you and who it is. There seems to be some money behind it. Don't worry, we'll get to the bottom of this." With that Mr. Livingston moved off to talk to some of his people.

Mr. Breaux leaned over and whispered. "He is a security nut, but the best in the country and most of Europe. Between Mr. Roux and Mr. Livingston we'll have this solved quickly."

"I hope so Mr. Breaux. I'm scared. I can't believe this is happening anyway. Why didn't Terry tell me about himself?"

"I don't know Toni. He had never been able to live a normal life because of the money he came from. When he came back to New Orleans, he had decided his previous life was over. That's why he had plastic surgery, I think. He really hadn't belonged anywhere and he just wanted to settle down. When he met you, it confirmed his desire to live like everyone else. The few times we got together over the years, I could tell he wasn't happy. He was great at making money. He enjoyed the intrigue of business around the world but it had no lasting enjoyment for him. To him, it was just another deal to be made. You made him happy."

"Thank You, I needed to hear that. I loved Terry completely. I feel a rage inside me. I want to find out who killed Terry and get them put away. I've never hated before, but I do now." Mr. Breaux patted me on the shoulder with understanding. I almost started to cry again. But Mr. LaFarge distracted me.

"Ms. Tucker, I've put a sandwich together for you. I know you haven't eaten today. Now come in the dining room and get some food in you. There's some tea, coffee, milk and juice if you'd like. Do you have an idea of what you'd like for dinner?"

"No, Mr. LaFarge, what ever you would like. Please don't make anything real fancy. I'm not use to a lot of rich food."

"Yes ma'am. I'll fix some thing simple. Now come and eat, you need it." With that he started toward the kitchen. It already looked like his domain.

I had finished the sandwiches and was sitting on the porch finishing my tea. A limo drove up next door. Mr. and Mrs. Ollivett were ready to go. The chauffeur took their bags. They waved to me as the chauffeur opened the door for them. "Have fun, I'll see you in a couple of weeks." They waved again as they got inside the limo. I was beginning to wish it was me leaving and not them.

The more I thought of the Ollivett's leaving the more I wanted to leave. But where on earth would I go? Who would I be running from? I don't think I could stand the fear in a place I didn't know. At least here, I knew how to get around and knew people that would help me.

Lt. Hanson made me jump when he said, "How are you holding up? I know there's a lot going on but everyone is working to protect you."

"I'm sure they are. Lt., what is the NOPD doing? I've only seen you and a few officers around. I haven't heard from Capt. LaSalle at all. Are you letting Mr. Livingston handle everything?"

"Well, sort of. The NOPD don't provide security or protection. We just don't have the manpower to do it. We are investigating Mr. Williams' murder. We will share with him and he'll share with us. We don't have the resources Mr. Livingston has but we are working to find the same thing. Don't worry, we'll take care of you."

# Chapter 11

At 6 PM, Mr. LaFarge announced dinner. He had the dining room set up for Mr. Breaux, Bailey, Demas, Livingston, Lt. Hanson and myself. He kept his promise of keeping dinner simple, red beans, smoked sausage and rice. The best meal there is. Usually this is a Monday meal. The beans would cook all day while the housewives did the laundry. That way two things got done at once.

Everyone enjoyed the meal and Mr. LaFarge was very happy. He had strawberries and cream for dessert with his special blend of coffee. I like the way he does the dishes. He has them put into bins and taken out to his panel truck to be done.

Once everything was cleared away, Mr. Livingston sort of called a meeting together. "Ms. Tucker, we do have some information but not a lot. I thought we would go over it together and see if anyone can add to it. Everyone ready?"

A nod of accent from every one was his cue to start. "We have found Bill and Jenny Williams. They don't live in Michigan. They are actors from New York City. It seems Terry had hired them many times through the years when he thought he needed live parents. Other than being hired by Terry they know nothing about Terry. We did a background check on them and they are just what they seem. So we can take them off the list of possibilities."

"Mr. Livingston, they had no idea why Terry wanted them to pose as his parents?"

"No, Ms. Tucker they didn't. It was an acting job for them and that was all."

Mr. Breaux stood up and Mr. Livingston sat down. "Toni, we've done a back ground check on your employees. Mr. Kingsly and Mr. Dryer are just who they say they are. I know they have worked for you a long time but with something like this we check everyone. Mary Robichaux is who she proclaims to be also. Now that brings us to Joey Clark. He isn't who he seems to be. We did the background check but there isn't any background."

"What do you mean. Joey has worked for Terry and I for years and before that he worked for Terry in his shop. He's only 25 years old, he went to work for Terry at 17 and he's lived here all his life. He has a back ground." I was indignant.

"No, Toni, he's not from here and he's not 25 years old. His name isn't Joey Clark either but we don't know what his real name is. Everything we've learned so far is that Joey hit town a little after Terry did. Right now that's all we know about him. It may take a while, but we'll know more soon. We think he's about 30 years old but it is just a guess."

"I can't believe this! At least John, Ben and Mary are who they say they are. Are you going to talk to Joey? When you do I want to be there. I've never given Joey much thought. He didn't go out with us on Saturday nights but Mary didn't either. He always did his work, was on time and was always there. What else can happen?"

"We thought we'd get you to help us when it comes time to talk to Joey. We were thinking maybe you could have all your employees over here for dinner tomorrow night. If Joey comes, we'll talk to him then. If he doesn't, we'll ask Lt. Hanson to get a warrant for his arrest. Then the interrogation would be an official thing. We'd like to keep this quiet but if we can't, we can't."

I looked at Lt. Hanson; "Do you have grounds for a warrant?"

"Yes, we can bring him in for questioning with out a warrant but we will have one in case he doesn't want to come in on his own. We don't know if Joey has anything to do with Mr. Williams' murder but his back ground just doesn't add up. It's like he didn't exist before he went to work for Terry. Do you mind if we call Mr. Williams by his first name?"

"By all means. Please do. Terry was very friendly and would have liked you to use his first name. Thank you for asking." It was good to use Terry's first name. "Are you going to wait until tomorrow night to see if Joey will come here?"

Lt. Hanson said, "I think that's the best way. We do have a tail on him to make sure he doesn't take off. So far he hasn't changed anything he normally does. We also want to know if he acts the same around you as he did before. That may help us when we talk to him. We'd like for you to call Mr. Kingsly and set up the dinner for tomorrow night. Are you OK with this?"

"More than OK. I want all this settled as quickly as possible. I'll call them now." John and Ben said they would love to come and that they would call Joey and Mary. They would come right after they closed the shop.

Mr. Demas decided it was time for him to talk. "Ms. Tucker, we want you to know we have security protecting your parents. They aren't aware of it but it is there. We thought you would want to talk to them and let them know about it. Just in case they should spot some one and become afraid. I don't know if you want to tell them everything but I think you should tell them something."

"I hadn't thought of them being in danger but it makes sense. I'll call them when we've finished here. Thank you."

The phone rang; it made me jump because it had been quiet all day. "Hello?"

"Toni, this is Mr. Visko. I just wanted you to know that your security people are here. I don't know how many are supposed to be here but so far I've counted five. Do I have the feed them? I don't have much food here. I don't know what to do for them."

"Mr. Visko, you don't have to do anything. We will handle feeding them and you too. I bet you would like some else's cooking for a few days, wouldn't you?"

"That would be lovely Toni. I do get tired of my own cooking. You are such a sweet dear. I've made them some coffee and they seem to be fine. I just wanted to ask what I needed to do."

"Thank you, Mr. Visko. We'll send some food over soon. Now you just do what you normally do and those men will do what their suppose to do. I'll call you tomorrow to see if you need anything. Good Bye."

"Good Bye, Toni."

"Mr. Visko says you have five men over there, Mr. Livingston. I hope they know how to deal with an elderly gentleman that will ask a thousand questions."

"Believe me, they will do fine. This is right up their ally. It's really a little quiet for them so Mr. Visko will be a pleasant change for them." Mr. Livingston chuckled.

Mr. Breaux stood up like a commanding general. "Gentleman, I think it's time we left and let Toni get some rest. Toni, there are nine men in and around the house. Since there has been activity here all day, I doubt anyone will try anything. But rest assured we have you very secure."

There was a knock on the door. Mr. Livingston started for the door. He opened it and said, "Hello Dr. Talmage, I'm glad you're here. We've talked to Ms. Tucker and she has agreed to the insertion of the device. Let me introduce you. Ms. Tucker, this is Dr. Vincent Talmage."

"It's nice to meet you Dr. I hope this isn't going to be very painful."

"No, my dear, you won't feel a thing. It's so tiny and I'll numb the area first. This will only take a moment. I under stand you have a wound in your left chest and left thigh. I thought those would be ideal for insertion. That way there are no new abrasions on the skin. Let me look at the thigh."

"OK, lets go into the bedroom." I lead the way. Mr. Livingston followed Dr. Talmage.

"It's our policy never to leave you alone with another person, no matter how well we know them. I hope you don't mind." Mr. Livingston smiled.

"I don't mind if Dr. Talmage doesn't mind."

Dr. Talmage just smiled and opened his bag. "Andrew, how many years have we worked together? Ten, fifteen and you still insist on security. I do admire you tenacity. OK, here we go. This is the device. As you can see it is less than an eight of an inch around. Now let me see that thigh wound." I dropped my slacks and pulled the bandage back. "That will do nicely." He brought out a spray can and sprayed the wound. It was very cold. "OK, now it's numb and you won't feel a thing." He took a small scalpel and made a tiny cut. He was right I didn't feel it at all. Then he inserted the device just under the skin. Next he spread a paste on the cut. "That is like Super Glue and closes the wound. The numbness will wear off in a few minutes. I'll show myself out."

I put the bandage back on the wound and pulled my pants up. Mr. Livingston and Dr. Talmage left the room and I followed."

"Vincent, thanks for coming so quickly. It's appreciated." I said, as he was ushering him towards the door.

"Any time Andrew, just give me a call when you're ready to remove it." Dr. Talmage left with Mr. Livingston watching him go.

"Toni, I think the rest of us need to leave and let you get some rest. Gentleman lets go. We all have work to do and Ms. Tucker needs to get some rest."

Mr. Breaux, Livingston, Demas, Bailey and Lt. Hanson left. That left Mr. LaFarge with a fresh cup of coffee. There were security men around the house. In the living room, upstairs bedrooms, utility rooms, kitchen and the study. Mr. LaFarge set up the coffee urn with fresh coffee and cups. "Ms. Tucker, I'll leave now. I've written down my beeper number. If you need anything just give me a beep and I'll be here in no time. Is there anything I can get you before I leave?"

"No, thanks. I'm fine. I am tired. What time is it?" I looked at my watch as I asked the question and answered myself. "I can't believe it 11:30 at night all ready. No wonder I'm tired. Good night. I'll see you tomorrow."

As Mr. LaFarge was leaving Jack was coming up the steps. "I'm surprised you're still up. I told Mr. Livingston that you might sleep a little better if I took the night shift. Only because we have already gone through one episode together."

"I think you're right. I will sleep better. There's coffee in the kitchen. I'm going to bed, see you in the morning. Good night."

# Chapter 12

Sleep came quickly. Around 3 AM I woke up. Listened to the sounds of the house. Talk about de'javu. Except this time I wasn't struck with fear. I heard the same floorboard squeak. The fear wasn't there but I did feel a sense of caution. I rolled over and opened the night stand drawer and reached for the gun. Sliding the drawer closed and the gun under the sheets. I relaxed a little with the gun close.

The floorboard squeaked again. That made me relax a little more. You wouldn't think that someone trying to be quiet would step on the same squeaky board. I was drifting off to sleep when the bedroom door opened. It startled me. I sat straight up in bed. It was Jack. He whispered, "Toni, get on the floor. The motion detector outside picked something up. I may be just a dog or cat but we need to be sure."

He was surprised I had my gun with me. I slide to the floor next to him. We moved over into the farthermost corner of the room, with him in front of me. It seemed like we were there for an hour but it was only minutes. One of the guards came to the bedroom door and told us it was all clear.

Jack asked the man, "What was it?"

The guard said, "A cat, dog or something. But it wasn't big enough to be human. Just big enough to set off the motion detector. We have it reset. Everything is clear. Good Night."

"Jack, I can't go back to sleep right now. I think I'll have some coffee and try to sleep later. Will you join me?"

"Sure. My station is the kitchen and dining room. I'll pour, have a seat." The coffee smelled good. I was wide-awake.

"How did you get into the business of being a body guard? Oh, I'm sorry, you don't have to answer. It's none of my business."

He smiled. "I did a stretch in the Army with Jose Castro. He was a Green Beret and we met in the gym. I have a Black Belt in Judo and we use to work out together. He taught me a lot about what the Green Berets do but I didn't want to reenlist to get into the school. Jose convinced me to get out with him and we would work as bodyguards. That's how I got here."

There were dozens of questions I had. "Do you only work in New Orleans?"

"No, Mr. Livingston has offices all over the world. I've been all over. Last month I was in Japan. Security there is a very serious issue. I thought I had learned just about everything there was to learn but I was wrong. The Japanese taught me more in 30 days than I had learned in a year here in the States."

"I know I'm glad you're here. I feel safer with you than the other guards that are here."

"I'm glad to hear that. Why don't you finish your coffee and try to go back to sleep. You're still recovering from some pretty bad wounds. Come on get to bed."

"OK, I'm going. I think I can go back to sleep now. See you in the morning. Sorry, see you in a few hours" I had put the gun under the pillow when I left the room before. I put it back into the drawer and crawled back into bed. I woke up at 7 AM and was surprised I'd slept so long and gone to sleep so quickly.

111

After a shower, I headed to the kitchen. Mr. LaFarge was there. "Good Morning, Ms. Tucker. How are you this morning?"

"I'm great, but please call me Toni. What delights do you have for me this morning? All I know is, it smells good. What is it?"

"Well, if you'll sit down, you'll see. Here's your coffee and orange juice. Now, how about some grits, soft poached eggs and crisp bacon? Please call me Jon."

"You are spoiling me. That sounds wonderful. I am starving this morning. Bring on the food." It came in China too delicate to use. I was afraid to touch it. The bacon was very crisp and perfect. The eggs had a small amount of butter melted around them in a small China dish. I expected some fancy flavored grits but they were plain with butter, just the way they should be. The biscuits were light and delicious. "Have you eaten yet?"

"No, not yet. I wanted to have yours ready for you."

"Well, fix you something and join me. This is delicious. How long have you worked for Mr. Breaux?"

He brought his plate to the table and sat down. "I've been with Breaux, Bailey and Demas for several years. They have a very large client base and I get a lot of people to cook for. Usually, it's for business meetings. I enjoy it. There's a lot of diversity with the people and the food I prepare. I'm glad you like my cooking."

"Liking isn't the right word. I don't know what the right word is but that one isn't it. Your fancy food is only outdone by your everyday food. Those Red Beans and Rice were super. I could have those every week."

"Thank you. Do you have an idea of what you would like for your dinner party tonight?"

"Not really. How about something with shrimp. Not too spicy. Mary can't eat a lot of hot spicy food. I think you know better than I do. I'll leave it up to you."

"All right, I'll think of something nice. Now I've go to get back to the kitchen for a while and order some items I need." With that he got up and left me with my coffee.

I took my coffee out to the porch and sat in my favorite chair. Mr. Visko came out his door waving at me. He made his way over to my porch and a chair. "Good Morning Toni. How are you feeling today?"

"I'm fine Mr. Visko. I hope the security people aren't bothering you. If they are, just let me know and we'll see what we can do."

"No. No. They're fine. I'm enjoying the company. I'm on my way to church; I'll say a prayer for you. Can I get you anything on my way back?"

"No thank you I've got everything I need."

"OK, I'll see you later. I don't want to be late. Father Alex doesn't like it if the door is opened after he has started the Mass. Be careful Toni."

"Bye Mr. Visko. See you later." I sat on the porch for another half-hour. As I was going back in the house, a man opened the gate to my house. The gate is not a quiet one so I turned around. I didn't know who he was, so I hurried into the house. Before I could get the door closed, a security guard was beside me.

"Do you know this person?" he asked.

113

"No. I've never seen him before." Just as he got to the steps the security scanner blinked a green light.

"He's OK. He has the right security scan card. I'll still check him out. Please go into the kitchen. There's another guard there waiting for you." He opened the door and stepped outside. "Excuse me, I need to see some identification, Please."

"Very well. Here's my ID card. I'm Frank Castle and I work for Mr. Livingston. I have some information for Ms. Tucker. May I come in?"

"Yes. Ms. Tucker is in the dining room. Through the door and to your left." The guard reset the scanner and went back to his post.

"Ms. Tucker, my name is Frank Castle. I work for Mr. Livingston. He sent me over with some information you might like to know." We shook hands. He had a very pleasant face. I guessed his age to be around 50.

"Hello, Mr. Castle, please sit down. Would you like some coffee?" He sat down and opened his briefcase.

"Yes, thank you." Jon had a cup ready for him before he sat down.

"You said you have some information for me." For some reason I was apprehensive of what he had to say. So I prepared myself as much as I could.

"Ms. Tucker, our contacts in Europe have discovered who and what Mr. Jules LeBriton was. Mr. Terry Williams used the name in France. He used it to buy arms from Russia. He dealt the arms to Pakistan. Everything was legal. It seems Mr. Williams was in the arms business for three years. He made a mint and got out of it. He did have to deal with the State Dept. from time to time but it was all legal. He did pass information for the State Dept. to Pakistan from time to time but nothing that could hurt the United States."

"Why didn't he use his own name if everything was legal?" I just couldn't see Terry dealing in arms but there it was.

"In Europe, if you're dealing in arms you don't use your own name. People that deal in arms have a tendency not to be the nicest of people. Mr. Williams was young and the opportunity presented its self and he took advantage of it."

"Could those people be the ones after me?" Just the thought of that made me cringe. Knowing nothing of that world didn't make me feel at ease.

"No, we've done a through investigation. All of that was eight years ago and totally in the past. There is no reason to suspect Mr. Williams' contacts in the arms dealings. Not only because of the time that has passed but the people he dealt with have moved on to other things or are dead. Arms dealing is not a healthy business to be in if you're not the one with the money."

"Is there anything else you have for me?" I did feel better. At least knowing what Terry did in the arms business was legal. I couldn't imagine Terry doing anything illegal.

"No, that's all I have. Mr. Livingston thought it best to let you know what we had learned as soon as possible." He stood up to leave. "I have to be going. Thank you for the coffee."

He left me sitting at the table. I just couldn't picture Terry dealing in arms. I was thankful that all that, was in the past and had nothing to do with today.

We still had to find out who Joseph Casio was. Why did Terry use that alias?

The phone rang. I answered. "Hello"

"Toni, this is John. I talked to Joey and Mary and they will walk over with Ben and I. Can we bring anything?"

"No, you needn't bring a thing. Everything is set up and I don't need a thing. So I'll see you at 6:30 this evening. Thanks for arranging this with Joey and Mary. It's been a while since I've seen them."

"You're welcome. We all have been wanting to come over but we didn't want to wear you out. Toni, I've got to go we have a delivery being made and Ben needs my help. See you later. Goodbye."

I kept thinking about Joey. Who is he? Where did he come from and why did Terry keep it a secret? He seemed to be just as he presented himself. I would never have thought of Joey as anything but Joey.

Lt. Hanson knocked on the door. A guard opened the door and asked for identification. When he was satisfied he let the Lt. in.

"Toni, I've come by to take you to the hospital. Have you forgotten you have an appointment to get the stitches out?"

"Yes, I had. Give me a moment and I'll be ready. Have a seat, I'll be right out." I needed clothing that would be easy to get off or just raised up. My favorite, as always, shorts and a T-shirt. "I'm ready when you are."

"Shall we go? I've got a couple of unmarked cars to be around us and there are some undercover officers at the hospital. See, we've tried to think of everything." He opened the car door for me and went around to the driver's seat. He took off. I noticed a car in front of us and behind us. We made it to Tulane Medical Center in just a few minutes. Lt. Hanson parked in a slot marked for police. We took the elevator up to the second floor to Dr. Johnson office. There were no other patients in the waiting room. The receptionist showed me into a little room to wait. Lt. Hanson was waiting out side the door.

"Ms. Tucker, how are you doing?" Dr. Johnson said with a smile. "You must be pretty important. We had to clear the waiting room for you. If you get up here on the table we'll remove those stitches."

I climbed up on the table and raised my T-shirt. Dr. Johnson said, "This looks very good. OK, be still and I'll snip these. It will only take a second. Now, did you feel that?"

"No, I didn't. It's done?"

"Yep, now lets see that thigh." He removed the small bandage and looked at the wound. "It looks good but there is a mark here I don't remember."

"I think I scratched it in my sleep."

"OK, there are only two stitches here. I'll remove them. Be still. All done. I want you to not bandage the wounds any longer. Let the air get to them. They both look good. Unless something changes, I'm discharging you from my care."

"That's great. I do feel pretty good. I'm not ready to run a race but I'm almost back to normal."

"That's all fine and good but don't push it too hard. Those muscles still have some healing to do."

I slide off the table and started for the door. "Thank you Dr. Johnson, I'm glad to be released. No offence but I hope I never see you again."

*Mickey L. Strain*

"I understand. I'm usually not someone you want to keep a long relationship with. Take care and don't over do." We shook hands and I left, almost running into Lt. Hanson.

"Well, lets go Lt.. I don't have to come back here again. Dr. Johnson has released me. I can do what I want just as long as I don't over do." I started off down the hall to the elevator.

"I guess you are ready to go. I'm glad you're feeling better and Dr. Johnson released you. Is there any place you'd like to stop on the way back to your house?"

"No, I can't think of anything. Mr. LaFarge has every kind of food you can think of. So that leaves out the grocery store. I don't need any medicines, so no need for a drug store. No. I can't think of a thing. I'll be glad to get back home. This has been the most activity I've had since I got out of the hospital."

Lt. Hanson opened the car door for me. Then he got in and we started off. By the time I got home I was a little tired. Mr. Livingston opened my car door.

"Hello, Toni. I hope everything went well. You look a little tired." I got out of the car and walked up to the front door. Mr. Livingston and Lt. Hanson followed me into the house.

"Mr. Livingston, do you have any more information for me?"

"No, I just came by to see how you are doing and to check on my men."

"I'm doing fine. Dr. Johnson released me. He just said not to over do anything. I feel pretty good but I do get tired quickly."

118

"Like I said I just wanted to see how you are. I'll be back around 6 PM, before your dinner guest get here. Before they get here I'll be stationed upstairs. We'll also have all the other guards hidden so your guest won't see them." We stood in the living room by the door. Mr. Livingston was ready to leave. "Don't worry about security, it will be air tight. If there is any way possible to get Joey to stay after the others have left please try it. We need to talk to him. I think you should try to talk to him first. If he isn't cooperative I'll come down and talk to him. Lt. Hanson and I that is."

"I'll think of something to make him stay. Just make sure you're here and can hear what is being said."

"Oh, we'll be here all right. Now we have to go and get a few things together. I think you better get some rest. It may be a late night. See you later." They left together. Talking together like children making plans. I don't know why but I felt safer with the two of them working together.

Jon was in the kitchen working up a storm. "Toni, I made you a salad and half sandwich for lunch. I'm preparing for dinner tonight. I sat out several wines for you to choose from."

"Jon, I don't know anything about wine. You'll have to decide which is best for what you're cooking. This salad is wonderful. What dressing is on it? It's great."

"Just something I whipped up for you. I'm glad you like it. Would that be alright for tonight's salad?"

"It will be just fine. What kind of spice did you use on the ham? It's not sweet but yet I taste something that is really good."

"You are tasting honey and ginger with a hint of soy sauce. I've got a patent pending on it. But a patent takes about a year to get. By the way you do look a little tired. Why don't you take a nap? I'll wake you around 5 PM so you'll have time to get ready."

"I think I will. Lunch was delicious, thank you." I went into the bedroom and decided to call my parents before I went to sleep. Dialing the number I was trying to think how to start telling them everything that has happened. Mom answered on the second ring, "Hello."

"Hi, Mom, it's me. How are you two doing." I was trying to be up beat so she wouldn't suspect anything was wrong.

"Hi, Honey. Is everything all right?"

"Yes, everything is fine. How's Dad doing?"

"He's doing fine. He's watching TV."

"Mom, ask Dad to get on another extension. I need to talk to both of you at the same time."

"Henry, pick up the phone. Toni wants to talk to us."

"Hi kitten, how are you doing?"

"Hi, Dad. I'm fine. I need to tell you a few things that have happened since you left. Now don't worry, everything is under control." First I told them about the money. If that didn't put them into shock, I told them about the break in when I hid in the closet and then the break in with the police in the house. At first, they wanted to hop a plane and get down here. I explained the security that I had here and that if they were here I would be more worried about them than myself. Then I told them about the security that was watching them. They were quite surprised. They hadn't noticed anything out of the ordinary.

"Mom, Dad, I don't want you to worry. I've got the best security money can buy and the same security for you. I hired a private investigator to find out who wants me dead. So far there isn't much to go on, but I'm sure everything will be fine. I think it would be better for you to stay home, but If you'd like to go some where, I'll get you there."

"Honey, don't worry about us. We'll be just fine. I think we will stay here. You've got to let us know if we can do anything." Dad always the strong one.

"Dad, I will. I just wanted you to know there may be some people around that you don't know and not to trust anyone. If I know your safe, I'll be able to sleep better."

"Kitten, we are fine. I'll take care of us. You make sure you're safe. Let's make a deal to call each other every day. That way we will all know were fine."

"That sounds good Dad. Let's not set a particular time to call except after 7 AM and before 10 PM. That way we'll be able to sleep without worrying. I've got to go I'll call you tomorrow. Goodbye."

"Goodbye darling, talk to you tomorrow." Mom did sound a little worried but under control. I hung up the phone and laid across the bed. Throwing a light blanket over me. With a full stomach and already being a little tired, it took no time at all for me to fall asleep.

Jon let me sleep until 5:30 PM. He knocked on the bedroom door and I was instantly awake. "Toni, its 5:30. I know I said 5 PM but you looked like you needed the rest. You have an hour before your guests arrive. I hope that is enough time for you."

"It is. Thanks, I must have needed the sleep more than I thought. I'll be out in a little while. Thank you." I got into the shower and it felt great. Taking my time, I found shorts and a T-shirt that went together. I'd been out of the hospital for about a week and there was a pile of laundry to do. I have to get back into doing things. I've got to start my life over, without Terry. The thought of Terry was crushing. Trying not to cry because I didn't want John, Ben, Mary and Joey to see me with red eyes. OK, little girl, get your act together. You've got things to do, now go do them.

Opening the bedroom door, I was hit with an aroma that was heavenly. Fresh baking bread wafted through the house. What a delicious smell. The dinning table was set for five. There was china and crystal I had never seen before. There were flowers placed at different places. All very low arrangements so as not to block the view from one diner to another.

Not being one used to elegant dining, I had to see everything on the table. There were saltcellars by each setting. Three crystal glasses of various sizes and silverware settings three deep on each side of the plates. It was the most beautiful table arrangement I had ever seen. As I was admiring the table, Jon came in.

"I hope every thing is to your satisfaction."

"Are you kidding? You will have to tell us what silver to use for what. This just takes my breath away. My guests tonight are used to hot dogs and potato chips in this house. They won't know what to do."

"Toni, I have a bar set up in the study, with a bartender. Your guest can ask for anything and it will be there. The waiters are very well trained. You won't know they are there. I think you'll be pleased. But please, let me know if something isn't right."

"I feel like I should change clothes to eat at this table."

Jon laughed. "You are perfectly dressed to have dinner in your own home. I've got to get back into the kitchen. We'll be ready when everyone arrives. Now, would you like something to drink?"

"Yes, some of that great coffee you make."

"Coming right up." Within seconds he was there with a cup of coffee.

"Thank You, I'll leave you to your work and go to the living room." When I got to the living room I found more flowers. They were beautiful with a light fragrance that you had to think about to really smell. I put the evening news on the TV and enjoyed my coffee. It seemed like only a few minutes had passed when the doorbell rang. I opened the door to my four friends.

"Hello, everyone. It's so good to see you." We all kissed each other and gave hugs. It was good to see them all. "I am so happy you all could make it. I'm sorry I haven't been to the shop but I really haven't been up to it. I just got released from my doctors care so I'm up and running.

Mary was holding my hand. "Toni, you do look much better than when I saw you last. I'm so glad there is no lasting impairment."

"Thank you Mary. I am a lot better. Time does heal all things." I looked over to Joey. He was always a quiet person, always in the background. "Joey, I'm glad you came. Give me a hug." We hugged. I could tell there was something wrong but I had no clue of what. But I was determined to know before the night was over. "Joey, Mary, I want to thank you for all your hard work at the shop. John and Ben have told me that they couldn't have done everything with out you two. I'm so lucky to have you as friends and employees. Your friendship means alot to me. Now, lets enjoy the evening."

"John, Ben, take a look in the study. I think you'll like what you see. Take Mary and Joey with you." As soon as Ben hit the door he let out a scream. "Girl! Are you moving up town or what? Are you sure you have enough booze here for John and I? Mary what would you like?"

"I'll have a Tom Collins, but on the light side, thank you."

I took Joey's arm. "What would you like?"

"I'll have a beer if you got one."

"What kind. I think there are about 15 different kinds."

"I'm a little hard to please, so how about a Miller Lite?" Joey smiled.

The bartender was pouring the beer in a tall frozen beer glass before I knew it. The bartender seemed to know Joey, but didn't say anything. I observed a slight acknowledgement between them as Joey nodded his head.

"I'll have a Bacardi Cocktail on the rocks." The bartender fixed it and handed it to me. It was perfect.

"OK, everyone lets go into the living room and enjoy our drinks." We made our way to seats. Mary sat in Terry's recliner, I in mine. John and Ben took the sofa and Joey took the last chair.

"I'm very glad you all could come. I know it's hard for you. It is for me too, but I know that life goes on. Terry would not want us to be sad. He loved you all just as I do. I know you have lots of questions and so do I. I'll try to answer what I can. You must know there is a lot I can't answer because I just don't know the answers."

Mary was never a timid person and wasn't now. "Toni, do the police have any idea who murdered Terry?"

"No, not yet. They are working on it. I've also hired a private detective to help them out. But right now there is nothing to go on."

John said, "Toni, how are you doing? I see the thigh wound. I'm glad you don't have to bandage it anymore. How is the chest wound?"

"It's going very well. I was released from my doctors' care, so that should say something. He just said not to over do it for awhile." We chatted for a while, but Joey didn't really join in. The bartender got a work out from John and Ben.

At 7:15, Jon came into the living room to announce that dinner is served. John laughed saying, "A chef of your own? Wow. I could get used to this."

There were nameplates at the settings Jon wanted us to sit at. John and Ben immediately stuck their little fingers out. We all laughed at them. Jon had the waiters bring out a small bowl of cream of cauliflower soup for each of us. Again Jon had created a culinary masterpiece. Mary was impressed and wanted to ask for the recipe. Ben was aghast at the mere suggestion of asking the chef for a recipe. That brought us all a good laugh. Any time we saw Ben mortified was of great delight. The soup bowls were gone by magic and a light salad replaced it. The salad dressing was just as good as it was at lunch. There was fresh wine between each course of the dinner. The salad plate disappeared just like the soup bowls. We were all waiting for the main course with great anticipation. We weren't disappointed. A plate covered with a large silver doom was placed before each of us. With each of us having our own waiter, the dishes were all uncovered at the same time. John and Ben had Shrimp Scampi over pasta. Mary had boneless Cornish Hen with Wild Rice Dressing. Joey and I had Prime Rib and baked potato. There was asparagus with hollandaise sauce for each of us. Everyone was thrilled with the chef's choice.

Mary said, "How did he know I didn't care for a lot of fancy food?"

"I told him you did not like a lot of spicy food. He listened very well. I hope you enjoy it. It does look good."

"It's better than good. I'm savoring this. My complements to the chef." Mary seemed so happy that she was thought of.

Joey had a big smile. "How did he know I love steak?"

That I don't know but, I didn't say a word. Mr. LaFarge had met John and Ben before, so I'm not surprised with their dishes."

The waiters were gone again. We all ate and laughed. Joey participated more in the conversation. As each of use finished our meal, the plates were removed. Coffee was poured for each of us. We lingered over the coffee. When we were just about to retire to the living room, dessert arrived. Each plate had a small slice of peanut butter pie a slice of key lime pie and an almond cookie. It was great. Everyone seemed to enjoy it all.

We made our way to the living room. Each taking the same seats as before. We were so full. It was so nice being there with friends. Having enjoyed an excellent meal and just relaxing. If we had sat there a few minutes more being quiet, we all would have been asleep.

John and Ben got up. "I'm sorry Toni but we have to leave. Were supposed to meet some people over at Papa Joe's. We had already made the arrangements before you called about dinner. I hope you don't mind?"

"No, not at all. I'm glad you enjoyed yourself. I'll give you a call tomorrow."

Mary got up. "I've got to leave also. Tonight is the weekly salvation mass at St. Louis Cathedral. I promised Father Alex I would be there."

"That's OK Mary. I know how fond of Father Alex you are. Tell him I said hello." I turned to Joey. He was about to get up.

"Joey, please stay a few minutes. Let me see them to the door. I'll be right back." We said our good byes with hugs and kisses. I went back and joined Joey.

"I'm glad you're staying a few minutes. I need to talk to you about Terry." It seemed like Joey was no longer happy to be here. "Joey, Terry had millions of dollars. Did you know that?"

*Mickey L. Strain*

"No, I did think he was well off but not a millionaire. Why do you think I would know anything like that?"

"Well, it seems that you have known Terry longer than the rest of us. That's why I thought you might have known. Where did you meet Terry?"

"I applied for a job in his shop on Decatur Street." Joey wasn't looking at me any more. He was staring at his feet.

"Joey, that's not true." His head whipped up.

"What do you mean?" There was fear in his face.

"I know Joey isn't your real name. What is your real name?"

"I don't know what you mean. Joey is my name!"

"No, it isn't. I had a background check done on you. Joey Clark didn't exist until he went to work for Terry, eight years ago. Something else doesn't ring true, your age. You're not 25 like you pretend to be. Joey, there have been a few things happening since Terry's murder. Right now you are one person that can answer some questions for me."

"I don't know what you mean! What has happened?"

"Well Joey, there have been some attempts made on my life. Two as a matter of fact. Do you have any idea about Terry's murder and why some one is after me?"

"Toni, I! Well, I! No, I don't know! I can't imagine! Toni, I can't tell you anything. I don't know anything."

"Let's start with first things first. What is your real name?"

128

"Toni!" Joey was ringing his hands like he didn't know what to do. "You've got to promise not to tell anyone."

"Joey, the police know about you not having a background. They have hit a dead end. I may be able to satisfy them but I can't do it without your help. Talk to me. I think you know you can trust me."

"I don't know. I guess. But Toni!

"Joey you've got to tell me, now."

"OK, OK, Terry was in France. We worked together."

"I know about the arms dealing Terry did."

"You do? OK then, Terry had hired me and my father to smuggle arms to Israel. Most of the dealing Terry did was legal; I'd say 99%. He had some friends in Israel that were in a bind. They were in a new kibbutz and having problems with Arabs attacking. They had the manpower to handle the attacks but they didn't have the arms. They were losing people at a rapid rate. Other kibbutz tried to help but they needed their arms just as badly." Joey got up to pace.

"Come on Joey, go on."

"My father and I decided the job would be safe enough. We had false papers. The arms were hidden in farming tool crates. Broken down so no one could tell what they were. Each box weighed about 500 pounds. We got spaces on a freighter for 20 crates and us. Terry paid for everything. Terry was going to pay us about $25,000 American each. Terry didn't force us to do it. We wanted to help him and his friends. You see we knew them too. We wanted the money too. My folks and I were poor. Terry paid us a fair wage for work done. Terry had helped us a lot." Joey started pacing again. He seemed to be feeling better about telling me about this.

"Go on Joey."

"Well, Father and I were on the freighter and we arrived in Tel Aviv. Everything went according to plan initially. We had a truck on the wharf to handle the crates. We were going to a kibbutz just north of Petah-Tigwa. Thats a 150 kilometer from Tel Aviv. We made our way through Petah-Tigwa and we were hit by an ambush. The terrain was rock and sand. The trucks were shot off the road and stuck in the sand. There were 20 men with the trucks but the ambush was too effective. I was hit in the shoulder and my father was killed. I pretended to be dead. I was lying under the dead driver of the truck I was in. They didn't check too good and missed me. The Arabs got the weapons and the trucks. The Arabs murdered the men that were still alive. They just went around shooting people in the head. Then they were gone. I lay there for at least an hour afraid to move. Afraid they would come back. I made my way to Petah-Tegwa and to a doctor. I was there for three weeks. Then I flew back to France with my fathers body." Joey stopped pacing and looked at me. "Toni, no one from there would be after you. Terry had cut ties there many years ago. Besides he was known as Jules LeBriton, with a complete back ground from birth to death. No one knew anything about what we did that one time. And that was the only time it was ever tried. Terry felt to bad about my fathers death and my injury he quit arms dealing right then."

"Joey, why didn't Terry tell me any of this?"

"He didn't think he should. It was in another life, another time. A time he didn't want to remember. I know I reminded him every day of it but I tried not to. Terry tried to give me a lot of money to make up for what happened. That wasn't what I wanted. Terry brought me to America and let me work for him. I'm not illegal. I did change my name. My old name was Francois Arcenaux. And I mean my old name. I am Joey Clark. I worked hard to get rid of my accent. It took two years of speech lesson but I don't sound like I came from France. I sound like I've live in the bayous of Louisiana. Toni, I'm sorry Terry didn't tell you but I think you can understand why. But there is no one after you from what Terry and I did in France or Israel, No one."

"Joey, why did Terry have plastic surgery to change his face?"

"That's another reason why no one would know. He did that as a precaution. He had made a trip back to France to make sure his face wouldn't be recognized. No one did. Even the people he dealt with directly didn't recognize him. Beside, everything he did was legal, except that one time." Joey looked exhausted. "I'm glad you know now. But you can be sure there is nothing from Terry's past that I know of that could bring you harm. I don't have a clue who murdered Terry and is after you. I have thought and thought but I don't know of any reason for anyone to have murdered Terry. Much less someone being after you. I'm sorry I couldn't help you."

"Joey, you helped me. More than you know. Now I can look in another direction. I don't know what that is yet but I'll find it. Thank you, Joey. I really appreciate it. I know it was hard for you. Please know that I had to know. I want to live and I've got to find out who and why someone wants me dead. I can't think of a thing I could have done to cause someone to do this."

"I've got to go Toni. I'm tired. I'm glad you know everything now but please keep it to yourself. None of it is illegal now but I just don't want to deal with it again."

"Don't worry, Joey. I'll keep it a secret. You and I will never mention this again. I can't think of a reason why we should. Thank you again. Go home and get some rest." I walked Joey to the door. We hugged and he was gone. I locked the door and went into the dining room and got myself some coffee.

It only took a few minutes for Lt. Hanson and Andrew to join me. They both grabbed a cup and poured themselves some coffee. We all took a seat at the dining table. We just looked at each other. Lt. Hanson started, "He is right. All this happened to long ago to allow any charges to be made. Beside, what kind of charges could I make? It was all in a different country. He hasn't done anything illegal. Changing his name is very legal. He must have done it in another state, that would explain why we didn't find it."

"Well, where does that leave us. I got Joey to tell us about himself. I did promise him I would keep it to myself. I hope you will honor that promise."

"No problem. It's none of our business. It effects only the direction we look for who is after you. Don't worry Toni, we won't tell anyone. Right Andrew?"

"Right."

"Now what?"

"We have to catch one of the people after you. I'm not sure how were going to do that but Andrew and I will find a way." Looking at Lt. Hanson, I could see the concern on his face.

Andrew nodded agreement. "We'll figure something out. It's late; we'll leave now. There are 15 men stationed around here so you'll be safe. We'll be back tomorrow and go over a few things and see what we can come up with. Thank you for your help Toni. I know we wouldn't have gotten that information from Joey. Only you could have done that. At least we know we have to go in another direction. Come on Lt., let's get out of here."

"I'm coming. I'm tired too." They both left me in the dining room thinking about what I had heard tonight.

I was tired too. I got up and went to my bedroom and got ready for bed. After I got in bed, I kept running over everything Joey had told me. Somewhere along the line I fell asleep.

# Chapter 13

I awoke again to the smell of the rich aroma of coffee. Looking at the clock on the nightstand. It was 7 AM. I'm getting pretty good at sleeping late. Laying in bed mulling over what has happened to my life in just three weeks. Losing Terry has been the hardest to handle. His lies, I still can't understand why he never told me about himself. I'm sure he wouldn't have thought I would want his money. Especially since I didn't know he had it. Why the fake parents? Did he think not having live parents was a problem for me? But why? All this just makes my head spin.

There still isn't any reason to come after me. I had nothing to do with what Terry did before we met. He never said anything about it. If what Joey says is true, there still is no reason to fear his past. I do believe Joey. He didn't have to tell me anything.

There is another alias that has to be checked out, Joseph Casio. Mr. Roux hasn't come up with anything yet. I need to call him today. I think we need to search the house and the shop. Maybe Terry hid something. At least, with me asking for a search I can get them to do it without destroying everything. I don't think I'll let Lt. Hanson in or the search. I don't know why, it's just a feeling I have. I have no reason to believe Terry has done anything illegal. But. There's that but again. I just don't know what to think.

Maybe I should leave town for awhile. I have no idea where to go. I can't go to my parents. They're already in enough danger, so I can't go there. I could go to one of Terry's condos but I don't know anything about those places. Besides not knowing anyone there wouldn't be to smart. With not knowing who or why someone wants me dead, I think I'll stay right here. At least here I know what is around me.

I've got to get out of this house for awhile. I need some fresh air and I need to do some walking. Exercise is what I need. That thought brought tears to my eyes. I use to tease Terry about all the exercising he did while I did none. Come on Toni, ole girl get your act together. Get up, get dressed and go have some of that great smelling coffee.

I got up and took a shower. Again a favorite T-shirt and shorts were donned and out I went for coffee.

In the kitchen I found Mr. Livingston and Lt. Hanson. I looked at my watch and it was 8:30. I must have dozed off. I couldn't have thought that long or been in the shower that long.

"Good Morning. How is everyone this morning?"

I must have startled them; they all jumped a mile. Lt. Hanson almost spilled his coffee. He laughed. "Good Morning. I wish I could have slept this late. I couldn't sleep. I kept running everything over in my mind. I didn't get to sleep until midnight and woke up at 5 AM. Habit I guess. I get some of my best ideas in the middle of the night."

"Well, did you have a good idea?"

"As a matter of fact I did. The last two days there has not been an attempt on your life. I asked myself why. What I came up with was there is too much activity around here. We've got to make it look like we're pulling out. Since the perpetrator knows about the roof entrance. We've got to make another way of getting into the house. And the two houses on each side. Mr. Visko's house has a common wall with the shop next to it. We need to talk to the shop owner and Mr. Visko about doing some remodeling. Now all we have to do is make some kind of passageway between Mr. Visko's house and yours."

"Your idea is pretty good Lt.. I like the train of thought but there is nothing but a page fence between the houses. The wall at the sidewalk that creates the courtyard only covers the sides only up to the house. I can't think of anything that could be used to cover people moving back and forth. Wait! The workshop in the back has a common wall with the building behind it. I think it's a business but I can't remember what it is. Or who owns it. That would be a good way to get people in and out. Unless they're on the roof and watching the back yard. What do you think?"

"Toni, I think you've got it. We can still keep extra men at Mr. Visko's. I'll find out who has the business behind you and next to Mr. Visko and make arrangements. Andrew you've been pretty quiet, what do you think?"

"I think it's a great idea. Why didn't we think of it? I'll check the Ollivett house and see if they have a common wall. Lt., I think you're right about too much activity here. That is surely the reason no one has tried again. I think we'd better go and get things started. Come on Lt. let's go and get this show on the road."

They didn't even finish they're coffee. The more I thought about it the more I thought it would work. This way I could leave the house and they could wait for who ever it is. I'd have to be seen during the day but at night I could leave and be safe somewhere else. I could go to a hotel or to John and Ben's. To have an evening that was normal again would be heaven. Just the thought of not waking up to every little noise that seemed out of the norm. I think I'll stay at the Hyatt. A room with a hot tub and a massage after. I'll rent a movie and drink some wine and enjoy a quiet safe evening. Just the thought of being alone and safe was delicious.

I wonder how long it will be before I can do it. There were permissions to get. Construction work to be done and done quietly. If I figured it right it would be at least four to five days.

The Ollivett's will be gone for another four weeks. Mr. Visko wouldn't be a problem. He's having too much fun. The men that have stayed over there have said he's like a two-dollar radio with a broke switch. Their only saving grace is he can't stay awake past 9 PM and he doesn't get up until 7:30 AM.

If everything can be rushed a little, I can have some peace of mind at least at night. There are so many things I worry about with out even knowing it. Who is doing this? Why are they doing it? The one conversation I heard said there is a man, The Man. Who is The Man? What does he want? I know he wants me dead but what will that get him? Until Terry's murder, I didn't have any money. We still don't have a reason for Terry's murder. I just don't know about any of this. I forgot to call Mr. Roux and to get him to search the house. Maybe, just maybe there is something here that I don't know about and he can find it to clear this mess up.

Well, there is no time like the present, so I called Mr. Roux. "Mr. Roux, can you come by the house this morning? I've got an idea I'd like to discuss with you."

"Sure, I'll be there in an hour. I've got some news for you too." Mr. Roux hung up. I wonder what he has for me. Maybe we won't have to search the house after all.

The coffee caught my attention again. I refilled my cup and went out on the porch to my favorite chair. It was another beautiful day. The sounds of the French Quarter were all around. There has never been a time that I didn't enjoy the sounds and smells. It just gets in your blood and you can't get it out. I think I'll talk to Andrew and see if I can take a walk to the shop today. I need to get out of this house. I want to have a stroll through the French Quarter for a couple of hours. Go down to the French Market and pick up some fruit. Stop by Café Du Monde and have some Beignets. Watch the Mimes in Jackson Square along with the artist and their work. I must be getting cabin fever with the way I'm thinking.

The front gate opened and Mr. Roux walked through. He seemed happy and excited. He looked like he had something to say.

"Hi, Ms. Tucker. I hope you are feeling better today. It is such a beautiful day. I couldn't wait to get over here. I found out about the name Joseph Casio."

# Chapter 14

"Joseph Casio! That's great. What have you got?"

Mr. Roux started with a big grin. "Well, you'll never believe it. Mr. Joseph Casio was in the Peace Corp in Peru. He was there for one year. He taught them sanitation, plumbing and irrigation."

"What! You've got to be kidding. Terry was a Marketing Major not an engineer. I didn't think he knew anything about plumbing."

"Well, he did. He secretly used his money for supplies. He built hundreds of toilets in Peru. He taught them how to build a sewer system that worked with natural bacteria instead of chemicals. Because, chemicals aren't accessible to them. He had some guy working with him for a while but he moved on. He showed them how to build irrigation systems for their farms and to use the cleaned sewage as fertilizer. He had books printed in their language with lots of pictures in them. Most of the people couldn't read so he taught them using the pictures."

"You're right I don't believe it. This seems so unreal. Why didn't he tell me? It seems so strange."

"Well it seems that in the middle of college he decided to take a hiatus. He wanted to do something. He was too young to be a hippie but he was trying to be one anyway. So he joined the Peace Corp. He went to a country that was backwards and in need."

"Well, you could knock me over with a feather. As long as I knew Terry, he gave to charities but within limits."

"That is probably because he felt the Peace Corp wasn't doing enough with what they got. He would ask for supplies. A few shipments would show up but others would disappear. He did his own investigation and found the supplies were being pilfered all along the line. He felt if they put some one with the shipments that the supplies would get to where they should. He felt the Peace Corp really didn't care. By his calculations, the money taken in by the Peace Corp and what was distributed didn't measure up. Everything he ordered himself and paid for got to him."

"You said he was there for only one year. What happened to make him change his mind?"

"It seems he had worked in two villages. The provincial government sacked both villages. He and most of the villagers hid in the forest. But the soldiers destroyed everything. It was like they didn't want anyone to be better off than them so they smashed everything. After that, he came back to the States and went back to college. He did set up a independent trust for the two villages that provides goods to them every Christmas."

"I'm in shock. At least this alias was used for something good. Being an arms dealer wasn't good. I'll have to call Mr. Breaux and make sure the trust is maintained. I just can't see Terry doing labor and teaching. I'm learning a lot about Terry I would have never thought of. Thank you Mr. Roux."

"You're more than welcome. I'm still working on trying to find out who is after you. So far I haven't had much luck. I'm trying to find out what relationships he had before he met you. I've talked to Joey Clark and

140

I'll talk to Mary Robichaux tomorrow. I'll let you know what I learn as soon as I can."

"You might want to talk to Mr. Breaux to find out where Terry has lived and when. He kept up with him because of the work he did for him."

"I've talked to him. I have started working in various places. It shouldn't take too long. Ms. Tucker, I've got to get going. I've some calls to make and the time zones vary with each call."

"Oh, I almost forgot. I was thinking about doing a search of the house. I was thinking that you would want to do it. To look for something that might help identify who killed Terry. I didn't want to talk to Lt. Hanson. I don't want the police to do it. Do you think it's a good idea?"

"It's a great idea. I thought about it but I didn't want to impose. If you like I can have two people here this afternoon to do it. Professional investigators that won't destroy the house."

"Very good, I'll be here. They'll have to have identification for the bodyguards to let them in. Call Mr. Livingston to set that up. Again, thank you for the information. You are appreciated, thank you. I'll be waiting this afternoon for your investigators." I walked him to the door and he was gone.

I'd better go through a few of my things. I can't think of anything I'd have that I wouldn't want some one to see. There are a few poems that I really don't want to share. I'll go get them and set them aside and tell the investigators not to go through them. I poured another cup of coffee and went up stairs.

The stairs were getting easier to navigate. The twinge of pain in my thigh brought thoughts of Terry. I had to think if I was ready to read some of the poems. Yes, I think I am. I miss Terry so very much it hurts. I wish I had known the other parts of Terry's life. Thinking of Terry as an arms dealer was hard. The more I thought about it the more I got use to it. He was legal. He didn't mean to get Joey's father killed. He was trying to help someone. His actions after Joey's father's death indicated the remorse Terry felt. And being in the Peace Corp was honorable. I would never have thought of doing something like that. Terry was always kind. I never thought much at the time but now I understand a little more of when he saw someone poor and gave the money.

I found my little mementos box in the closet. My mother had made it years ago before I went to college. It had pictures of the family on the top. It was a special picture with my brother in it when we were a whole family. Mother had painted it and embossed pictures of me at various times of my life. She was always creating something.

Inside I found Terry's poems. Each was so sweet. He always had a way with words. I found the first ring Terry had given me. It was a slight band of gold with a small pearl. Very simple and elegant, like he was. He had given it to me only a few months after we met. He had taken me to the La Petite Theater to see 'The Death of a Salesman'. We enjoyed the play and went out for coffee afterwards at Café Du Monde. It was there he gave me the ring. He had said he just happen to see it in a store window and it reminded him of me. Looking further, I found an old diary of mine. One that I had when I was in college. Opening it I found my list of things I wanted in a man. It made me laugh. I hadn't seen it in years. The list started with; 1) Good Looking, that was Terry. 2) Good in business, Terry was great in business. 3) Generous, He was more than generous. 4) Patience, With me he always was. 5) Cultured, Terry was that too. 6) Rich, Well that one is an understatement. Terry filled my entire wish list and I didn't even know it. We had been so compatible in everything. If I had ever read this list while Terry was alive, we would have had a great laugh over it. Terry was the answer to all my dreams. I'm sorry I didn't know it when he was alive, as much as I do now.

I found pictures of my first boyfriend. I don't know what I saw in him. But when you're 15 years old what do you know. Anyone that pays attention to you at 15 is a dream. There was also a picture of girl friends from high school and college.

At the bottom of the box I found an envelope I'd never seen before. How did this get here? It was sealed, I turned it over and in Terry's hand writing it said 'For Toni, In case of my death. Do not open otherwise.' Terry had to of put it there but when? I was afraid to open it. It could contain all the answers to my questions or it could be something I don't want to know about. I closed up the box and put it on the bed. Taking the letter and my coffee cup I went down stairs. The envelope was thick and legal size. I laid it on the dining room table. Looking at it I wasn't sure I wanted to open it. Thinking about the envelope I almost dropped my coffee cup. The cup was almost empty so I went to the kitchen to fill it. I wanted to open it but I was afraid of what I might find. Terry had so much in his life he had never told me about. Is this something else to surprise me with? Can I take being surprised again? Sitting at the table I just stared at the envelope. I don't know how long I stared at it but the doorbell ringing brought me back to reality.

A bodyguard came from the study to answer the door. I had forgotten about the bodyguards being there so I was startled when he appeared. He answered the door and let two men in. "Ms. Tucker, these men work for Mr. Roux. They say you are expecting them."

"Oh, yes, I almost forgot. You must be the men to search the house." They wore jeans and T-shirts on. The T-shirt had AJ's Plumbing. There was even a van outside with the same logo. Each had two toolboxes with them.

"Yes. Ms. Tucker we'll start up stairs and work our way down. The toolboxes have the tools we need. If we feel the need to remove a windowsill or door jam. We'll start in the attic and go from there. This may take more than one day. Don't worry about a mess, there won't be one. If we take something apart we'll put it back together. We've done this many times and know how to put things back. Not like the police who don't care how they leave things."

"Thank you. That's why I talked to Mr. Roux about the search. Did he tell you what to look for?"

"In essence. We will be looking for anything related to Mr. Terry Williams that could identify who or why he was murdered. We've done this a few times and know what we're doing. We'll sit down with you when we are finished and go over what we've found. I'll let you know everything and what we think will be of help to Mr. Roux in his investigation. Don't worry, we work for you."

"I guess you want to get started. There is coffee in the kitchen, so help your self."

"Thank you, we'll have some later." Both men donned surgical gloves and started for the stairs.

"What are the gloves for?"

"Oh, sorry. If we find something that we think should be finger printed, we don't want our prints to mess anything up. I know the police didn't find any prints after the break-ins but we might."

"OK, thanks. I'll stay out of your way. Let me know if you need anything."

The men started up stairs. I couldn't imagine what they would find. I thought about the break-ins and hoped they would find something about them. Maybe, just maybe, they would find some evidence to find out who broke in and who hired them.

Then I thought about the letter on the table. If I can get the nerve to read it, I may not tell them about it. I'm just not sure I want to read it. But, at the same time I want to know what Terry has to say. I went back to the dining room table and sat down. The envelope just sat there and so did I. I took a deep breath, which caused a little pain in my chest. With a grimace I took the envelope and started to open it. I noticed the envelope was old. It had started to yellow. Wonder why I hadn't noticed that before. How long has it been there? I finished opening it. There were about five or six pages. Unfolding it, a key fell out. A bank box key. We didn't have a bank box. God another mystery. I didn't want to go any further but my curiosity was stronger than my fear.

*Mickey L. Strain*

Dear Toni

If you're reading this, I must be dead. I'm sorry, honey. I didn't want this to happen but I knew it could. There's a lot to explain and I'll do my best. I'm sorry I'm not with you. I love you with all my heart. I'm sorry I put you in danger. Just being with me put you in danger but I couldn't live without you. I thought in the beginning that I should leave you but my love for you was too strong. Forgive me, my selfishness. You made me happy and you made me feel complete. You made my life worth living.

By now you've met my lawyers. You can trust them implicitly. They have worked for my family for over 30 years. Please listen to them. They know what is best for you.

I know you must be shocked with the wealth I have. I was born into money and I'm sure Jeffery, Mr. Breaux has told you how I increased the family wealth. I made choices in my life. Some I'm proud of and some I'm not. I'll try to explain the best I can so bear with me.

One of my good choices was joining the Peace Corp. while in college. I was sent to Peru to teach sanitation, plumbing and irrigation. The Peace Corp. taught me what I needed to know. I was sent to Tennessee for training. That took about three months. When I arrived in Peru and

146

found the village I was assigned to, I found abject poverty. Something I didn't know how to cope with initially. The money from the Peace Corp was of little use because it was such a small amount. I immediately contacted Jeffery for what I needed. I taught what the Peace Corp wanted. The tools used by the locals worked but I had to learn to use them. I learned more from them and not just tools and how to use them. The natives are peaceful and full of love. As you know, I was there only a year. I became disillusioned with the Peace Corp. Every time they sent supplies they were missing more than half the order. What was received had been picked over by government officials all along the way to the village. Despite the lack of supplies from the Peace Corp. we didn't accomplish a lot. Jeffery would send me things needed from time to time. I worked in two villages close to one another. When the sanitation systems were functioning and the irrigation system was in place the government came and smashed all of our work. I fled with the villagers to the forest until the soldiers left. After that I came to the United States. You'll find I have set up a trust for the villages I worked in. I only send things there at Christmas. I hope you will continue the trust. I'm sure you will. I believe I know you well enough to know you will keep it going.

You probably know about my time in France. Yes, I was an arms dealer. I thought I could do some good by getting weapons to parts of the world that needed them. People that were striving for freedom. I'm sure you've talked to Joey by now. I told him that if anything happen to me, that you would help him. Please do. I am the cause of his fathers' death. I owe him so much, I know I can never repay him. The guilt I feel about his death is still overwhelming. I sent Joey and his father to Israel to smuggle guns to a friend. They were ambushed and many died. I want to take care of Joey. He has never asked for anything. He doesn't know how wealthy I am, but even if he did, he wouldn't ask for anything. I quit dealing in arms while the deaths occurred. But I had lost faith not only because of what I had done but I found weapons were not the answer. No matter how many weapons there are, the people striving for freedom won't have enough. After the smuggling incident I realized I had caused many deaths by dealing arms. I had to leave it. You know by now that I had plastic surgery. I had to. The people you deal with in the arms trade are not people you just walk away from. I had my face done. Afterward I went back to France to make sure no one would recognize me. No one did.

I decided to come to New Orleans and live like a normal person. I was tired of living the jet set life. People there only want your money or what they think you can do for them. Having my face done helped with that too. I went to New York where I'd spent some time. The people that I knew before didn't know me either. So I knew I could live in New Orleans without fear of being found by anyone of my previous lives.

I opened the shop using my money. After that I lived on what I made. As you know it makes a nice living. Not rich but enough to live well and to do as we pleased. I'd had the shop for three years before I met you. Meeting you has brought nothing but joy to my life. I'm sorry I deceived you. I am so happy with you. Our life together has been the happiest time of my life. I was afraid to let you know about my wealth. I didn't want anything to change our life together. At first I kept it a secret because I wanted you to love me for me and not my money. Later I was afraid you would hate me for deceiving you. But the real reason was I just didn't want anything to change between us. I have loved you so completely. Toni, I'm sorry for my deception but I hope you understand.

I assume you have found the bank box key. The box is in your name. I got you to sign the card without your knowing it when we first opened the T-shirt shop together. It's at the Valley Bank on Dryades Street. Inside the box you will find some records.

Before I met you. Along time before I met you I was engaged. I had met her in New York. Her name is Collette Dapolito. She was of Italian decent and connected with the Mob. Her connection was by birth; her father was well connected. Her family was well off at one time. Her father had fallen from grace with the Mob.

149

He hadn't broken any major rule to be killed over but he was being punished financially. I was in love with Collette and I would have done anything for her. She was in a hurry to get married. I didn't care because I loved her.

At the wedding rehearsal, I heard her talking to her father. "Daddy, once Terry and I are married there will be enough money to get back his prior position. It doesn't matter what it cost because Terry has the money. Daddy, after you get your position back we can deal with Terry as we see fit. I'll inherit the money and then we can do anything we want." When I heard this, I walked out the door. I went to my condo, packed a bag and started traveling. I bounced around the world for a couple of years. I settled down in Hong Kong for a while. Her family found out where I was. They made an attempt on my life. That's when I moved to France and got into arms dealing. The people I had around me in France were very security minded. So I was safe there for a while. About the time of the Israel incident, I discovered they had found me again. It was another reason to have plastic surgery. After the surgery I went back to New York to make sure no one would recognize me. They didn't so I thought I was safe. That is also why I hired fake parents. The Terry Williams they were looking for didn't have living parents. I thought it would help to get them off my trail. Since you're reading this, I was wrong.

The records are of the Dapolito Mob involvement. I had an investigator find everything he could on them. Everything is in the bank box. I think they should be turned over to Jeffery. He will know what to do with them. He's not aware of what has taken place. I didn't want to involve him. I didn't want to put him and his office in jeopardy. Talk to him, he'll know what to do. The records are old. It's been at least 8 years since the investigation.

I'm sorry I didn't do a very good job of protecting us. Please forgive me. I should have taken action a long time ago but I'm not like those people and can't do what they do. I've already caused enough death in this world. I don't know how they found me. I figured enough time had passed but I was wrong.

Toni, just know that I love you. I've made mistakes in my life but you weren't one of them. You have made me happy and whole.

All My Love

Terry

All I could do was cry. It didn't seem possible that something so long ago would come back to haunt him. I reread the letter. I put the key in my pocket and refolded the letter. Terry had lived with this threat and never told me. I was a little angry with him for not telling me but at the same time I understood.

When the search was completed, I'd show the investigators the letter. Maybe they can use it to find

151

the Dapolito's and see if it was them who murdered Terry. Why would they be after me? I had nothing to do with that part of Terry's life. If they kill me they still can't get the money. What would be served by my death? There has to be something or someone else. It just doesn't make sense after all these years.

It made me cry more to think of Terry and how he felt about me. If I'd only realized that he answered all my dreams and that I did the same for him. I guess as relationships go couples tend to forget to tell each other how they really feel. Anger flared within me. I will find out who did this and make them pay. If the Dapolito family is responsible, they will live to regret it. I promise Terry, someone will pay. They don't know what revenge is. But they will.

# Chapter 15

Sitting there with the letter in my hand and waiting for the search of the house to be complete made me angrier. This was a cold fury that wasn't going to go away. It was something that had to be satisfied. I felt hard and cold inside. It was nothing I had ever felt before. Now I had to decide what to do about it.

At first, I didn't have a clue as to which way to go. Then I starting thinking of the people I have met in the past few weeks. There were the lawyers. Terry had said to trust Mr. Breaux implicitly and without question. OK, I'll do that. I have to assume that goes for Mr. Bailey and Demas, since the firm has been with the family for 30 years. OK, I'll do that. But with caution.

Lt. Hanson didn't know Terry at all, so that leaves him out. Mary is just who she pretends to be, according to Mr. Roux. So that leaves her out. Now Mr. Roux didn't know Terry before all this happened. So that leaves him out. Mr. LaFarge didn't know Terry, according to him. I'll ask Mr. Roux to check that out for me. Joey knew Terry but from the letter, Terry trusted Joey. That leaves Joey out. Mr. Livingston didn't know Terry. If I remember correctly, Mr. Livingston hadn't worked for Terry at all. I'll ask Mr. Roux to verify that before I decide on him. None of these people would gain from Terry's or my death. So who could it be? I don't have any questions about John or Ben. My neighbors wouldn't have any reason to hurt Terry or me.

153

The Dapolito's have a reason. Even if they kill me, they won't get their hand on the money. You would think that eight years time, that would be enough for them to forget about it, but I guess not. I'll talk to Mr. Roux and ask him to investigate the Dapolito's. Maybe they left a trail to and from New Orleans.

Of all the people involved, Mr. Roux is the only one I can think of that had nothing to do with Terry before his murder. He makes money only if I'm alive. I hate putting all my eggs into one basket but the other baskets may have holes in them.

I'll have to set up a meeting with Mr. Roux outside the house. With all the bugs in here, I don't want others to know what I'm doing. When the men have completed their search, I'll slip them a note for Mr. Roux.

I went to the study for pen and paper. Again, surprised by the bodyguard being there. I guess you tend to forget they're there after a while. I returned to the dining room table. It has lots of room around it and I could cover what I'm writing before anyone could get a look at it. What did I want to say?

Mr. Roux

I am writing this to ask for your help. I know you are already hired to investigate Terry's murder via Breaux, Bailey & Demas for me. But I think I want the information you find to be just between you and I. If this is problem for you, please let me know. I don't want to create a conflict between you and the lawyers.

To start with I've made a list of the people I've met in the past few weeks and made some assumptions. With my life in danger, I don't want to assume anything. I'd like to set up a meeting with you but it must be outside the house. The house is bugged for my protection. I don't want what we talk about to be picked up by the bugs.

Terry has left me a letter. I found it today and it is quite surprising. There is information in the letter I think you should know about. I want to keep this between us only. Another name has come up that hasn't been mentioned before. I think it will require additional resources, of which I'm ready to support.

We have to find a method to talk as soon as possible. Please notify me of how and when. I'll be ready.


Thank You

Toni Tucker


Rereading the note for Mr. Roux made me feel better. At least I felt like I was doing something, other than hiding. I put the note in an envelope and sealed it, putting "Mr. Roux Only" on the front. If I am making a mistake by selecting Mr. Roux as my confidant, it will be a big one. I just prayed my analysis is correct.

The men searching the house came down stairs. They were carrying their toolboxes. "Ms. Tucker, we've finished upstairs, we'll start down here now."

"I think I'd like for you to come back tomorrow and finish." I walked over to them and handed one of them the envelope. I pointed to the front of it and motioned to my lips not to speak about it. "I'm a little tired today. Would tomorrow be alright?"

"Sure, we'll be back in the morning." He took the envelope and nodded that he would deliver it. "What time would you like?"

"Is 8 AM to early?"

"No, that will be fine. See you in the morning. Good bye Ms. Tucker." They took the toolboxes with them as they left.

I was praying I'd made the right decision. It would be a while before I knew one way or the other. "God, please let this be the right decision."

I went upstairs to see if they had mad a mess. I looked the same as when they had first come in. I could see minor things, like a chair cushion not quite in place. Other than that nothing was out of place. I forgot to ask them if they found anything. Boy, am I on the ball or what? Wait, I'm glad I didn't ask, with the bugs everywhere. I'd like to know without everyone else knowing.

I wish I had a clue who was after me. Not knowing who to trust was getting on my nerves. I should be able to rely on Mr. Livingston but I can't take the chance. He has protected me, but will he continue? Maybe I know something I don't know I know. Just listening to myself, I sound paranoid. "Hold on girl, keep it together." I didn't want to spook myself, there's enough already to spook me.

I looked at my watch and it was 2 PM. No wonder I'm hungry. I opened the refrigerator and found lots of stuff to snack. Mr. LaFarge had made several things to keep me and the bodyguards fed. There was a tray of finger sandwiches, another of cut vegetables, with fresh dip and large bowl of cut fruit. I made myself a plate with a little of everything and sat down to eat. Everything was very good and fresh. I went back for a little more fruit. Mr. LaFarge has some kind of sauce mixed in the fruit with a hint of sweetness. I think I could get use to having food ready for me when I want it.

Of course I do like to cook. I think I'll make some pralines and cookies and take them over to the shop. I wonder if Mr. Livingston has made arrangements for me to take a walk yet. I'll call him in a little while and see when I can go to the shop. I've got to get out of this house and do some walking. I'll have to see if I have everything to make the pralines and cookies in the pantry. I'm sure Mr. LaFarge has stocked everything.

I'd forgotten about making an entrance into the workshop in the back and another in Mr. Visko's house. No one has said anything and I haven't seen any work trucks on the street. I hope Mr. Livingston doesn't think I don't need to be kept informed. That would not make me happy. I want to know what's going on and when. I'll call him now while I'm thinking about it.

The phone was in the dining room. I had to keep in mind that the phone is tapped. Trying not to think about it, I dialed the number. "Hello, may I speak to Mr. Livingston, please."

"May I ask who's calling?"

"This is Toni Tucker."

157

"Yes ma'am, one moment please."

Almost instantly Mr. Livingston was on the line. "Hello, Toni, what can I do for you?"

"I was wondering if you'd made arrangements for me to have a walk yet? I'm going stir crazy in this house. I've been in here too long."

"As a matter of fact I have. How about tomorrow at noon?"

"That would be wonderful. I'm looking forward to it. Who do I have to wait for to come and get me?"

"I thought Jack would be good since you've been seen with him before. Who ever might see you together may think he's just a friend or they'll know not to mess with him. I don't want to know the agenda for your walk. We'll have you covered every minute. Don't worry, you'll be safe. How does that suit you?"

"Thank you. I can't wait. I'll be ready to go, so tell Jack to put his walking shoes on. I may not get back till dark. Thank you again. Bye."

Now I was excited. I had something to look forward to and I was going to take full advantage of it. First the shop, then the Moonwalk, Café du Monde, a stop by the cathedral, then some ice cream and a drink at Pat O'Briens should do it for my first outing. I was feeling like a child waiting for a surprise. Even knowing what was going to happen didn't diminish the excitement.

The phone rang. "Hello."

"Hello, Ms. Tucker, this is Lafitte Roux. I thought I'd come by tomorrow if you don't mind?"

"Hi, Mr. Roux. I'd love to see you tomorrow. I'm going out tomorrow. Would you like to meet me at Café du Monde around 1 o'clock?"

"Hey, that would be great. I haven't been there in a long time. I'll be there at one and have a cup ready for you. See ya then. Bye" That quick and he was gone.

At least I know he got the message and he responded very quickly. That made me feel a little better about my decision. Better but not comfortable. I felt for the letter in my pocket again. I just wanted to have it close to me. Some how it made me feel closer to Terry. I'll show it to Mr. Roux and see if he can find out anything about the Dapolitos. I'll have to go to the bank box pretty soon. It just has to be worked out so I doesn't look like I'm going for something. Maybe Mr. Roux can already be in the bank and I can pass the records to him there. I'll ask him to have them scanned onto a computer disk and E-mail it to me. Just trying to think what could be in those records didn't make me feel any better.

Oh, I'd forgotten about the computer. I can get on the internet and search for Dapolito's in New York. Maybe I can get to the public records and see if there are arrest records. The letter didn't say what Collette's father's first name. I'll do some sleuthing on my own.

Logging on to the internet is easy. But finding what you want can take some time. And time is what I have a lot of. I accessed the New York City White Pages of the phone book. There must be over a hundred Dapolitos. Let's see, her name was Collette. Yep, there's one on 43 rd Street. Now are there any other Dapolitos on 43 rd Street. Oh, there are three at the same address, Vincenzo, Carlotta and Collette. Well that was pure luck. I printed out the names, address and phone number for Mr. Roux. I got into the public police records database. There were several pages on

159

Vincenzo Dapolito. He had been arrested many times for racketeering, suspected in several fraud cases, classified as having Mob connection, and just a down right nasty guy. He scared me alright. I hope all this will help Mr. Roux.

I decided to look in the society pages of the New York Times. Low and behold there she is. Not bad looking. Collette's face was there with several other socialites. They were posing for some charity they were working with. That went to the printer too. What about a photo of Vincenzo. There had to be some picture on the steps of a justice building. I looked and looked and finally found one. It was at least a year old. Vincenzo Dapolito was around 55 years old, about 6 feet tall with a slender build and olive complexion. A rather distinguished looking man. The article said he was involved in a murder cover up. He was charged with accessory after the fact in the murder of three people. The paper said it was a Mob hit and Vincenzo Dapolito had helped the murderer to hide from the police. Boy, this is some kind of nice guy. I hope it isn't him I'm dealing with.

I could only hope they would find him guilty and put him away so I don't have to deal with him. But from what Terry had said about Collette, I don't want to deal with her either. I pray all this can be cleared up quickly.

With any luck, it's not the Dapolitos I'm dealing with at all. But who? So far there hasn't been anything else to look at. All this just makes my head spin and doesn't help at all. I printed out the pages on the Dapolitos for Mr. Roux. I turned the computer off. I'm tired of searching for answers and not knowing if I'm going in the right direction.

I wonder if Mr. Roux has found out anything in any other areas. He was suppose to talk to Mr. Breaux about all the places Terry had lived. But I'm beginning to think that the letter from Terry says more than I initially read. Maybe Mr. Roux will find something I didn't see in it. Between the letter and what I found on the internet about the Dapolitos, Mr. Roux will have a direction to go on. I just pray it's the right direction.

I want all this to end so I can get my life back. It won't be the same because Terry isn't here but I've got to get some semblance of order back in my life. I was starting to feel sad and depressed with all that is happening. I'd better get up and get moving or I'll set here all night and cry. Come on girl, get out of this funk. Don't sit here, move. I got up. I heard someone in the kitchen and decided to see who it was.

"Hello, Mr. LaFarge, how are you?"

"Jon, remember? I'm just over to make sure you have a good dinner. You haven't eaten yet have you?"

"No, I don't even know what time it is." I looked at his watch, only to see it was past 6 PM. "Now that you mentioned it I am hungry. What do you have in store for me this evening?"

"I thought you might be in the mood for some Trout Almondine, with some sautéed mushrooms and potatoes. Maybe some asparagus on the side. You said you liked my salad dressing so I brought some with me."

"That sounds great. Will you join me?"

"Don't mind if I do. It's easier to cook for two than one and I'm hungry too. I was hoping you'd ask. But I really came to make sure you had something to eat. You've been quite distracted lately and not paying attention to your diet." He moved around the kitchen knowing where everything is. "I thought I'd make a few things for the bodyguards too. I see the coffee urn needs to be redone. I'll do that first so you can have some fresh coffee."

"That sounds good. Can I help you with anything?"

"No, but you can keep me company. I like to chat while I'm cooking. Drag up a chair and relax."

There's a bar stood in the corner of the kitchen so I brought it over by the counter but yet out of the way. "Terry and I enjoyed cooking. Terry and I used to take all the cooking classes offered at the various restaurants. We'd laugh because when we tried to make something at home it was never as good as it was in class. We did have some interesting meals."

"There are little tricks of the trade that sometimes don't get passed out to the classes. That's what keeps you coming back to the restaurants. You've got to remember that chefs are businessmen too. If not they won't stay in business long or be able to run a kitchen effectively. It does take years of training in both cooking and business to know how to balance the two."

"I never really thought of it that way, but it makes sense. Then having the right people working for you is a must. A bad waiter can ruin a great meal. Have you ever thought of opening a restaurant for yourself?"

"I've thought of it, but I like what I'm doing. I don't have to be in the kitchen everyday. The people I have working for me can handle a lot of things for me. Breakfast is an easy meal at the office. Most of the time the lawyers only want toast and coffee at their desk. Only about 50% of the lunches are done at the office. Most of the time they have lunch meetings all over the city. There is rarely an evening meal to prepare. Only when business requires it. Usually, there is not much notice but I like that too. I can whip up a gourmet meal pretty quickly. Of course that takes some prior planing. I always have fresh meats and vegetables ready for anything. It does cause a lot of waste but it is worth it for the finished product. And prepared food is a product. If the product doesn't meet the expectations of the customer it can cause many problems. Mr. Breaux uses me the most and when he wants me, he wants everything to go perfectly."

"How long have you worked for the firm?"

"Lets see, I guess I've been there about seven years. The hard part is not getting into a pattern of making the same food over and over. If I did, I wouldn't be working there long."

"What about what you've done over here? Have you had to do this before? Or is this an unusual case?"

"It's happened a couple of times through the years, but not often. Actually, I like it. It gets me out of my usual surroundings and into something different. It also becomes a challenge using someone else's kitchen and still create food to be enjoyed. By the way, you have a very complete kitchen. There is not much I can think of that I would add or even move. You must have listened in the classes you went to."

"Thank you. We both liked to cook so we tried to make it like the professional kitchens we visited." It was pleasant sitting here and just chatting. I'm really glad he came over. He has helped and gotten me out of my funk.

"Here's your coffee. Nice, fresh and piping hot. I'm glad to see you know how to enjoy coffee. I never could put sugar or cream in my coffee. I tried a few times, but to me it just ruined it. That's not to say I don't like cappuccino but even with that I don't put sugar in it."

"Thank you. I love cappuccino too. Like you I can't stand sugar in my coffee. I do put it in my tea but never my coffee."

"I could make you some cappuccino if you like."

"No, this is fine. Maybe some would be nice after dinner."

"OK, we'll be eating in about 20 minutes. I'll set the table. I have a nice white wine in the refrigerator if you'd like for dinner."

"No, I'm not one for wine. I like to have one glass of wine but I don't enjoy a second glass. So it doesn't really pay to open a bottle for me. But please, it you'd like to have it, please do."

"I think I'll stick with the coffee. Since I came up with this blend of coffee I can't get enough of it."

"I would love to have a couple of bags of it here after all this is over. Could I talk you into making me some?"

"Sure. I'll make you some and give you the names of the beans I use and how much of each. OK, dinner is served, my lady. Won't you join me?"

"This is beautiful. I sat there and watched you and didn't really see you perform your magic. I thought I was paying attention. It smells great and I'm starved." We sat down and started to eat. It was heaven. "You have out done yourself again. Your salad dressing is just as good this time as it was before." We ate and chatted and it was nice and relaxing. "Thank you very much, this has been wonderful."

"Thank you, I'm glad you enjoyed it. I'll have the kitchen cleaned up in a minute. Would you like a cappuccino now?"

"That sounds good. Can I help you clean up?"

"No thanks, I have my own system of doing things, but thank you. Here's your cappuccino, I hope it's like you like it.

I took a sip. "Great. That blend of yours makes great cappuccino. I can't decide which way I like best. You should market your blend." It seemed to only take him a few minutes to clean the kitchen. His system for cleaning worked very well.

"I'm glad you enjoyed the dinner. There's a full urn of coffee and some snacks for the bodyguards. I've got to go. Tomorrow I have an early morning."

"Thank you. I really appreciated dinner, coffee and most of all the company." I opened the door for him and thanked him again. Closing the door, I decided it had been a pleasant dinner and chat. I was feeling better. I need to send him a Thank You card. He was just what I needed.

I turned on the TV. There was a public TV program I wanted to watch. A bodyguard came out of the library, heading for the kitchen. "Excuse me. I got a whiff of that coffee and had to have some."

"Help yourself. It's freshly made. Mr. LaFarge made some snacks for you. They are in the refrigerator."

*Mickey L. Strain*

"I'm going to hate for this job to end. I've never had better coffee or been fed so well. I bet I've gained 5 pounds. I'm sorry. I know you want this job to end. I didn't mean anything."

"It's ok. I understand what you mean. I'm going to miss it too." I know I'm not going to miss the rest of it. Oh well. I'm going to bed. Maybe tomorrow there will be more information and maybe this can end."

# Chapter 16

At 7 AM the smell of fresh coffee and biscuits woke me up. I was feeling much better. I took a quick shower in anticipation of the biscuits. Trotting out to the kitchen I wasn't surprised to see Jon. "Good morning. I see I'm the early morning you were talking about. The biscuits smell wonderful. Are they ready?"

"Just coming out of the oven. Have a seat and I'll have them there in a jiffy. There's some apricot preserves on the table. I made it myself. Would you like anything else besides a cup of coffee."

"I think that will do it. Come join me. I bet the best thing of all is to enjoy your own work? So come join me."

"Thank you, my lady, I will. There is also some fresh homemade butter in that little brown crock."

"You are spoiling me. I'm really excited today. I get to go for a walk. I can't stand this house anymore. I'm going out at noon and I won't be back till dark. I've missed all my friends and the shop to long. I want to see them and just enjoy being outside for a while."

"That sounds good. What about dinner. Would you like for me to prepare dinner for you?"

"No, I think I want to go over to Brennan's this evening. I have a lot of friends over there and I'd like to see them. Most of the time I eat in the kitchen with them. Thanks anyway."

"No problem. If the firm doesn't have anything for me, I'll spend a quiet evening at home. Well, two biscuits are enough for me. I'll clean up and be on my way."

"Don't bother. I'll do it. I need something to do while I wait for noon to leave. Besides, all that's left to clean is the baking sheet. I think I can handle that without any problems. Go, and I hope you have a good day. Thanks again for the biscuits."

"You're more than welcome. I'm glad you like them. Maybe I'll see you tomorrow. I hope you enjoy your walk on the outside. Bye."

"Bye." I was on my third biscuit with preserves. That man can really cook. After the dishes, I have to decide what I'm going to wear while I'm out today. My excitement was building again. I'd been wanting to go to the shop for some time now but just being out was the most important.

It felt good doing the dishes. It just didn't take long enough. Going to the bedroom to decide what clothes to wear I passed another bodyguard. I was beginning not to notice them at all. I guess that's what happens after a while.

At exactly 12 noon, Jack rang the doorbell. I was walking on cloud nine to answer the door. "I am so glad to see you. I've been like a drop of water in a hot skillet, just bouncing around and not being able to sit. Unless you need something in the house, let's go."

"I'm ready if you are. Do you have a plan you want to follow?"

"I'd like to go to the Moonwalk first, then to Café du Monde. "I'm going to meet Mr. Roux for coffee at 1 o'clock. Then I'd like to go to the shop and visit for a while.. After that I think I'll have wonder lust. Are you ready?"

"More than ready. I'm with you. Would you like to lead the way?"

"Yep, I hope you can keep up with me."

He laughed. "I'll do my best."

I left him standing there and bounded down the steps. Swinging the gate open like I was leaving a prison. I felt high as a kite. We walked on Conti Street towards the river. Everything smelled so good, even the garbage that hadn't been picked up. We passed Jackson Brewery going behind the building to get my first look at the river. It gets in your blood to see the Mississippi River. The beauty and power of it will always draw you back to it. We sat on the steps that descended to the river at the Moonwalk. The sights and sounds of the river felt like home. Jack and I didn't talk. I think he understood how I was feeling. The sun felt so good.

"Toni, it's 12:50. Shall we go to Café du Monde?" We got up and started walking towards the café.

"Yes. This was so nice. I could sit here all day. Let's go. I want to talk to Mr. Roux. Jack, I'm going to need some time alone with him. Is that a problem for you?"

"No, not at all. I'll get me a cup of that famous coffee and sit at another table. Far enough away not to hear what's said, but close enough to watch and provide protection. Enjoy yourself and take your time. I'll be ready when you are."

Mr. Roux had a table close to the front. There was already coffee and beignets there for me. "Hello Mr. Roux. I'm glad to see you. Thank you for meeting me."

"It's good to see you too. But please call me Lafitte. My I call you Toni?"

169

"By all means, please do." It felt great being here again. Several of the waiters stopped by to say hello and gave their condolences for Terry. That got to me and I had to hold back the tears. "Lafitte, did your searchers find anything in the house that would help? I know they only got to do the upstairs, but they said they'd be back today to finish."

"Toni, they found a few things. I've got a report to go over with you. They found a large envelope in the attic. Inside there were some pictures and papers. The papers refer to a Mr. Vincenzo Dapolito of New York City. They indicate a mob connection but nothing we can use as evidence. Now I've already contacted my office in New York City to initiate an investigation of Dapolito. The men also found a fireproof box hidden in the second bedroom upstairs. It was hidden in a wall unit for hiding things. It's not a safe but you have to know what you're looking for to find it. You probably would never have found it. It was a professional job installing it. I'll show you where it is so you can use it if you want."

"Every time I turn around, I'm learning more about Terry. What else can there be? I stay in a state of suspense of what will be next."

"The box contained some deeds and land titles within the city and other cities. According to my men, there's at least 200 properties identified. All are completely paid for and the taxes have been paid for 20 years. There are accounts for each property and each has a different management company handling them. They all support themselves and gross a profit that goes into the various accounts. The properties are mostly in New York City, New Orleans, Dallas and

San Diego. They are worth millions and I mean millions and they're not apart of the accounts or properties handled by the law firm of Breaux, Bailey and Demas. It seemed he wanted something that only he knew about.

"Oh no. More money? I can't handle this. You know what the law firm handles is almost a billion dollars. Now, there is more? I can't believe this."

"Well, you're the beneficiary on all of them. Each are established so the inheritance tax will be paid out of a tax account. A strange thing is that a lot of the property in New York City now are occupied by this Vincenzo Dapolito. I'll know more about that tomorrow. The New York office is working on it. We're not sure of the Dapolito connection."

"Well, I am. Although I just found out myself yesterday. I found a letter from Terry to me. It seems he knew he was in danger but thought it was in the past. He had taken some precautions to protect himself but they didn't work. It explains the Dapolito connection. This man is in the mob and Terry jilted his daughter when he found out they were just after his money. Here's the letter. Lafitte, I want it back. Maybe we can get a copy of it over at my shop and you can use it. I want to keep this letter. It's the last thing I have of Terry."

"Great. I'm glad you found it. Maybe it will help us in our investigation. When I gave the name to my New York office they did know the name. They didn't tell me a lot but they did indicate he is not the best of character."

"Lafitte, I want to keep this investigation between you and me. I don't know why but I feel I should keep it this way for a while. If the lawyers or security people ask you about it, don't tell them anything. I'm putting a lot of trust in you and I hope it is not misplaced. Can you work just for me on this?"

"Of course. I thought that was the way it was from the beginning. The firm has referred me to clients before but they have never made inquiries about the work once I took the case. Toni, I don't work for them, I work for you and you only in this. I have other clients that I work for but each case is independent. Don't worry, you'll be the only person I talk to."

"The security people have put bugs in the house. Because of that I don't want to talk at the house or on the phone. I have to make arrangements for me to leave the house each time I want to go out. Right now I think that is necessary or I wouldn't be doing it. So we have to make arrangements on our own. I can schedule an outing whenever I want I just have to give them enough time to get the security people in place. I can sure thank Terry for the money. Otherwise I wouldn't be able to pay for any of this. We made good money with the shop but nothing that would cover all this. I can't even think in the realm of money Terry has left me."

"I bet it is a shock. I think you'll get use to with time. Let's go make a copy of this letter and I'll get back to work. Are you ready to go?"

"More than ready. The shop is just across the street. Come on." As we got up, Jack appeared like magic.

"Hi, Toni! You ready to resume your walk about?"

"Yep. Let's go over to the shop so I can say Hi to everyone. Lafitte, why don't you come with us a moment. I've got the papers you wanted at the shop, OK?"

"Sure."

The three of us walked over to the shop. You would have thought I'd been gone a year with the reception I got. Hugs and kisses. Joey kept the customers happy until John took over for him. He gave me a hug and kiss. It was great to see everyone and to be back in the shop. At the first opportunity I made a copy of the letter and gave it to Lafitte. As soon as I did he left. I spent two hours in the shop with my friends. Several of the shop owners on the square came over to see me. Of course all gave their condolences for Terry. After the two hours I was ready to resume my outing. We all said good bye with hugs and kisses again.

Once outside again, I got a little teary. It was good to be with my friends again. All the shop neighbors were sweet and kind but I needed to get out of there. The sadness was getting to me.

Jack and I walked over to Pat O'Briens for a drink and to chat with some of my friends there. We sat in the Garden Bar. I felt like a queen with everyone paying court. I ordered a Hot Buttered Rum and Jack ordered a soda. Everyone said they had missed me and wanted to see more of me. Those that could take a break did and we talked about what had been going on since I had seen them last. This time Terry was brought up only a little. I must have looked like I didn't want to talk about what had happened. I only had one drink but I knew I'd had one. I'd forgotten I hadn't had any alcohol in weeks.

We left and headed over to Brennan's for dinner. After more hugs and kisses we were lead back to the kitchen for dinner. Jack said, "Why are we in the kitchen?"

"Jack this is a place of honor for dinner. To be allowed into any kitchen for dinner in the French Quarter is reserved for only a few people. I've been coming here for years and know every one that works here. Terry and I use to come here at least once a week. As time goes by, I'm sure I'll start coming here weekly again. It may take me some time to do that but I'm sure I will."

"Sorry, I didn't understand. I guess there are few people that are allowed back here. I will say one thing, these people are busy and don't stop at all. They earn their money, that's for sure."

"That they do. Not only is the chef one of the best in town, but the service is also the best in town. Being a tourist restaurant of high quality requires the service to be the best there is. It keeps people coming back."

Dinner was wonderful. They went out of their way to make it special. By the time we finished our coffee I was tired and ready for bed. It was only 8 PM but I did more today than I'd done in weeks. Jack walked me to the door and said good night. I was glad he didn't want to stay, I was too tired.

It only took me a few minutes to get ready for bed and fewer minutes to fall asleep.

# Chapter 17

Another morning with the smell of coffee. I was getting used to this. But now I didn't have to rush because I knew it would still be there when I got out of the shower. After the shower I smelled something else, bananas. Now what was Jon doing with bananas for breakfast?

"Good Morning Jon. What wonders are you fixing this morning? It smells great and sure makes me hungry."

"How about some banana pancakes? Hot off the griddle. Mr. Breaux likes these from time to time. I made enough batter to take to the office. I've got to go. One of my helpers will clean up and then come to the office. See ya later Toni."

Jon left as soon as he put a plate full of pancakes in front of me. They were wonderful. Of course everything he makes is. Who ever taught him, did a bang up job. I had just finished the pancakes when Jack walked in.

"Good morning Toni. How are you this morning? Thank you for a nice day yesterday. I talked to Mr. Livingston about further outings. He's made security arrangements for you to go out with just two hours notice. I told him it would help your recovery."

"That's great. I'll go out every other day. Taking basically the same walk. Those are my favorite places to go. Thanks for asking and getting it set up."

"You're welcome. I have some news for you. All the arrangements have been made to put a door into Mr. Visko's house and in your workshop. As a matter of fact it started yesterday. Mr. Visko is on cloud nine. The men working over there want to give him sleeping pills everyday. Mr. Livingston has every thing going well. He has a crew working around the clock to get it done."

"This is great news. This means I'll be able to leave without anyone knowing it. I'm almost use to the bodyguards but not quite. I'm amazed."

"Mr. Livingston has contacted Mr. and Mrs. Olivetti and they have agreed to allow us to put a door in their house too. The three businesses were a little hard to convince but like all things, money does some loud talking. We had to redo their security systems for them and sign a contract to fix every thing back the way it was. We were lucky. All three of the businesses have an area for the construction that is not seen."

"How are they getting the bricks and wood out of the stores and getting the stuff they need inside?"

"The debris is broken down and taken out in boxes. The boxes are put in panel delivery trucks and taken away. Pretty smart, huh? They look like merchandise that's been sold. The wood for the doorframes is a little harder to get in. The Olivetti's have a shed behind their house too. We've made it look like some work on the shed is being done. The store next to Mr. Visko is always doing construction so it looks normal for them. The store behind you was great. We took an entire load of everything that is needed through their garage."

"How long will it take to get it finished? I can't wait to sleep in a hotel without worrying about someone getting to me."

"Would you believe tomorrow night? We've made arrangements at the Hyatt for you. We thought you might like to go the first available evening."

"This is great. I can't wait."

"You need to be aware that you can't go to the restaurant there. You'll eat here before you go and the room will have every thing you need. The suites are very nice. Of course there is always room service. You'll still have protection. We've got the suites next to yours and the one across the hall too. So you don't have to worry about a thing."

"This is unbelievable. This could possibly end soon. I just hope it works. If who ever it is after me thinks I'm alone again, maybe, just maybe you can catch them. If you do, how are you going to get them to tell you who they are working for?"

"Well there are ways. Since the police have let us handle every thing it will be easier for us. Don't worry, we don't beat people up or torture them. But there are many ways to get what you want. We're not bad guys? We are professionals and know what we're doing."

"I just want this to be over. The sooner the better. I don't want to live like this much longer. I understand it, but I sure don't like it. That was a mistake, I don't understand any of it."

"Well, Toni. I've got to go. I have the late shift tonight and I need to get some sleep. The next time you see Mr. LaFarge, please tell him we really appreciate all the food he makes for us. I'm still gaining weight." He has a nice smile. I was always comfortable with him.

"Thanks Jack. I really appreciate the news and can't wait. Sleep well. Maybe I'll see you tonight. Bye Jack." Out the door he went.

The thought of being able to get out of this house and not worry about someone coming after me for a night or two was heaven. I've never stayed at the Hyatt. He said a suite. I've never stayed in a suite before either. This is going to be fun.

I keep forgetting that I can afford a suite, bodyguards, construction and all the other stuff. All I really want to do is get back to my normal life.

The phone rang. "Hello."

"Hi honey, it's Mom and Dad. How are you doing? We hadn't talked to you in a couple of days and we were getting worried."

"I'm fine. Every thing is going well. My wounds are doing fine. Yesterday I got to go out to the shop and have dinner out. I only have a little soreness in my thigh but it is really doing very well. My chest doesn't hurt at all."

"Has your private detective found anything out yet. We are so worried about you. Thank God you've got protection."

"Don't worry, there are six men here all the time. There are additional men in the houses on each side of me. Mr. Roux is working hard and Mr. Livingston has provided great security. By the way, how is your security? Do you see them?"

"Yes, we see them all the time. Our neighbors don't know what to think and the police have increased their drive byes. They also have a couple of men here at the house. Only one is in the house and one is in the garage. They are so quiet, we forget they are here. We'll be glad when this is all over."

"Me too, Mom. Everyone here is working on it. So far I've gotten a few reports that look promising. We still don't have a clue who or why yet, but we will."

"Honey, how are you handling Terry's death? I know this is a hard question but we worry. Can we do anything for you?"

"No, I'm fine. I don't think I'll ever stop missing Terry. Some times it gets really hard but I try to think of the happy times we had. That hurts too, but it also makes me feel better. Some times I feel so close to him I forget he's gone. I expect him to come walking through the door and have to remind myself he won't. Time has helped but I don't think I'll ever get over it. Dad? I know you're on the extension. I'm so angry. I want revenge and I want it to be hard. I know I shouldn't feel that way but I do."

"Baby, that's normal. I'm angry too. Knowing how you are hurting. We hope you know we loved Terry too. We can't believe he's really gone. But be angry, it's all right. Maybe it will help you to solve this."

"Thanks for calling. I'm glad you two are safe but please be careful. I couldn't handle something happening to you too."

Mom always ended conversations. She really doesn't like to talk on the phone. "Sweetheart, we are worried but we're confident you'll be fine. Don't worry about us we are fine. Call us in a few days will you?"

"I will Mom. Y'all take care and I'll call soon. Love you both. Bye." They both said good bye and hung up. It was good to hear from them. I was worried about them but I guess it was in the back of my mind. I'll make a point of calling them every other day until this is over.

Back to the thoughts at hand. If the construction is finished by tomorrow night, maybe I can really sleep somewhere else tomorrow night. I was feeling like a kid again. The anticipation was building. Today I'll pack a small bag to take with me. I won't need much. It should all fit in a small tote bag.

The house seems so quiet. I know the bodyguards are here somewhere but I really don't notice them anymore. I don't hear any work going on in the workshop. Maybe I should go out and see what it looks like with a large hole in the wall. 'No, what are you thinking? You can't go out there. Terry died there. I don't know if I'll ever be able to go out there.' Then I thought, that's the way I'll have to leave the house after dark. It will be dark in there too. I do have a night light out there. Just the thought of going out there made me cringe. I don't know how I'm going to do this. Terry would say, 'I'm not there I'm in here.' Pointing to my heart. Terry I'll try my best to keep that in mind.

It was time for lunch. I wonder what Jon has stored up in the refrigerator. The last time I raided it, there were some great finger sandwiches. The coffee smelled good as always. I got a cup of coffee and took it to the dining room table. I opened the refrigerator and there was a Styrofoam box with my name on it. I took it to the table and opened it. Inside was a beautiful Cesar Salad. I was chock full of all kinds of things. I just really noticed the size of the container, it was surely more than I can eat but I was going to try.

After lunch I went out on the porch. Mr. Visko was on his porch. I usually didn't talk to him too much. I was feeling obligated because of the men in his house, the danger I was putting him in and the hole in the side of his house. "Hi, Mr. Visko." I yelled.

"Hi Toni, how are you feeling? You're looking beautiful as usual. Would you mind if I came and joined you on the porch?"

"That would be nice. Would you like a cup of coffee?"

"Absolutely. Give me a minute and I'll be there. I'm just a little slow but I haven't stopped yet."

"Take your time. I'll get the coffee. If I remember, you take it black."

"I sure do. Why ruin a good thing." He was making his way down his steps when I went to get the coffee. By the time I got back, he was making his way up my steps. He really is a sweetheart, so lonesome.

"Here you go, take this seat. The coffee is very good this morning. How are you feeling, Mr. Visko?"

"Oh, I'm going great for 86 years old. I make it to church everyday. I do my own shopping. Well, usually. Those men have done all the shopping. I'm eating things I can't even pronounce. They are a great bunch of guys. They have some great stories and they listen to mine. They have been great company."

"I'm glad it hasn't been hard on you. I was worried but I can see I shouldn't. Can I help with anything over there?"

"No, not a thing. Toni, look at those tourist in that carriage? That was the only way I traveled around New Orleans when I was young."

He's so cute. He tells me that every time I'm with him and a carriage goes by. I guess at 86 years old you can repeat what you would like. "Toni, the constructions is almost finished. I think they'll be finished tonight. Those boys work so quiet they don't even wake me up at night. When I get up in the morning I'm amazed at what's been done."

"Mr. Visko, I really appreciate your permissions to do this work or your house. You know we'll put it all back the way it was when were finished?"

"I don't want it back the way it was. I'm glad it will be different. That room needs painting and I can't do it anymore. The house is falling down around my ears and I can't do a thing about it. It's hell getting old. I use to do all the house repairs. I was good at it too. I look at these young people now and they just don't know how to do things any more. All the new fangled stuff they use today, I just don't understand it"

"Mr. Visko, didn't Mr. Livingston tell you that we plan to redo your entire house for you?

"No, he didn't. Toni, you don't have to do that. That old place is just fine the way it is. Besides, it costs too much."

"I know I don't have to do it. But I'd really like too. Please, Mr. Visko. What you're doing may just save my life. We don't know when we'll find out who is after me and without your help, our search would be harder. Mr. Visko, I thank you very much. I'll make sure everything is just the way you want it. We'll have them do one room at a time so as not to make too much of a mess."

"Child, what kind of neighbor would I be if I didn't help. You'll find out who it is and you'll get them. Toni, I've got to go to church now. See you later."

"Be careful Mr. Visko on those steps. I think tomorrow you and I will get with a contractor and see what we can do with your house. May I help you with the make over?"

"You can do anything you like. It's your money but I still think you shouldn't do it."

"Mr. Visko, I really want to. Would you like it as it is or more modern?"

"We'll talk later, I've got to go. You know how Father Alex is when I'm late. I always need his prayers. So I can't be late." Mr. Visko was trying to hurry out the gate. I knew he wouldn't be late but he had a tear in his eye and didn't want me to see it.

I think I'll get Mr. Breaux to look into Mr. Visko's finances and see how they are. I've never given it much thought how he was really getting along. Looking at the house I can see, it does need a lot of work. With a really good look I can see it needed more that just normal work. He's been retired for a very long time. You can't live in the French Quarter on Social Security alone. Yep, that's what I'll do. I'll try to do my first good deed with this money. To someone who gave me something and asked for nothing in return. Mr. Visko, you better look out. Great things are going to happen for you because of your kind unselfish deed as a neighbor.

I went to the phone and called John. "John, don't you have a friend in building remodeling here in the French Quarter?"

"Yes, I do. He is highly recommended. I've seen the work he has done and he is very good. I can show you a few places around here he has done, if you like?"

"No, If you say he's good, that's good enough for me. With the security here, could you bring him by?"

"Sure, I'll find him and we'll be over in just a little while. See you in a few. Bye." John was never one to wait on anything. I think that's one of the reasons we got along so well over the years. Knowing John, he will have this guy here in a couple of hours.

I was getting excited about it. It felt good to be thinking of something other than the mess I'm in. Mr. Visko deserves this done. He has been a good neighbor since I've been here. I really felt close to him when he allowed the security guards in his house. Again when he allowed a hole to be put into the wall. He has no clue I have all this money and that even makes it better.

Since he has really enjoyed having someone in the house, I'll see just how long we can make this project last. He'll have plenty of company for as long as I have anything to do with it.

The day was beautiful. The humidity is at its normal high but with a slight breeze to take the edge off of it. There was something I was going to have to do that I didn't want to do. I had to go out to the workshop. Strength was not my problem, it was sadness. Anything that brought the sadness of Terry's death created an ache in my heart that at times was unbearable. To help save my life, I was going to have to walk through the workshop. Even though Terry didn't really spend any time out there, he did die there.

I was trying to talk myself into this. I'd rather go out there during the day than at night. But night was when I would leave the house. OK, Toni, go do it. The first time will be the worst. Do it while you're alone. The thought of going out there with some one was too hard. Just do it.

There was no time like the present. I got up and walked through the house, into the tiny cement square called a yard. Standing in front of the door took my breath away. I reached for the door. As I opened it, it made that same squeaky noise it always had. Some how that was comforting. It was always dark in the shop no matter what time of day you were out there. I switched on the light. Dad had done a good job. Everything was in its place. There was no apparent signs of what had happened here. Thank you, Dad. I didn't feel as sad as I thought I would. My last project was on the bench waiting for me to work on it. I walked around the shop, looking at everything. I just noticed there was a noise in the middle of the wall. Running my hand across the wall to feel the vibration to determine where the new door will be. Yep, right in the middle. There were a couple of shelves where they wanted to come through. It wouldn't be to much of an impact.

I started moving the stuff from the shelves, finding other places for the things. Before I knew it I had the area cleared and I knew where everything was. On a handy tablet I started writing down some supplies I needed. Taking a small inventory of paints, brushes, canvases, and cleaners. There were a few other things I moved, to have better access to the back wall. I also combined the contents of cans that could be combined.

Before I knew it, several hours had passed. The sadness I feared was not there as long as I didn't dwell on it. Maybe I was healing.

Just as I left the shop and opened the backdoor, John and his construction friend were there. "Hi, you startled me. I was just out in the workshop seeing how things were. My Dad did a great job."

"Toni, this is Charles Guidry. He's the contractor I told you about. Why don't we go to the dining room so he can show you pictures of his work."

"Hello, Mr. Guidry, it's nice to meet you. Would you like some coffee?"

"No thank you and please call me Charles."

"Very well, Charles. I have a neighbor that is 86 years old that I want to do something for. I've decided to remodel his house. I do have a few quirks about this that may seem unusual but I think are necessary. Have I driven you off yet?"

"No, I'm interested. What kind of quirks?"

"Mr. Visko is a lonely old man. Company is important to him. He's had a couple of workmen over there the last few days. His days with them have given him life, a spring in his step. The quirk is unusual, I want you to go slow. We'll set down with him and figure out what he would like. There is no limit to what he can have. The cost of anything, can not be brought up to him. I'll handle all the funding. I need you to stagger your work schedule on the house. What I mean is, work on one room at a time, cleaning up every night. When a room is finished this is what I want done, spend some time measuring, selecting paint, wood molding, accents, lights and so on. The additional time between rooms should take at least a week, while the actual work on each room will take twice as long as normal."

"Are you serious?"

"I'm more than serious. Mr. Visko has done something for me and I want to do something for him. He needs his house repaired, remodeled or what ever and I want to do it. Because he doesn't have anyone to visit him, this construction will be that for him. He'll get more than a remodeled house, he'll get some companionship for a while. After everything is done, I'll worry about other companionship then. It will be a couple of weeks before you can start on the house. First of all, are you available now?"

"I'm completely yours."

"OK, start collecting the stuff you need to present to Mr. Visko. Let me know when you need to look at the house. Like I said it will be a couple of weeks before we can get started. I assume you work by project and not wage. What is your normal income, for your business, on a weekly bases."

"Toni, I have six men working for me. I just finished a job yesterday. If it's going to be a couple of weeks, I'll take another job in between. But I'll be ready when you want me. My normal weekly business income runs around $7 - $8,000 a week. That covers my payroll, insurance and equipment."

"Charles, let's do this, if you don't mind. I want you to start to work for me tomorrow. I'll pay you $10,000 a week until you start the job. You and I will meet and negotiate the actual contract of the work in a couple of weeks. Take a week to 10 days vacation and tell your men to also. I know this sounds nuts but I do have my reasons. Is this acceptable to you for now?"

He looked at John with a amazed look on his face. "If you're serious, so am I. You don't want me to do anything for at least 10 days?"

"That's right. You don't need to come and look or measure or anything. You can ask John if this is for real or not. I assure you it is. I'll write you a check right now for three weeks. I just need you available in about 10 days. I don't want you to lose any money and I need to know I have some one I can call and get here the next day." I wrote the check out for $30,000 and handed it to him.

"Now I've seen it all. Getting paid for not working and then getting paid to do a job slow. I may have to retrain my men after this job. Thank you. Here's my card with all my numbers on it. Shall I call you in ten days or what?"

"No, don't bother. If the wait goes over three weeks, I'll send a check to your office. Now, Charles I'm glad we can do business. Go and enjoy yourself. Your men are going to love you for this job."

John laughed at Charles. "I told you that you were in for a treat. I had no idea it was going to be this good. Man, you owe Ben and I dinner at the best place in town. Toni, I've got to get back to the shop. I'll take Charles with me so he can get use to taking a vacation. I'll call you later." John gave me a kiss and Charles shook my hand. I think I saw Charles still shaking his head a block away. I had to giggle.

This felt good. When this is all over, I'll try and make a habit of this.

# Chapter 18

If everything worked out today, I'd be sleeping in a hotel tonight. If nothing could get me out of bed, that would. Just the thought of sleeping somewhere else was exciting. For some reason, I just laid there and looked around the room. A few things I saw I wanted to take with me. I had slept well last night but I'd wake up sometimes from different sounds. But tonight will be different.

The shower was calling. I got up and enjoyed a nice long hot shower. I love my morning showers. Today was going to be hot, so shorts and a T-shirt was what was called for. I was beginning to think that's all I had to wear.

In the kitchen was that wonderful coffee again. I was getting spoiled. I was pouring a cup of coffee when Jon came in. "Good morning Jon. How are you this morning?"

"I'm fine, what about you?"

"Couldn't be better. Today the door will be finished in the workshop and I can leave this house and sleep some where else. I'm getting excited."

"Toni, just remember you can talk like this in the house but be careful else where. You never know who's around so be careful."

"Thank you Jon. I do forget. It's been so safe in the house for a while, I forget about what is happening. I'll be so glad when this is done and over with."

"It will be. But I know for you it isn't soon enough. No one has any idea who is doing this?"

"Not right now. There are some plans in place to try and find out who. I just don't know who or why. Even if I do find out I'll never really understand why. Nothing is worth taking a life. No one got anything from Terry's death but me. And I didn't even know about what he had until he died. Believe me, it has been a shock and a half. I don't think I'll ever get used to it."

"Not to change the subject, but what would you like for breakfast. Anything you want and it will be here in a jiffy."

"Actually, I'd just like some toast and coffee. I think I had better start watching my girlish figure. With you around, I'll be five by five in no time."

"The toast will be here in a moment. As far as gaining weight you don't have to worry. What I cook is as close to being fat free as it can be. I keep track of the calories and carbs and all that stuff. The only thing I can do for you is to reduce the portions. Consider it done."

"That's rough but that would be the best. Thanks for the help, I need it."

Jon worked in the kitchen for a few minutes and the toast was ready. He brought it with a cup of coffee for himself. "I've got a business lunch to do today. Would you like me to prepare a lunch for you?"

"No thanks. I think I'll do a little cooking myself. You've got everything stocked so I'm sure I can find something I want. I must admit I do like my own cooking."

"OK, I've got to go. I hope you have a good day. What about dinner?"

"No, I'm going to go out tonight for dinner. I don't know where yet, but some where I haven't been in a while. I'll see you tomorrow."

"Goodbye, Toni, see you tomorrow." Jon left like he was in a little bit of a hurry. I wonder what he was fixing for lunch today and for who. I can see that he could be highly in demand. The firm has a great asset in him.

I took my toast and coffee out to the porch. The way the porch is, you can't see who is on the sidewalk in front of the house, accept as they pass the gate. But the view of Royal was great. All the shops were getting their daily orders in. It made me miss the shop. The early deliveries and the quiet shop. Watching Jackson Square slowly come alive in the mornings was always nice.

The gate opened and Mr. Livingston walked through. "Good morning Toni. It's a beautiful day. One I know you're looking forward to. Everything will be ready before dark and we can get this investigation moving along."

"I know, I'm really excited. How many people are you going to have at the hotel and here?"

"I think six men at the hotel and six here will do it. We have all the electronics set up here so we should have plenty of advanced notice of anyone coming here. At the hotel we'll put some devices on the windows and the door. There will be surveillance on the street. Don't worry, you'll be fine."

"How are we going to do this?

"Today we'll make a small production of our leaving. We'll have some new people with Mr. Visko and in the Ollivett house. They will look like customers going into the adjacent shops. After dark, we'll move you out through the workshop. Before that we'll move some people in. We have a woman that looks a lot like you. She's been watching how you do things so she can act like you. You do have a little routine you do and she'll do the same things."

"I'd like to go out for dinner tonight with John and Ben. Can you make the arrangements for me? I haven't called John or Ben to see if they are free for dinner but I'm pretty sure they are."

"Not a problem. That may work in our favor. Maybe someone will try to get into the house while you're at dinner. We'll have our stand in go back into the house instead of you. We'll have to figure out where to do the switch but this may just do what we want. Would it be all right if I leave some clothes for you to wear tonight?"

"As long as you make it nice and slacks. Sure. I like blue. That helps, and I wear a size 8." I smiled.

"There will be a package here in a couple of hours with a matching outfit for you. I think this will work very well. Do you ever wear a hat?"

"No, never a hat."

"Fine, we'll work it out. Do you know where you're going for dinner?"

"No, where would you suggest?"

"How about The Rib Room in the next block over. That place is big enough and we'll make arrangements to have another change of clothes for you there. What size shoe to you wear?"

"6 ½ regular. I'll pack an overnight case to be taken out the back. I'll put it in the utility room. That way I'll have the things I need."

"Since you're familiar with Jack, we'll have him bring it to you. I've got some plans to make. I'll be back around 4 PM so our little game can get moving. I'll pull all the men out. Or shall I say the ones that are known to be here if someone was watching the house. I'll get Lt. Hanson in on this too. I'm sorry to rush off but there's a lot to do in a short time. Goodbye Toni."

"Goodbye, Mr. Livingston."

The thought of tricking whoever is after me is exciting. I bet it will work. I haven't been out but once since I got out of the hospital. I just hope the production of the bodyguards leaving isn't so fake that no one will believe it. I'd better go over to talk to Mr. Visko so he'll understand what is really happening. I let the bodyguard in the library know where I was going.

It only took a moment for Mr. Visko to answer the door. He was happy to see me. He couldn't get the door open fast enough. As I stepped through the door he was asking if I wanted anything to drink and heading for the kitchen. I had to grab his arm to stop him. "No, Mr. Visko. I have something to tell you. Since the hidden doors are done we are going to use them today. At 4 PM Mr. Livingston will come and take the men away. No one will know that they have been replaced by men coming through the door in the wall. When they leave, just go on the porch and wave goodbye. We don't want to make to big of a show. If any one is watching we want them to think they have really left."

"Don't worry child. I'll make it look good."

"Mr. Visko, we hope this works. With any luck we can stop all this confusion and get back to a normal life again."

"I've enjoyed it. It made me feel I was doing something for a change."

"You've done more than just a little something. I don't know how to thank you. But I'm thinking. I've got to go. I'll see you later." I know he wanted me to stay longer but I knew if I got him started I'd never get out of there. I gave him a hug and left.

Thinking of the carpenters work being planned still gave me a nice warm feeling. Mr. Visko needs it done and I'm sure I can talk him into it.

No sooner did I walk into my house than different bodyguards started showing up. Several I'd seen before, while others were new. The ones I'd known before were showing the new ones the house. Since there wasn't going to be many lights on when I left, they all needed to know everything in the dark. It seemed so strange setting a trap for someone we know nothing about. But there just isn't another way.

The clothes from Mr. Livingston arrived. It was a beautiful pant suit of royal blue with white trim. I couldn't have chosen this well myself. Maybe I should let him do all my shopping. There were shoes to match and a small handbag. This was going to be very nice. No sooner did I get out of the shower when Jack showed up. It still took me 20 minutes to get ready. The overnight bag was packed and put outside the bedroom.

Jack was in the kitchen having coffee. He dressed in slacks and sport coat and was quite handsome. "Hello Jack. Are you ready for our evening of what Mr. Livingston calls The Game?

"More than ready. Where did you have in mind to have dinner?"

"I thought I had told Mr. Livingston The Rib Room. Is that OK?"

"More than OK. They have some of the best food in the city. It also has the best area for a swap of people. I hope we do it after we eat and not before."

"It will be after. I've been wanting to eat there for two weeks. Their chef makes the best Italian bread you ever ate. It's so good I could make a meal of it. But they know that It can't be brought to the table until after the entrée. I usually have it for dessert."

"Dessert? How come?"

"Because I'm usually to full to have dessert and the bread is so good, it's better than dessert. Besides, whatever is left on the table I bring it home. It makes great toast. The taste of Italian bread is not like any other bread. Not even French bread is as good."

"If you're ready Ms. Tucker, may I take your arm and see you out?"

"By all means Mr. Armond." We laughed as we headed for the door. The Rib Room is just a block from the house. The evening was beautiful. A light breeze to cool the feel of the humidity. The street lamps giving off a warm glow. It took us about three minutes to walk to The Rib Room. The doorman opened the door and gave me his hand to help me up the steps.

Mr. Livingston had made the reservations and had done very well. The table was in a far corner away from the windows but it was still the best table in the

195

house. There was champagne already at the table for us. I could tell from the way the waiters and busboys were working that this was going to be a long and expensive dinner. I can't imagine what Mr. Livingston has ordered for us.

Dinner was an experience. It took four hours and worth every minute of it. We were lingering over the coffee when I decided it was time to do the switch. I picked up my handbag and excused myself to the restroom. Jack stood up as I did and pulled my chair out. The restroom is not in the restaurant but in the lobby of the hotel. It was elegantly decorated. As I walked through the door I saw a door in the back of the restroom open and my duplicate walk through. It was amazing how much we did look alike. I walked through the door she came out of and she closed the door. I was in a utility room with a deep sink, mops and brooms. On a hanger was clothing for me to change into. There was a bare bulb in the utility room. I changed clothes and shoes. There was a scarf for my head and some glasses with clear glass in them. After I changed, I opened the door and went into a stall to wait for someone to pick me up.

I was there for only a moment before someone came for me. The woman came into the restroom and made sure she and I were the only ones there. "Ms. Tucker? Please come with me."

We went out the restroom door and down the hall to a stairwell that lead to the parking garage. There was a limo waiting for us. We slid in and the car drove off. I'd never seen the woman before or the driver. But Mr. Livingston set this up so it must be OK. The limo turned left out of the parking garage. The windows were tinted so I couldn't see out very well. We went down Chartre's Street and turned left on St. Louis Street. Now having seen these two people before I was getting a little nervous. Something was putting me on edge but I didn't know what. When we got to Rampart Street we turned left, just like we were suppose to.

It only took a few more minutes to get to the Hyatt Hotel. We drove into the parking garage and stopped next to a stairwell. The woman opened the limo door for me, then the stairwell door. She lead the way up to the seventh floor. Before she opened the door she looked through the window in the door, up and down the hall. There was a bodyguard standing by a door down the hall. The woman opened the door and hustled me toward the guard in the hall. Once we reached him, he opened the door and we all went inside. It was the most beautiful suite I'd ever seen in my life. I hadn't seen anything like it even on television. The two bodyguards spoke into their radios and excused themselves. They closed the door behind them and I was left alone.

Looking around I was in shock. I didn't think places like this really existed. The entry hall lead into a living room that was so posh I couldn't believe it. The furniture in this one room cost more than what I had in my entire house. There was a white Baby Grand piano in front of the picture windows. The leather sofa and chairs were a color I couldn't describe. It was close to teal but not quite. The tables around the room were endless. There was something on each one of them, something very expensive.

There was a bar that had everything you could possibly ask for. There was Crystal glasses of every size and shape. The paneling of the cabinets was carved with a tropical theme. It was absolutely the most exquisite carving I'd ever seen. I was almost afraid to touch it.

There was a hallway to the left of the room and one to the right. I chose the left. It lead to a kitchen that was set up for a chef not a cook. It was very large, with a grill, double ovens, microwave ovens, and all other appliances built in the walls and counters. There was another door but it was locked from the inside. The refrigerator was huge and fully stocked. On the middle shelf was a platter of fresh cut vegetables and finger sandwiches with a note, "In case you get hungry. Jon". I had to laugh since I'd just eaten at The Rib Room. At least I knew Jon had been here and that made me feel more at ease.

Making my way back to the living room, I went down the other hallway. There were three bedrooms. Each very large and very well decorated. The master bedroom was like an apartment of its own. There was a bar in one wall with a small refrigerator, sink, crystal glasses and soft drinks. The television was mounted in the wall and was one of those digital televisions that are flat with a 46 inch screen. Next to the bed was a remote to handle the TV, stereo, lights and window shades. Across the room was a desk with a computer that could do everything. The bathroom was as large as my living room at home. There was a large tub, glassed in shower, double sinks, massage table and the toilet was in another room by itself.

My whole house could fit in this hotel room with room to spare. I made my way back to the living room and found the television. It was another digital television but it had a fish tank displayed on it. It really did look like a tank of fish. I switched on the news to see what was going on in the city. I realized I hadn't seen my overnight case in the bedroom so I went looking for it. It was in the closet and had been unpacked for me. I found my PJ's in the dresser drawer and changed into them.

I could get used to this very easily. I fixed myself a soft drink and went back to the news. There was the typical political in fighting stories and sports. Then there was a reporter breaking in on the sports. The reporter was standing outside Mr. Visko's house, "Tonight there was a shooting on Conti Street. The police have determined it was a drive by shooting. The house being shot at belongs to a New Orleans businesswoman that has been in New Orleans all of her life. The police think whoever did this was on the wrong street and shooting at the wrong house. The only damage is a few broken windows and some plaster walls. The way the house is situated a person in a car or on the sidewalk can only shoot up into the house and not level with the windows. Causing all the bullets to almost hit the ceiling. The home owner refused to make a comment but sent word that it must have been a mistake." Then the station went back to the sports news. The phone rang, which made me jump a mile.

"Hello?"

"Hi Toni, this is Andrew (Mr. Livingston). I bet you just saw your house on television."

"That I did. Is it true that only some windows and some plaster was damaged?"

"Yep, that's it. The best part is that the game is working. We'll have a bodyguard here tonight so they can be seen. Tomorrow, you'll step out on the porch and tell them to leave. We will be ready for them. Sleep tight."

Sleep tight? Was he nuts? He was having fun, to much fun for me. I was praying that this little game will work. I also wanted to know what all had been damaged and if I could get Charles over there tomorrow to fix it.

It took me a while to find my address book. Since I'm not used to having someone unpack for me, I didn't know where to look. I found it in the desk. I looked up Lafitte's phone number and dialed it. "Mr. Roux, I mean Lafitte, this is Toni. Did you see the news this evening?"

"I sure did. It doesn't look like to much damage was done. You don't think it's the Dapolitos do you?"

"I'm not sure. Can you check it out for me. I'd like for you to have some of your people in New York City to check into what they've been doing the past few days. I'm just curious. I'd also like to know who shot up my house. I just want to make sure it's the same people or not. There is just to much going on. Do you understand what I'm trying to say?"

"Sure, Toni. I agree, we need to know if it's the same people or not. It could have been a mistake like the police said on the news but we'll make sure. I'll let you know something when I do. Now don't worry and get some rest. I'll call you tomorrow. Good night Toni."

I sat there for a while thinking about why anyone would want to kill me. It couldn't be the money. My parents would get it if something happened to me. I didn't take Terry away from anyone. According to Terry, he hadn't been serious with anyone for at least a year before we met. Only Joey knew of Terry's money. No, that's not true the lawyers knew about it. Still, they wouldn't get any of it, other than the fees of settling his estate. None of this made any sense. If the Dapolitos are behind it, what could they dream of achieving? OK Toni, stop this. Let it go. Let the people that know about this stuff do their jobs.

A late night talk show was on the television. I switched the channel to a life science program. Now I used the television as a sleeping pill. If the program was mundane I can fall asleep quickly. I moved my drink to the bedroom and shut everything off in the living room. I noticed there were lights along the wall next to the floor that made walking around safe. The entire suite was aglow with soft indirect lighting. Yet it was soft enough not to keep you from sleeping. I should have this at home.

The bed was a over sized king with silk sheets and about ten pillows. I fluffed up some pillows and started watching television. The program was about what the FBI does with trace evidence. It was quite interesting. Maybe some of this stuff could be used to solve my problem. Now I was grabbing at straws to make this stop. I've got to trust the people working for me until they show me a reason why I shouldn't.

I settled down into the bed. It was so comfortable it only took me seconds to fall asleep.

# Chapter 19

The phone woke me up. It surprised me but it didn't frighten me. I saw the clock as I found the phone, it was 9:20 AM. I'd slept so soundly I didn't realize the sun was up. "Hello!"

"Good morning, Toni. This is Andrew. How did you sleep last night?"

"Would you believe, the phone woke me?"

"I'm sorry. I thought you would have been up and at it. Jon should have been there at least two hours ago. Have you heard from him?"

"Naturally not, since I was asleep. But I know he is here because I can smell that special blend of coffee. Did you find out anything about the shooting last night?"

"Not much. It seems there were two men involved. Would you believe Mr. Visko saw them and got a license plate number? That man is a kick. He keeps a set of binoculars by his front window. Mr. Visko said he couldn't sleep, so he got himself a beer and went out on the porch to listen to the evening. He happened to take his binoculars with him. He said he likes to view the streets at night with them. Mr. Visko had just gotten himself settled when he noticed a car driving down Conti Street very slowly. It was a rental car so he wasn't too concerned. He became concerned when he saw it again and again on the street. About every 10 to 15 minutes he saw the car. The lights weren't on at your house so he thought they might be thieves. He wrote the license plate number then he started looking at the men in the car. You came home or who he

202

thought was you and turned the lights on at your house. Mr. Visko saw the car coming again but he couldn't get into the house quickly enough to notify the bodyguards. He was standing at his door when the shots were fired. The men stopped the car in front of your house got out and just started firing. Mr. Visko said they didn't seem to be aiming at any thing accept the house."

"Is Mr. Visko all right?"

"He's more than that. He's excited as heck. All that action took ten years off of him and he's running around like a kid. The police were there with him all night. He has given them a detailed description of everything. Who ever these guys are, they weren't too smart. The police have the car rental place staked out and they have very good descriptions of them. I've got some of my men at the airport looking for them. They won't be on the street to long."

"I'll have to go over to see Mr. Visko today. He'll be so pleased that he could do something to help with all of this. He has been feeling guilty about not being able to do more. He doesn't understand that letting us use his house is a big help."

"When do you want to go to the house? Every thing is set up for you but if you know of a time it would be helpful."

"How about noon? Mr. Visko and I can have lunch together at my house."

"That sounds good. I'll let my men know. Got to go Toni. I'll stop by your house later today. Have a good day Toni. Goodbye."

The smell of the coffee was becoming over powering. I got out of bed and headed for the shower. I still couldn't believe I slept so late. I guess the stress was getting to me and I didn't even know it.

The shower was huge with shower heads on three walls. I may have to get one of these for the house. The way I've been thinking, my whole house will be remodeled.

Thinking about remodeling, I'd better give Charles a call to fix up the house. Maybe he'll have some ideas on how to fix it without having to redo everything. I just hope the crown molding wasn't damaged. I'll have a heck of a time trying to match it. That molding must be over a hundred years old.

As I laced up my sneaker there was a tap at the door. I opened it and it was Jon with a cup of coffee. "Thanks. I've been trying to hurry a little so I could get to this coffee. The aroma this morning was hard to take. I wanted some before I took my shower but I wasn't going to come out in my PJ's."

"You're very welcome. I almost brought it to you earlier but decided to wait. Knowing that you shower in the morning, I thought I should wait. I'm sorry, did the phone wake you?"

"Yes, but I'm glad it did. I haven't slept this late in a long time. I guess I needed a change of environment that was considered secure. I don't think I moved a muscle all night. What else do I smell?

"I thought you might like a couple of biscuits this morning. There's also some strawberry jam to go with them. I just took the biscuits out of the oven and your place is set in the kitchen. Unless you'd like to eat in the dining room."

"The kitchen is great. Did you make enough for both of us?"

"Yep."

"Great. I want to eat and go home. I need to see the damage that was done and visit with Mr. Visko."

"That old gentleman is a kick. I believe if he'd had a gun with him last night, he would have shot those guys."

"He is a character. He's been very sweet to me. I hope they didn't scare him to much. He is 86 years old and that could have scared him to death." I was worried about him but I bet he enjoyed himself being the center of attention.

"Jon, these biscuits were great. Thank you. I've got to call Mr. Livingston and get me back to my house."

"You're welcome, I'm glad you like them. I'll clean up and be out of here in a few minutes. Would you like for me to come and fix dinner for you?"

"No, I think I'll get room service and pamper myself with a bubble bath."

Gathering up the things I wanted to take with me, I called Mr. Livingston, Andrew to come and get me. It only took ten minutes for a bodyguard to knock on the door. They took me down the service elevator and out to a van with dark windows. In just a few more minutes we were driving into a parking garage on the opposite side of my house on Conti Street. We drove to the back of the garage and into a walled off area. Before we got out of the van a door was closed behind the van. We got out of the van and walked through a door into my workshop. It seemed so strange. Like walking into another world.

I started to go out of the workshop when I was stopped. "Wait Ms. Tucker. We have to wait for your double to come out here. That way no one will know you have a double. We have everything covered but you never know and we don't want to take any chances." Just then my double walked into the workshop wearing a bathrobe. She took it off and handed it to me. I donned the robe and headed for the back door of the house. Once inside I took the robe off and hung it by the back door.

I went directly to the living room to see the damage. Nothing was as I expected it. There was no damage and no broken windows. The smell of paint was in the air along with window putty. Everything had been repaired. Everything. How they matched the color on the wall I'll never know. You couldn't tell anything had happened. Andrew had been in the kitchen and I must have walked passed him and not noticed. He came into the living room.

"Toni, how does it look?"

"I'm shocked. I expected the windows to be broken and wall damage and I see none at all. How did you do it?"

"Well you had put that guy Charles on retainer so I thought I'd call him and get some work out of him. He was glad to do it. There was one problem of getting a glass company to open up but Charles found one. I'll say one thing, he sure knows what he is doing. It didn't take him but about four hours to get everything done."

"I'll have to thank him and let him know we think he did an outstanding job. I'm still amazed. I'm going next door to visit Mr. Visko. How is he doing this morning?"

"He's great. I think he only slept about four hours last night. He was so excited I didn't think he would ever calm down. I know he wants to see you."

I walked out the front door to meet a beautiful day. Walking out to the gate I noticed the garden needed some work. Maybe I could do that today. The French Quarter was bustling outside my gate. Making my way up to Mr. Visko's porch only to find him there waiting for me.

"Mr. Visko, are you all right? I heard about last night. I understand you gave the police and Mr. Livingston everything they need to catch these guys. Thank you."

"No thanks necessary child. It was fun. That car kept driving in front of the house very slowly about every 15 to 20 minutes. It was a rental car. I saw the sticker on the bumper. You know all those company's do that. Advertising or something. That's how I spot all the tourist with my binoculars. I knew something was going on, I just didn't know what it was until it happened. Toni, they shot at your house. I'm sorry I couldn't do anything to stop it. I tried to get to the bodyguards for them to stop it but it happened to fast."

"Mr. Visko, I'm just glad you're not hurt, you could have been. The information you gave the police is more that anyone could ask for. I bet that's the most excitement you've had in years. I'm sorry this had to happen and I'm very glad to see you're well."

"You're right. It was exciting. The police were here until 2 AM asking questions. I gave them good descriptions of the men and the car. It won't take them long to get them behind bars."

"Thank you for everything. If you need anything, please let me know. Now you be careful. I've got to go back to the house and get some things done. Thank you again. I'll come back later today to see you. I think you better get some rest. You didn't get much sleep last night." I gave him a hug and left. His eyes had a sparkle in them. It was nice to see. I was going to ask Mr. Visko to lunch but I think I need to see Lafitte for lunch.

As soon as I got back to the house I called Lafitte. "Lafitte, this is Toni. How are you doing today?"

"Great. I was just going to call you. Would you like to meet me at Brennan's for lunch. I called and made reservations for noon. Can you meet me?"

"Sure. It's one of my favorite places. I'll be there. Goodbye." I wonder what he has? We know not to talk on the phone. It's still bugged by Andrew. I wanted to keep as much as I could away from the police as I could. Since Andrew and Lt. Hanson were still working together. That reminds me, I haven't heard anything from Lt. Hanson about anything. What about last night? Why hasn't he called me? I may not have been here but it is my house and my life that is in danger. He also hasn't called me about Terry's murder or the attempts on me. I think after I talk to Lafitte I'll give him a call and ask him why. I was getting angry at the Lt.. Toni, calm down. Anger won't get you anywhere. Keep the anger in check but available.

Looking at my watch, I noticed it was 11:30 AM. Just enough time to change into slacks and a blouse. I hadn't worn anything but shorts and T-shirts for so long, I didn't know what to wear. Black slacks are always right with a spring business blouse. My feet didn't like the black pumps, but they'll get use to them. It felt good to dress up a little bit. I'd forgotten I was comfortable in these clothes.

I located the bodyguard in the kitchen and let him know I was leaving. I was assuming that Andrew had taken precautions. He had because the bodyguard knew I had plans to leave the house. I'm leaving and I'll lock the door behind me.

The walk to Brennan's took less than two minutes. As I walked in, Arthur the maitre'd saw me. "Toni, It's so good to see you. How have you been? Would you like your regular table?"

"Hi, Arthur. I'm fine as usual. I'm meeting someone. A Mr. Lafitte Roux has a reservation."

"Yes, he's here. We gave him the corner garden table. He said he wanted to have privacy for a business meeting. Are you up to monkey business?" He laughed.

"No. Not me. I'll see you later." Knowing the restaurant as well as I do, I didn't need an escort to the table. I loved the garden area of the restaurant. I found Lafitte writing feverishly in a notebook.

"Hello Lafitte. What are you writing? You were going so fast I didn't want to disturb you."

"Hi Toni. I was just taking some notes on a call I just got. If I don't write it down quickly, I'll forget. Just give me a moment and I'll be finished." He started writing again.

I ordered some iced tea while I waited. It was peaceful in the garden area and I always enjoyed it. The waiter started to come to the table but I waved him off. Lafitte was still writing. It took another five minutes before he was finished.

"I'm sorry Toni. I find as I get older I have to write everything down. I've got more notebooks than I know what to do with. Now what would you like for lunch? I think I'll have the Caesar Salad and a Shrimp Cocktail, what about you?"

"I think I'll join you. That sounds good, they always have the best salads. Now Lafitte what do you have for me?"

"Let's place our order first, I want some more tea." The waiter came over and we placed our order.

"Lafitte, you're driving me crazy. What have you learned?"

"OK! OK! It seems that Collette Dapolito was in Biloxi last night. There were two men with her. They flew into New Orleans yesterday morning, rented a car and drove to Biloxi. They registered in a casino hotel about two and half hours after landing here. Which means they didn't have time to stop in New Orleans to do anything. That doesn't mean they couldn't have made arrangements to talk to someone in Biloxi. The people in Biloxi that work for me say the three of them didn't leave the hotel or casino. They played the tables, ate, drank and left today at nine this morning."

"What would they be doing down here? Atlantic City is so close to New York City. Do you know if they met with anyone?"

"No. They played the tables for a while and then went back to their rooms at 2 PM. They stayed in the rooms for about two hours then left to go eat. They had changed clothes but we couldn't tell if they met anyone in the room. They rented three rooms, all of them connecting. After they ate they went back to the tables. They played the tables until 2 AM, then went to bed. This morning they packed, ate and drove to the airport here in New Orleans. My men watched the rooms when they went to eat last night and didn't see anyone leave except them. They didn't use the hotel phone but they could have had cell phones."

"Do you think they hired the men that shot up my house?"

"I don't think so but they could have. Have the police come up with anything about the guys that shot up your house?"

"Not that I know of. Actually I haven't heard from them. I know they were there last night but they haven't talked to me yet. As a matter of fact I'm a little annoyed with them. I'm going to call Lt. Hanson when I get home and ask him what's going on. Maybe he thinks that Andrew is keeping me up on things but I think it is his job to keep me up on things. Andrew does let me know everything but I still think the police should let me know what they are doing."

"I know what you mean. I thought they would have talked to you. I'm sure they just thought Andrew would tell you everything."

"Do you think it could be someone here in New Orleans? I don't know but something isn't right. There are so few people that knew about Terry's money and even if they did, killing him wouldn't get them any of it. I just get more confused the more I think about this. Have you found out anything about Mr. Dapolito? Maybe he's up to something. Lafitte, I just don't know what to think anymore. Let's talk about something else for a while and enjoy our lunch."

"I'm for that. Would you like something else to go with your salad?"

"No, this is very good. Starting with the Shrimp Cocktail was a good idea. I will save some room for dessert. I want some Peanut Butter Pie."

"I think I'll join you. How is your shop doing. You haven't mentioned it in a while."

"It's going well. I don't know what I would do with out John and Ben. Those two have really helped me. Joey and Mary have too but not like John and Ben. I'm glad you said something. I'll give them a call later or take a walk over there. I'd also like to spend some time with them. I have neglected them. Thanks for the reminder." It was true I hadn't thought of the shop for a long time. I did need to apply more attention to it.

"I just thought you'd like to direct some of that nervous energy in another direction. Besides, my investigation of the four employees has cleared all of them in my mind. If I didn't feel comfortable about you being with them I would let you know."

"Thanks, I appreciate your concern." It made me think about my need to apply more attention to John and Ben also. Spending more time together as soon as things get back to normal..

"Toni, I'm glad we had lunch together. I'll be contacting my New York people later today. There are a few things around here I want to check out. I'll call you later, goodbye."

Lafitte stopped at the front of the restaurant and paid the bill. I lingered over my coffee enjoying my surroundings. When I was ready to leave I stopped and chatted with some of the employees I know. It felt good just to chat about nothing.

As I left the restaurant, I looked around to see if I recognized anyone. I did, Mr. Castro was across the street sitting under a tree at the Wildlife and Fishery Building. I made a point of not making any movement that could be construed as recognition of him. Once I got to the house and unlocked the door I noticed that the house looked like no one was there. But there was, about five bodyguards.

I thought about Lt. Hanson again and decided to call him before I forgot. "Lt. Hanson, this is Toni Tucker. I'd like to know what you've come up with about last night?" The tone of my voice indicated I was not happy.

"Ms. Tucker, it's good to hear from you. We've been working on it. I don't have much but I'll be happy to pass what we've got to you." I could tell he understood that I wasn't going to be pacified.

"Lt. Why wasn't I contacted last night by the police? I know you're working with Mr. Livingston, but I'm the person these people are after. I hope in the future you'll keep me informed of all developments." Again I kept my voice with annoyance in it.

"I'm sorry Ms. Tucker. I thought Andrew was keeping you informed, but I understand what you mean. I'll speak to you personally in the future. Again, I apologize." Lt. Hanson started being conciliatory. He finally got the idea I wasn't going to let this go.

"Lt. you must understand. Yes, Andrew does work for me, but I don't want any information filtered through anyone else. Even if it's not intentional, it happens. In the future, unless Andrew is with you, I want to be informed first of all events. By the way, has anything come up about Terry's murder? I've heard nothing and I want to know what is being done by the police."

"Ms. Tucker, there are few leads but each are being pursued extensively. We don't have a suspect yet but the investigation is active. The ballistics report is still pending. We sent the bullets to the FBI and that takes several weeks to get back. There were no finger prints but there was some fiber evidence and some trace evidence being tested. I'll let you know as soon as the reports are available."

"Thank you Lt.. Please let me know if I can do anything to help. I have resources not available to the police and I'm willing to use them. Just let me know and we'll use them." This was my way to let him know that I wasn't going to let this go at all. He must understand that if the police don't solve this, I will.

"I'll keep that in mind. Right now were waiting on reports. If I need anything I'll let you know." He sounded like he was getting the picture, so I felt a little better.

"Thank you Lt.. I expect to be hearing from soon. Goodbye."

"You will, goodbye."

The thought of not solving Terry's murder was hard to take. There is no way that I could let that happen. No matter what it takes, it will be done. I need to set something up with Mr. Breaux and my parents that if anything happens to me they will continue the search.

# Chapter 20

We had been shuffling back and forth to the hotel for about three days. The shooting the first night was the only thing that had happened. It was almost a routine. A routine I was tiring of. What do people do when they don't have the money to hire the people I've hired. I couldn't imagine. I was getting accustomed to the fear. It was second nature to watch my back. I had learned to really see people around me. I still couldn't pick out my bodyguards on the street but I knew they were there.

I had talked to Andrew about trying to go about my normal daily routine, of going to the shop in the mornings. Staying an hour or so then coming back to the house. At first Andrew wasn't for it. He said he couldn't control the people coming into the shop. I told him I'd go to the office in the shop and close the door. If need be I'd lock the office door and give a key to John and Ben. There are no windows in the office and the desk was set to the side so shooting through the door wouldn't work.

Wait! I'm not thinking right. If I go to the shop, I'd be putting everyone there in danger. Not just John, Ben, Joey and Mary but customers too. That settles that. I've got to find something to do.

I'll get Andrew to get a car and take me to my art supply stores and I'll work in the workshop. At least I'll be doing something. Andrew will have to get someone to walk around the house, to pretend I'm in the house. Usually when I'm working in the workshop I lose track of time and stay for hours.

Now I only had to decide what I was going to do. I had been painting a picture of the St. Louis Cathedral. I don't think I can go back to doing that right now. To many memories are tied into that painting. I haven't done stained glass in a while. My art goes in cycles from painting, stained glass, wood carving, clay sculpture and welding sculpture.

Stained glass would be my medium now. It was easy to spend hours cutting glass and soldering them together. I just had to think of what I wanted to make. There were several patterns out in the workshop but nothing I wanted to do. I know. Terry and I had talked about replacing the top panes of glass at the store with stained glass. We had talked about making them about the French Quarter. There are hundreds of scenes that could be made. I liked what was painted on the roof slates that are sold at the shop and around Jackson Square. The window dimensions were out in the workshop. That's it. It was something that Terry and I had talked about and doing it would keep me close to Terry. Having them at the shop would always keep Terry a part of the shop.

I called Andrew and told him where I needed to go. Within an hour a car was there for me. I told the driver where I wanted to go and away we went. Shopping in a craft supply store is something you don't hurry doing. I knew the colors of glass I wanted and about how much solder I needed. Of course there were several other things you know you just have to have. By the time I finished shopping the driver had to take two trips to the car to load everything. Every time I picked up something I needed for the windows, I became excited about doing the project. It would take weeks to do five windows with two panes each. Just doing the designs for ten panes would take more than a week or two.

When I got back to the house, Lafitte was sitting on the porch. I hadn't talked to him in several days. I was surprised to see him. Usually he calls before he came. He must have found something out that he wanted me to know right away.

"Hello Lafitte. What's up? I haven't heard from you in a while. What do you have for me today?"

"I just found out the police caught the two men that shot up your house. They aren't the smartest guys in the world. They were still driving the same rental car. It shouldn't take Lt. Hanson to long to find out who hired them. Both of them live in Mississippi. Just outside of Gulfport."

"This is great. At least I don't have to worry about them anymore. Where were they caught and when?"

"I thinks it's only been a couple of hours. They were in Chalmette trying to buy a boat. The salesman got suspicious when they wanted to pay cash for the boat. He called the police and they were arrested. They had about ten thousand dollars on them and neither one has a job. The rental car was sitting in front of the store. There was an APB out on the car and the men. The store is in St. Bernard Parish so they are in jail just a few blocks from here."

"Now where would they get money like that from? Do they have a criminal history."

"More than just a history but a Rap sheet a mile long. My source say these men are typical white trash from the sticks. Making a big score for not doing much. They think of themselves as big shots but that won't last long. From their record they always end up spilling their guts. Who ever hired them will know pretty soon."

"This is the best news I've heard in a long time. Will the police let you talk to them?" I was so excited I couldn't sit still. There hadn't been a smile on my face for the longest time but there was one now.

"No, but I have sources that will let me know what they say. We need to wait and see if they take a public defender or if someone hires a big time lawyer for them. That could be another lead to the mastermind. When you talk to Lt. Hanson, don't let him know you already know about the arrest. I'd like to keep my sources private. I've got to go. There's more to be done and I need to get to it. I'll talk to you later. Bye Toni."

"Goodbye Lafitte and thank you very much. You have made me a happy woman today. Don't worry about your sources, Lt. Hanson won't know a thing." Lafitte was gone in a flash. I was standing on the porch and the driver had his hands full waiting for me to open the door.

"I'm sorry. Here I'll get the door. Please take the packages out to the workshop out back. It shouldn't be locked. If it is, just put the stuff down by the door and I'll get it later." Again it took two trips to get everything I bought out of the car. The bodyguards stayed hidden from the driver. The driver tipped his hat and was gone.

Closing the door I noticed the phone message light was flashing. I bet that's Lt. Hanson or it better be. I listened to the message and it was Lt. Hanson. He asked me to call him back as soon as I could. It helped knowing what he was going to say before I called him. But I need to act surprised and happy about the events.

Before I called Lt. Hanson I got some coffee and walked out to the workshop. My supplies were there, still in the boxes and bags. I cleared the cutting bench and started to layout the supplies. Looking at what I had to work with would help me design the panes I wanted. It would take more than a week before I'd finish the designs and drew out the patterns. It was very relaxing thinking about designing the panes and not about my safety. I'd better go call the Lt. or it would be hours before I thought of it again.

It seems so unreal to have several bodyguards in the house and not to notice them. I would have never thought that would happen. As I walked into the house it seemed they were present then just melted into the woodwork. Refreshing my coffee I called Lt. Hanson.

"Lt. this is Toni Tucker. I got your message, what have you got?"

"We arrested two suspects. They have admitted to shooting up your house. The interrogation will go on for a while longer. We want to know who hired them. They are from Gulfport, Mississippi but were caught here in the New Orleans area. They were trying to buy a boat with cash. Neither one of them are employed and they couldn't explain the ten thousand dollars cash they had. For crooks that is kind of stupid."

"Lt. this is great. Did they say why they shot up my house?"

"Other than they were hired to do so, nothing. Who ever hired them did it by phone. We are going through phone records of the various places they hung out at and their home. They had been hired the day before the shooting. Being the good ole boys they are, they didn't travel much outside of their immediate area. I think we should have a phone number pretty soon."

"This is getting better by the minute. Do you really think you've got a good lead on who hired them? How long do you think it will take?"

"Slow down. This does take time. It may take a few days but we'll get the number. These guys can't stop talking. Who ever hired them didn't know them very well. As soon as I get something I'll give you a call. I've got to call Andrew now. Toni, bear with us, we'll find out who's behind all this."

"Thanks Lt. I'll be waiting to hear from you. Goodbye." Well, the Lt. did have more information than Lafitte, but not much. I was excited. Maybe, just maybe, this will be over with soon.

Well this was good news. I even got a little information that Lafitte didn't have. If the phone records prove to help identify who hired them. Could this be one of the first steps to the end of this? I could only pray that it is.

Being quite satisfied with the information and seeing some progress I decided I could work on my glass and relax a little. The weather was warm so I got a glass of lemonade to take out to the workshop with me.

With all the glass laid out so I could see the colors, I put my mind to the task of designing the window panes. There were several books in the workshop with some New Orleans art and several of the roofing slate paintings. Setting them up on my bench I started to design the panes. There was one with a crab and crawfish, another with various seasoning, another of a

Mardi Gras mask, another of a saxophone and trumpet, another of a courtyard, another of trees with moss on them, another of a Mardi Gras float and the last, of St. Louis Cathedral. The concept for each pane was written down. Now I had to start drawing the pictures. When you design stained glass the pieces can't be to small. The lines between the pieces are thick which can change the presentation of a picture. It's not easy but it is fun. There is a lot of thought that goes into the designs. If you use a large felt tip pen, the size of the lead lines it helps. Even with that you have to put the picture on a wall at least ten feet away to see the real picture.

I had been working on the first pane with the crab and crawfish when Jon appeared at the door. "Toni. It's 7PM and you haven't eaten yet. What are you doing out here?"

"Hi Jon. Actually, I'm having fun. I've had this project in mind for a long time and decided to do it. I didn't realize the time, but now that you mention it I am hungry. What's for dinner?"

"First of all, the picture is very nice. As far as your dinner goes, it's sitting in the hotel kitchen waiting for me to put it together. I've been waiting for you and decided to come over here to see what was going on. I didn't mean to stop you from your project."

"That's OK. I am hungry. Lets go in the house and you leave through the front door and I'll leave through the workshop. I'll be at the hotel in about 15 minutes."

Jon showed himself out while I got a few things ready to take with me. I needed my sketch pad, pencils and eraser. I put on a robe and went back into the workshop. I went through the door in the back of the

221

workshop and my stand in took the robe. With in minutes I was on my way up the service elevator to my suite. My bodyguard checked the hall and lead me to my door. Once inside the door I could smell that Jon was already busy.

Now a days the kitchen was my favorite place to be. Jon was at the stove with a wok. He knows I love Chinese food. He does make the best Fried Rice and Beef Broccoli. "Jon, how did you know that is what I wanted? Or is it because the smell of it makes me want it. Either way, I'm ready. I hope you will join me."

"Of course, why do you think I went to get you? I'm hungry." We both laughed at that. I felt that Jon was becoming a good friend. We had fun together during our meals. He was really the only person I talked to who didn't involve murder or the attempts on my life. We didn't talk about it. We talked of food and plays. Sometime art or cooking. He was a great stress relief.

# Chapter 21

The doorbell was ringing. At first I couldn't figure out what the sound was. Not being awake, the sound was confusing. It took a moment for me to figure out what it was. The doorbell in the hotel doesn't sound anything like mine at home. Once I realized what it was I jumped out of bed. Grabbed a robe and went to the door. I almost opened it without looking. Just as I was about to turn the knob I thought of what I was doing and stopped. I looked through the peep hole. It was Mr. Breaux. What was he doing here this time of morning and here.

"Mr. Breaux, what are you doing here. I take it Andrew told you where I was. There isn't any coffee ready yet, but there will be in a moment. Come on in. Let's go to the kitchen."

"Good morning Toni. I'm sorry to wake you but I've been going through some of Terry's accounts. I've got most of them transferred to you but there are still some I've got more work to do. The inheritance tax is going to be murder." He had a shocked look on his face. "I'm sorry I didn't mean to use that word."

"It's OK, I knew what you meant." I felt sorry for him. The coffee was ready and I poured us both a cup. He didn't seem interested in the coffee. The stress he was feeling wouldn't let him do anything but focus on what he had to say.

"I'm really sorry, Toni. I'll try to think before I speak from now on."

"Forget it, I understand. Now Mr. Breaux, what was it you needed to tell me?"

"Oh, please call me Jeffery. As I was saying I've got most of the accounts transferred over to you. Terry had many accounts across the world. My office has records on all of them and it will still take months to get everything done. The problem is I've found discrepancies in several account. Toni I don't know how this has happened but I will find out." The look on his face was one of deep sorrow. This was really hurting him.

"Are you telling me that someone was stealing from Terry?"

"Yes. I don't know how or who yet but I promise you I will. The accounts involved are foreign accounts. So far I've found three accounts and I'm looking into others. The dollar amount I've come up with so far is over fourteen million dollars. It seems the accounts have been tapped over a three year period."

Jeffery was very upset. He was wringing his hands. He really looked like a little boy caught shoplifting a candy bar. I don't believe he could have felt worse.

"Toni. I'm the only one in the firm that knows about this so far. I didn't want to tell my partners until I could clear this up. I've hired a private auditing company to go over all the accounts, even the ones I've already looked at. I found this totally by accident. Who ever did this knew what they were doing. It doesn't look like it's from inside the firm but I can't be sure. Until I am, you and the auditors will the only ones to know about it. I've got to keep this from everyone at the firm and act like I've found nothing. If it is someone in the firm, I don't want to let them know that I've found the missing funds. I've figured out a way to get all the accounts to the auditors without raising suspicion. I'll say the State Inheritance Tax Office wants to total everything up. Everyone is use to the tax offices requiring entire account records. We've done it many times, so it shouldn't be a problem. As long as I don't give it away I think it will work. The State Inheritance Tax Office usually keeps records for months."

"It sounds like you've got a plan. Do you think it may be more? When do we bring the police into it?" I was full of questions but for some reason I wasn't upset. Never really having money before I didn't know what to think. The number associated with the money I had still didn't seem real. Jeffery seems to be really concerned.

"Toni, if we contact the police now it will hit the papers and who ever is doing this could be gone. I don't know about you, but I could live very well on fourteen million dollars in a country that doesn't have an extradition agreement with the United States. No, I think we should wait and try to catch them on our own."

"What about a private investigator?"

"I thought of that, but that would mean having someone come into the office and there would be to many question." Jeffery was still wringing his hands.

"What if we get Mr. Roux? I could get him to do some outside investigating. Like who in your firm has come into some additional money."

"That may work but we do internal investigations of all the personnel that work for the firm every few years. It's been a while but I don't want to initiate one now. It wouldn't look right with the records going out of the office. I might tip someone off. What do you think"

"I think you're right. I'll contact Mr. Roux and ask him to do some snooping. Maybe he can track the money without alerting anyone. I'll call him this morning but I'll need more information about the accounts in question. Bring me a copy of a couple of the files and I'll get to work on them."

"Toni, I don't know how this happened but the firm will make good on everything. I've never lost a dime in the thirty-five years. The firm will do its best to regain your trust. I would understand if you decided to move to another firm but I hope you don't. I want to thank you. You've taken this so well. I didn't know how to tell you or what you would do once I did."

"Jeffery if I felt in the slightest that you weren't earnest about finding out what happened, I would move everything. I'm willing to wait and find out who is responsible and then take action. You have convinced me you've come up with a plausible plan to solve this. I'll wait and see what happens. I agree that the police shouldn't be told anything until we've solved this."

"Thank you. Please rest assured that everything will be done to correct this. I'll go now and get this going. I'm really sorry Toni, but I'll make it right, I promise." Jeffery left, leaving his coffee untouched. Trust is the backbone of his business and he feels it all may slip away because of this. His shoulders were slumped and his walk wasn't as quick as it was before. For some reason I have faith he will make it right.

Starting my second cup of coffee, I heard Jon coming in the service door of the suite. "Well, good morning. I'm surprised to see you up. Couldn't you sleep?"

"I slept very well, thank you. It was just time to get up. What do you have in mind for this morning?" I didn't think he should know about Jeffery being here. One never knows where information can be passed on, even by accident.

"I was thinking of Holy Eggs."

"What are Holy Eggs?"

"You'll just have to wait and see. Would you like ham, bacon or sausage this morning?"

"I think I'll go with the bacon this morning. Just remember I want it to be crispy, crispy. I hope you are joining me. I'm not sure I want Holy Eggs by my self."

"Like I would forget. I'll join you for breakfast. I assure you, you will enjoy it. Why don't you go get dressed and by then breakfast will be ready."

"Do I have time for a shower?"

"Of course. As long as it isn't thirty minutes long."

"It won't be. I'll be out in fifteen minutes." Never being one for a lot of makeup makes my getting ready in the morning was quick. I've always liked just the natural look with just a hint of color.

I was back in the kitchen in fifteen minutes. As I poured a fresh cup of coffee, Jon was putting the plates on the breakfast table. It took a moment to figure out what he had made. It was pan toasted bread with a hole in the middle and an egg inside the hole. Each of us had two slices of toast with the egg fried in the middle of it.

"This is Holy Eggs? This is neat. I've never seen anything like this. Where did you come up with this?"

"Actually, it's a Boy Scout recipe. They use it while their camping, but I've always enjoyed it."

"Me too. You get your toast and egg together. If you cut it like a pizza you get both in every bite. I really like this. We can have this again. Thanks for the crispy bacon. This would go very well on a restaurant menu. Of course, the name would have to be different."

"The Boy Scouts have been teaching this for years. It seems as we grow up we forget some of the good stuff we did as kids. Everything is done in one skillet so clean up is easy too."

We enjoyed our breakfast. While Jon was cleaning up, I was getting my things together to the trip back to the house. Thinking about what Jeffery has said gave me cause to wonder. It didn't seem possible for any one outside the firm had access to the accounts. No one knew about them but the firm.

After I got to the house I put a call in for Lafitte. He wasn't in his office, as usual, but they assured me he would be in touch with me soon. That gave me time to go out to the workshop and look at my designs. I'd worked on them last night until one in the morning. Looking at them in the morning light I liked what I saw. This was going to be fun.

I looked up and Jack was at the door of the workshop. "Hi. What are you doing here?"

"Mr. Livingston thought I should come by. He said I should make an appearance every now and then in case someone is watching the house. This way if I should show up from time to time it would seem normal."

"Well it's good to see you. Pop in any time. You've saved my life a couple of times already so I don't mind."

"I'm just here for a minute. Got to keep up appearances. I've got to go. I'll stop by again in a few days. Maybe we can go out to dinner again."

"That would be great. You choose the place this time. Jack I don't know if I ever thanked you for saving my life so I'd like to now. Thank you."

"You're welcome but it wasn't necessary. I've got to go. See ya." Jack was out the door and gone. He really is a nice person. I hope when this is all over we can remain friends.

One of the bodyguards came to the workshop to let me know that Mr. Visko was at the front door. As soon as I heard his name I felt guilty for not seeing him in the last few days.

"Hi, Mr. Visko, how are you. Come in. Would you like some coffee or lemonade?"

"No dear. I just came to see how you are. I haven't seen you in a few days and I was concerned."

"I'm fine. I started a project in my workshop so I've been staying out there. How are the bodyguards treating you? Are them being there becoming a problem for you?"

"No, no. Their fine. As a matter of fact I've haven't eaten so well in years. Those guys bring in all kinds of stuff and share it with me. I was keeping soft drinks for them but they started bringing them too. I've really enjoyed them. I hope your troubles will end soon but I'll miss them when their gone. But life goes on. I've got to go, it's time for me to go to church. You know Father Alex doesn't like for me to be late. You take care dear. I'll come by again in a few days. Goodbye Toni."

He is such a sweet heart. I need to call the carpenter and make sure he is still waiting to do Mr. Visko's house.

I hadn't thought of the Olivetti's in a long time. I'd better find out when their cruise is over. I wrote it down some were. I just hope I don't have to ask them to stay away longer. Maybe I should call them and see how the trip is going. They should be able to come home if they want to. I just want to make sure they are safe.

I called Lafitte, but he wasn't in his office. His secretary took the message that I needed to see him. With Lafitte not available, I called Mr. Breaux's office. When his secretary answered, I was surprised that no one was in the office but her. Well everyone was out today.

This means I get to work in my workshop for awhile. Taking the phone with me, I got excited about working with the glass. The designs were done and it was time to start cutting the glass. The crab and crawfish would be the first ones to cut. I selected three different colors of red to start with. Both the crab and crawfish have several shades of red with maroon as the shaded areas. The pane is thirty-six inches by twenty-four inches. To make the portions right the crab would span twelve inches from point to point. A Blue Point Crab is usually about eight to ten inches from point to point.

My design was pretty good so I laid it out on the bench. The first piece of glass was going to begin the real project. There were thirty-six pieces in the crab, with seven in the top shell. The center of the back being the largest piece. Making the first cut and breaking it alone the scribed line was perfect. Some minor trimming and it fit the pattern, just like it's suppose to.

Just as I was ready to cut the second piece the phone rang. "Hello".

"Hi, Toni. I just got your message. What can I do for you?"

Lafitte always sounded pleasant on the phone. A voice with friendship in it. "I've got two things I need to talk to you about. When can you meet me at Café Du Monde?"

"How about thirty minutes?"

"That would be great. See you there, Goodbye." With the phone being tapped there was no reason to tell the bodyguards that I was leaving, they already knew. I had to change clothes then I'd leave. It took a few minutes to clean up the broken glass. By the time I'd changed clothes it was time to leave.

The walk to Café Du Monde took less that ten minutes. Lafitte was not only there but he had coffee for both of us. "Hi Lafitte. I hope I didn't take you away from something important."

"Not at all. Actually, I was doing paperwork. When I do paperwork, I turn off the phone and let my secretary take messages. If I don't, I'd never get it done. You really saved me."

"Good. I've got two problems I need your help on. The first is getting in touch with the Olivetti's. I think their cruise will end sometime next week. I need to talk to them. With still trying to find out who's trying to kill me, I don't want them home, unless there's no other way. If they go somewhere else, it would be great. I'll send them to wherever they want to go. I just hope they don't mind not coming home."

"That won't be hard to do. The ship should have cell phones on it. I should have a number for you tonight. I think their several hours behind us, so even if I get it late it should be a reasonable time to call them. What else do you need?"

"This is a little tougher. It seems that several foreign accounts that Terry had are being used by someone. Mr. Breaux came to see me this morning and told me. It involves several million dollars. Mr. Breaux is doing an internal audit. He's doing it like a normal annual audit so as not to alert anyone. He doesn't think it's someone on the inside because no one else knew about the accounts. I'll get you the account numbers and where they are. I'll also get you a list of everyone that works at the firm. I don't have a clue where to start. Mr. Breaux and I will be the only two you can talk to about this."

"This is some second item. Toni, I hope you understand this won't come cheap. I'll have to get my European offices on this, plus some extra manpower on both sides of the ocean."

"Lafitte, I don't care what it cost. I won't have someone stealing from Terry."

"I think you mean you."

"Oh! I keep forgetting. I'm not use to all this being mine. I still think of it as Terry's. It feels like someone is hurting him instead of me."

"I understand. I think it would take me along time to get use to it too."

Well, I think that's everything. We absolutely do not want to talk on the phone about this. How about if we meet everyday at Pat O'Briens's garden bar at 2 PM. I want to know every thing. Is every day OK?"

"I'm sure it will be. If I don't have anything new to report I'll call around noon to say I'm just checking on you. Would that be OK?"

"Perfect. I think I'll get a cell phone so we can have a private conversation once in a while. I'll give you the number and to Mr. Breaux. I think that covers everything. I've got to go. I'll meet you tomorrow. Thanks for the coffee." We shook hands and I decided to walk over to the shop.

When I walked into the shop Joey was at the register He took one look at me and tears came to his eyes. We hugged, then we both had tears in our eyes.

"Toni, I'm sorry I haven't been over to see you. It's been so hard. Terry was as close to me as my father. Terry always felt responsible for my father's death so he tried to replace him. He couldn't do that but he did everything else and then some. Forgive me?"

"Of course. I know just what you mean. It seems only you, Mary, John and Ben understand just how deeply it hurts to be without him." There seemed to be a little relief in his eyes. Mary came out of the office and was surprised to see me. Again there were hugs. Mary had a smile (a mile wide).

"It's so good to see you. Your looking well. What have you been up to?"

"Well you see those windows up there? Terry and I had planned to replace the panes with stained glass. I started cutting the glass today. Since I have to stay

233

home, I thought I'd do something other than sitting there. I think you'll like them. Where's John and Ben? Are they off today or did they do the morning shift?"

Mary said, "They were here this morning and then they did the books. I think they went to the bank then on home. They have been working very hard. I think you'll find everything in order and I think we're even turning a profit of about fifteen percent or more. John changed some of the stock to some local handmade jewelry and it's really gone well. We think you'll be happy with it." She seemed so excited about the changes, I couldn't help but feel the same way. Mary showed me a couple of the new displays and they were beautiful. Those boys sure know what their doing.

The three of us chatted between customers for a couple of hours. It felt good to be in the shop again. But knowing my being there put them in danger I left with getting hugs again.

By the time I got back to the house it was time to go to the hotel. Grabbing my bathrobe I walked out to the workshop so my stand in could wear the robe back into the house.

As I walked into the hotel suite I could smell boiled seafood. I hope it's crawfish. I haven't had them in a long time. On the table was about ten pounds of boiled crawfish, boiled new potatoes, whole garlic, corn on the cob, carrots and mushrooms. All on the standard table cloth of several layers of newspaper. At each of our chairs was a nice stack of paper towels. Jon came in carrying the butter and crackers. It was a Cajun feast.

"Wow! This is great. I haven't had this in ages." We dug in. Spreading the boiled garlic on crackers and

234

peeling crawfish. I thought I knew how to peel crawfish until I saw Jon do it. For every one I did, he did three or four. But no matter how fast he was, I wasn't going to starve. It may take me longer but that just makes them taste better.

After we ate, Jon cleaned the left over crawfish. "In a few days you'll have Crawfish Bisque."

"Oh, I love that. Jon, you are spoiling me. I may have to steal you away from Mr. Breaux."

"That would be pretty hard to do. But I appreciate the thought. It makes me feel good. I really just like to cook for those that enjoy it."

"Jon, I've only really worked with Mr. Breaux. Mr. Bailey and Dumas have been to some of the meetings but I really don't have a feel for them. Tell me about them, please."

"Well, Mr. Dumas is the fine Southern gentlemen. I've never heard him raise his voice. He's the only one that really enjoys being in court. He has four legal aides that he keeps hopping. In his forty years of law, he's case winning average was excellent. It's because of his research and preparation. His aides come from the Tulane Law School and rank in the top ten percent. They usually stay about five years, then go out on their own. I don't think you could find a more honest or tenacious lawyer."

"He sounds like he enjoys what he does. Has he ever worked outside the firm?"

"I don't think so. His commitment to the firm is one hundred and ten percent."

"What about Mr. Bailey. In meetings he participates but defers to Mr. Breaux.. What's his story?"

"Sometimes he's a mystery to me. He's very vocal in the firm meetings, but when a client is present, he's quiet. His client level is less that the others. The ones he does have aren't to difficult and usually selected for him. He hasn't done any client searches in a long time. A few years ago he had a scare of cancer, but it proved to be false. That's not to say it didn't scare him, it did. After that he got a divorce, moved into a condo in the River Walk and started to travel more. He just doesn't sound happy too me. The three of them set up the firm thirty-five years ago. Back then all three of them were go getters. Don't get me wrong they still are. I wouldn't tangle with them. Most of the other firms in town won't unless there is no other way."

"Are any of them extravagant in any way.?"

"No way. I think they all still have the first nickel they ever made. Each of them have more money than they know what to do with. Mr. Bailey lost some in his divorce but believe me, it was as little as possible. They do have a lot of money but none of them are really tight. They just want the true value for the dollar." While we were talking Jon had cleaned up everything.

"I noticed you haven't had any of your helpers over here. How come?"

"I just thought it would be safer. The fewer people that know where you are the better."

"Thanks. I haven't learned to think that way all the time. I'll be so glad when this is over. I just wish I knew who and why all this is happening."

"I wish I could tell you but I don't know anything. I've got to go, it's getting late. I'll see you tomorrow some time. Have a good evening. Good night."

After Jon left, the suite seemed so quiet. Turning on the television was some help. The suite had a television in every room. Including the bathroom. I ran water in the hot tub, poured a glass of wine and relaxed. The hot tub was great so I watched a movie and became a prune. When the news started I got ready for bed. After the hot tub sleep came in minutes.

# Chapter 22

The phone woke me. Glancing at the clock it was three A.M. "Hello!"

"Toni, this is Andrew Livingston. I'm sorry to wake you but I thought I should let you know there has been another attempt on your life."

"How is my stand in? What happened?"

"Your stand in is fine. Our security equipment picked them up before they could do any harm. We let them get into the house and make their attempt. They went directly to your bedroom. We had to let them shoot into you bed to get them on attempted murder. We even have them on tape. There shouldn't be any trouble getting them to turn on who ever hired them. It may take a while but we'll see."

"What should we do now? Should I stay here in the hotel or come to the house. I don't know what to do. I've got to think. I'll put some coffee on. Please come over. Have you called the police yet?"

"No, I wanted you to know first."

"Is it against the law to hold them for a while? We need to talk and try to figure this thing out. Can your men interrogate them before we call the police?"

"I'm sure it is but we'll do it any way. Let me get things started here and I'll be over as soon as I can. Goodbye."

This was becoming more dangerous than I thought. My stand in could have been hurt. What if the electronic equipment hadn't been working right? We've got to do something to stop this, and quickly.

The coffee had just finished dripping when the doorbell rang.

As I got to the door I thought about looking through the peep hole to make sure it was Andrew. It was. "Come in Andrew. The coffee is ready in the kitchen. I don't know what to think about all this. What do you have?"

"Toni, these men aren't from here. They are from up north. The ID's they had on them were from New Jersey, so that confirmed it. They are not talking at the moment but my guys are really good. I'll call Lt. Hanson before I leave here and meet him at your house. From what I can tell, they aren't part of the mob. They are mob wannabe's. I think they got the job third handed. Between us and the police, I think we'll get what we need out of them." Andrew sounded so sure of what was going to happen. I wish I could feel the same way.

"Andrew, if these guys are from New Jersey and the ones before were from here. Are we dealing with threats from two different directions? What can we do to find out? I'm so tired of this and scared someone is going to get hurt I can't stand it. If someone got hurt because of me, I don't know what I'd do. Andrew we've got to get a handle on this."

"Toni. Maybe if we made it look like you were hurt in the attack and in the hospital and would be there for some time, we could set up an area in the hospital even more secure than we have your house. And it would look even more passive than the house. What do you think?"

"How would we do this. What would I do during the time we waited for something else to happen? Will the police go along with it?"

"We can do it. We'll put it out that you were gravely injured but will recover with extensive rehabilitation. That will cover you not being seen and establish the hospital façade. I'll talk to Lt. Hanson when I get to the house."

"What about the men that tried to kill me? They'll know that they didn't get me. What will we do about them. They'll talk to who ever and make this not work."

"Toni. We can keep these guys under cover. We'll put out that they were killed by a bodyguard you had on duty. Let me call Lt. Hanson and get this going." He reached for the phone and rang Lt. Hanson's cell phone. After a moment he answered. "Lt. Hanson, this is Andrew Livingston. We've had another attempt on Toni Tucker's life tonight. I need to talk with you before you call your office and get officers over to her house. We think we've thought of a way to trap the instigators of this." The Lt. said something to Andrew and the call was over.

"I've got to go. The Lt. will be there in a few minutes and we can get this thing started. I'll let you know what were going to do."

"Andrew, should we play this for everyone involved? The lawyer, my employee's and everyone else? Wait, everyone but Lafitte Roux. I have business with him I need to continue. This also means I won't be seeing Jon anymore until this thing is finished. That will be hard to take but I guess I'll handle it. I'll wait for your call. Goodbye."

As soon as Andrew left, I called Lafitte. "Good morning, Lafitte. I'm sorry to wake you but I need to see you right away. Can you come to the hotel?"

"Sure. I'll be there in a few minutes. Just let me get dressed. Shall I bring some donuts with me?"

"No. I'll fix some biscuits. Some things happened this morning and I need to talk to you. We've got some work to do and fast."

"Give me fifteen minutes and I'll be there. I'll also use the service elevator so no one will see me. Bye."

The thought of scaring everyone didn't make me happy, once I thought of it. If I could think of another way, I would. It wouldn't be safe to tell John, Ben, Mary and Joey and trust them not to make a slip. Maybe Andrew can tell them just enough to stop them worrying. I'll have to talk to him.

I started on the biscuits and was just taking them out of the oven when the doorbell rang. It was Lafitte. "Come on it." Taking him into the kitchen, I started telling him what had happened and what we hoped to do. We ate the biscuits, drank coffee and Lafitte listened. After I'd told him everything that had happened. I could see his mind was working overtime. There were a few minutes of silence before he said anything."

"Well, this is different. Threats from two different directions. A fake serious injury. Hospital security and the story of you being out of commission but recovering. I think I need to step up my investigation in a few places. I brought you a cell phone for us to talk on. It's listed under my name so there shouldn't be any connection that could be made to you. I also picked up a beeper for me and you will be the only person to have the number. Here's the phone and my beeper number. You should call your parents and let them know what's happening. That way they won't worry. Just make sure they don't come to New Orleans. Make something up that would prevent them from coming. I'll set up an Uncle to come see you in the hospital to make it look like the family is interested. I'll talk to Andrew and get this worked out. Sit tight and I'll keep you posted. I'll give Andrew the cell phone number but no one else will have it. OK, let me get started. I'll head over to your house now and let you know what has been done." Lafitte got up and headed for the door. "Toni. Be sure not to answer the hotel room telephone. Just in case someone that knows you were here will believe the story. Just disconnect them, that way they won't bother you."

I walked around the suite disconnecting the phones. With one in every room, it took a while. I read the booklet on the cell phone so I'd know how to use it and set up the charger for it. With the size of the suite, I'd have to carry it with me all the time. What was I going to do stuck in the hotel? Sitting and stewing over things isn't the way I do things. This time I didn't have much choice.

Mom answered the phone. "Hi Mom. How are you doing?"

"Honey, is everything OK? It's 6 AM and this is early for you to be calling."

"Mom, I'm fine. There have been a few things happening I need to talk to you about." I explained what had happen and what we were doing about it. "Mom, I need either you or Dad to pretend to be sick."

242

With further explanation she understood what I needed.

"I think it should be your Dad. That way I can keep him in the house and treat him like a king. Otherwise he wouldn't go for it." She laughed. Dad loved to be waited on and Mom did it all the time. He wasn't going to like being stuck in the house. "We'll let your Dad out on the porch but we'll make it look good. You know we'll do anything we can to help."

"Thanks Mom. I really appreciate it. You'll be getting some calls later today so we can get the phone records to match what were doing. Just so you'll know the person talking to you is with the investigating team, they'll use the word "Triangle.""

"Triangle? Where did that come from?"

"I don't know, I just thought of it. I don't even know how it can be used but it will be. At least you'll know who you're talking to is safe. Remember, the two of you are still under surveillance and protection. Has anything happened since I last talked to you?"

"No. Everything is fine. We'll be expecting the calls. Don't worry, we'll handle it. Do you have any idea when this will be over, Toni? We just want everything back to normal and for you to be safe.?

"I know Mom. We're hoping we can find out who is behind this and get this over with. I'm tired of it too. I'd love for things to be normal again." As I said that, the realization that it would never be normal again without Terry swept over me. "Mom, I've got to go. Remember the word is "Triangle". I'll call you in a few days and let you know how things are going. Love you. Bye."

243

I almost didn't get the phone disconnected before I starting crying about Terry. It seemed that little things would trigger the loneliness of not having him with me. Missing him was only a small portion of it. The loss and pain of losing his love and gentleness was overwhelming sometimes. This was one of those times.

I was laying on the sofa when I heard the kitchen door open. I rolled off the sofa on to the floor. The only person who had the kitchen key was Jon. I didn't want him to know I was here. I prayed it was Jon but I really didn't know until I heard him collecting some of his kitchen utensils. I remained hidden on the floor by the sofa until he left. Thank goodness he didn't go through the suite. I don't think I could have moved around the sofa without him seeing me. Once I was sure he was gone, I went to the kitchen to make sure he got all of his stuff. He had, so I put the dead bolt on the door and the safety chain. Then I went to the front door and did the same thing. My nerves were beginning to fray. I wasn't sure I was going to be able to stay in the suite alone until this thing was over with. When Andrew called, I'd tell him I want Jack to come and stay with me.

It seemed reasonable to think that who ever was after me didn't know about the hotel suite. So I guess I didn't have to move out of here. The more I thought about staying here the more I didn't like it. If I could think of something else I'd do it, but there wasn't a thing I could think of.

After I took a shower I turned on the TV. The local morning news had just started. A report of the shooting at my house was on the screen. The reporter was standing outside the garden wall. First the reporter said that I had been gravely injured but that I was expected to recover in time. He also said the two men who tried to kill me were killed by a bodyguard. Just then two gurneys came through the gate to waiting coroner vans. It looked like bodies were on them. The reporter said I'd been taken to Tulane University hospital and that I was in intensive care but expected to recover. He said the nature of my wounds would require many months of rehabilitation but that I was expected to fully recover. The police have started their investigation into the shooting. Lt. Hanson was in charge of the investigation and expected a quick closure to the case. He said the assassin's had left many clues to the source of who hired them and that he expected warrants to be issued soon.

I was hoping he was right but I knew it was a rouse to make the real people behind this make a move. All we could do was hope it all worked. If this could work, maybe just maybe I could start living again. Fear was a companion that I was tired of living with.

The day passed slowly. Waiting for Andrew or Lafitte to call was nerve racking. I knew I shouldn't call them but it was hard to do. Around 3 PM, Lafitte called. "Toni, I'm almost at the hotel, I'll be there in a few minutes. Goodbye."

He sounded like he had something to say but wanted to wait until he got here. I couldn't imagine what it could be. Just the thought of making progress was exciting. The doorbell rang. Looking through the peep hole, I was happy to see Lafitte. When I opened the door he rushed in with a big smile on his face.

"This has been some day. You are officially in the Tulane University Hospital and the two attacker's are officially dead. Lt. Hanson does have some good information about the two men. They haven't started talking yet but they will. Right now they think they've been left to hang because no lawyer has come to their aid. We've only got forty-eight hours before they have to have access to a lawyer. Let's see, I've got lots to report to you. I think I'll start with today's events. The information we have so far is that the two men had just come into town yesterday from New York. We have tracked their flight and were working on a money trail. Toni, you got a beer?"

"Sure, hold on a minute." I got him the beer and he started telling me more of what he'd found out.

"Remember the two guys from Mississippi? Well we did track some phone calls from a cell phone belonging to Colette Dapolito to one of the hang outs of those fools. It took my guys in New York to get the phone records. That was a great step forward. Now we have both groups traced back to the Dapolitos. If we can get the evidence together, the police will be able to get warrants for them."

"Lafitte, this is great. I'd really like to know why she is still after me. It doesn't make any sense. Killing Terry after all this time and going after me just doesn't make any sense."

"What can I say? A person that is a killer doesn't make sense. I've gotten a report from Switzerland. It seems that one of your accounts there was tapped just a few weeks ago. The bank makes tapes of all phone calls that makes withdrawals. The tapes are placed in a security vault. They do it on all withdrawals done by phone and they take video's of those done in person. The security officers keep the tapes for three years then they dispose of them. We have to provide a voice print of Terry's voice and a picture of him to them. If they match with what they have that opened the account, they won't tell us anything. If they don't match, then they'll share information. They'll help us to prosecute or they will ask for extradition of them. If they have been fooled you can bet they'll ask for extradition. Because of their banking system, they'll handle it quietly and if found guilty they'll put them in jail for life. The firm had sent a voice print and video of you after Terry died. We think the last withdrawal was done just before they got your information."

"Do they have any idea who it was? How long will it take to find out? Should we go there? What do we do now?"

"Hold on lady. This will take some time. As soon as I know something, you'll be the first to know. I've got to go. There are some things I have to do today. And to top that off, I've got to get a little sleep. I'll call you in a couple of hours if I have anything new to report. Don't worry, we'll get this settled as soon as we can. Toni, don't stew, I'll call as soon as I can."

"OK. Just remember I'm sitting here and I've no one I can talk to and no where I can go." Lafitte nodded his head that he understood and aimed for the door.

After he left, I was left with my mind whirling. Now we have information that indicates the Dapolitos are the ones. I wonder if Collette's father knows what she has been up to. I bet he does. Those people don't miss much and he's probably helping her. Now I was thinking about what a District Attorney would think of the information we have. Would it be enough to get a warrant on them? What else do we need to make sure they would be arrested? How would we get them to New Orleans and in jail? The information may be coming in but could it really be substantiated enough to get a conviction? Their lawyers are probably very good and expensive. I was getting to excited and expecting a quick closure, yet knowing this would take months if not years to complete.

If the Dapolito's are arrested and make bond, what would happen then? Would they come after me harder than they have been? How long could I hide from this? That answer was quick, no time at all. Not because I couldn't disappear, I could. It's just not in me to hide. Now I've got to think of how to meet this head on. Between Lafitte, Andrew and I, a plan could be made to trap the Dapolitos into making more mistakes.

I'm driving myself crazy. My mind wouldn't stop going in every direction. My thoughts and emotions were bouncing all over the place. If I kept this up, I'd go bonkers. Maybe if I sit down and write all this out I'll get a better idea what is happening and where. Then maybe I'll know who is doing what. I'll figure this out and get it over with or it just may kill me. I wasn't going to give them the satisfaction of killing me. Anger flared. The kind of anger that makes one fighting mad. The kind of anger I needed to make things happen. Now was the time to plan and to put a plan into action. That's what I needed more positive action.

The coffee pot was empty. While making coffee, I ran through the people who could possibly want to kill Terry and for what reason. Taking a cup of coffee to the dinning room table, I started making a list of people. What they did for a living, where they were in Terry's life and possible reasons why they wanted Terry dead.

Collette Dapolito was jilted by Terry, almost at the alter. She was very angry. All she had wanted was access to Terry's money to get her father back on top in the Mob. I wonder what she told all the invited guess of why the wedding was called off. Because Terry disappeared during the rehearsal, she could have said anything. With Terry not being from New York and not having any permanent ties, she could have said he died. No one would have known better. Besides, who's going to argue with what someone in the Mob is going to say?

Vincenzo Dapolito expected his daughter's plan to work. From what Lafitte said, he had already started to make noises in the Mob. The anticipation of almost a billion dollars all but in his pocket was hard to lose. The noises he had made were nothing but hot air and his standing dropped a few pegs more. He needed to save face, with the Mob and his daughter. Not knowing anything else about him, that was all I could think of.

Joey Clark had known Terry during the arms dealing days. He and his father had helped Terry with most of the arms deals. All three of them worked together but independently. When Terry's friends in Israel were in danger and needed weapons, he wanted to help. That part of the world always being on edge and not knowing when violence was going to break out didn't help. When his friends called and asked for help, Joey and his father volunteered to take the job of getting arms into Israel and delivered. The delivery was several hundred miles inland from Tel Aviv. Some how someone knew about the shipment and hi-jacked the weapons, killing Joey's father. Terry had felt so guilty that he became a substitute father to Joey. Bringing him to the United States and setting him up with a job. Joey didn't want charity, so a job was all he wanted.

No one has been named during Terry's time with the Peace Corp. The government of Peru was involved with destroying his work but nothing since then. Besides the different name he used, it's doubtful they knew anything really about Terry. Maybe Lafitte could find something but I doubt it.

The legal firm of Breaux, Bailey & Demas knew of all of Terry's money, property and stocks. But how could they benefit from Terry's death? Maybe some legal fees for changing everything over to me, but that didn't seem reasonable. They made more taking care of everything. There's no way they could know if I would stay with them or not.

Mr. Jeffery Breaux was the lead attorney. He knows more about Terry's affairs than anyone. He already has plenty of money. Maybe the firm isn't doing as well as he thinks. Maybe he found out something and is trying to hide it, but I doubt it. There doesn't seem to be a real reason for Jeffery to orchestrate all this. Putting the compassion that he has shown me aside, I just can't think of a reason. Maybe Lafitte will learn something that may change my mind, but I hope not.

Mr. Bill Bailey has always been quiet during the meetings. His reputation is spotless, according to everyone I've talked to. A tiger in the court room and worshiped by his aides. Mr. Bailey has enough money not to need Terry's. He negotiated most of the property deals for Terry. What if he isn't as conservative as he appears, that may be a question. Again there doesn't seem to be a reason. Again, maybe Lafitte will learn something that may change my mind.

Mr. Baily does seem like the odd man out. A dirty divorce. Excessive spending after the divorce. Purchasing a condo in the River Walk. He to has enough money to not need any more. Even though his wife tried to take it all. He had hidden more than half of it from her and only had to split the other half with her. His investments since the divorce have been great. The other partners let him do some investing for them and they all did very well. He does most of the accounting for the firm. Jeffery said that their books are fine, but how do you know for sure. Maybe I'm trying to find something that isn't there. Again, I'll ask Lafitte.

I almost forgot Mary Robichaux. According to Lafitte, she's just who she says she is. Living alone in Chalmette and having worked in most of the French Quarter business over the years. Terry didn't know her before he opened his shop. She didn't know anything about Terry's money. Knowing about it wouldn't have helped her get any of it.

The phone rang and it made me jump, I thought I'd unplugged all the phones. I missed the most obvious one, in the living room. I almost picked it up, then I remembered I'm suppose to be in the hospital, not here. As it rang, I went over to the Caller ID box to see if I knew who was calling. The number was Jeffrey's. Not knowing if he knew I was here or not, I didn't answer. When I got back to the dinning table, I made a note of the time and number that called. I don't know why but it just seemed the right thing to do. My train of thought was interrupted so I went into the kitchen for more coffee. The phone must have rung twenty times before it stopped. I would never have thought it was hard not to answer a ringing phone, but it is.

When I got back to the notes I'd taken, my cell phone rang. Since Lafitte was the only person that had the number, I answered. "Hello!"

"Toni, I thought you'd like to know that I got in touch with the Ollivett's. I explained that you needed them to stay away a little longer. You should of heard them laugh. With the treatment they are getting, they may never come home, they said. I offered another destination if they wanted and they said no. They want to take the cruise again. I know you wanted to talk to them but I thought this was best."

"I agree, since I'm suppose to be in the hospital. Lafitte, the phone rang here. I looked at the Caller ID box and it was Jeffery Breaux's number. I didn't answer it, but I was surprised he called here. If it was him."

"I'm glad you didn't. I know he was informed that you were injured and in the hospital. He's tried to see you there but we have handled it. What time did he call?"

"Not five minutes ago."

"I'll find out where he was, five minutes ago. If he wasn't in his office, we'll have a clue of someone else being involved. We'll find out, one way or the other. I almost forgot. The two men have started to talk. Not anything yet but were getting close. Would you believe Lt. Hanson has cooperated completely. He has those guys in a section of the jail that should have been condemned. There is no hot water and the toilets aren't that great. Their cells are across the hall from each other, so they can talk and see each other. We have cameras and microphones all over the place. The cop Lt. Hanson put there during the day should get an Oscar for his performance. Humphery Bogart would cower from him. Those guys are shaking in their boots. It won't be long before they start to sing."

"I'll sure be glad when this is over. I want my life back. At least as much of it as I can get back. Of course, it will never be the same without Terry. I'm not even sure I can go back at all. Lafitte, what about those other two guys? What have you found out about them?"

"You know we connected them to the Dapolitos. They are talking, but they're so stupid. They don't know who hired them. I can't imagine the Dapolitos hiring these guys. Both of them will be put away for twenty-five years. They are going to plead guilty for a minimum security prison. The case will go to court next week and those guys will be gone. So put them out of your mind while the courts put them in prison."

"Thanks Lafitte. I needed that. Now if we can just get to the bottom of this and get it stopped, I'll be happy. It's beginning to get to me. I don't want to be paranoid any more."

"Well, stick with it kid. I don't think it will be long now. Were getting closer every minute. My agents are working all over the place. I should be getting another report from Switzerland some time today. I'll keep you posted. Toni, I've got to go. I'll call you as soon as I can. By the way, I decided not to give your phone number to Andrew. I just thought it best for now."

"I understand. He's worked for the law firm for a long time. I'm sure he wouldn't mean to let them know where I am, but you never know."

"Right. Talk to you later. Goodbye."

I felt better after talking to Lafitte. Maybe it's his way with words or just being a normal person that I like so much. I have put a lot of trust in him. So far, it's been well placed.

My coffee was cold and I was getting hungry. Looking through the refrigerator I found some Crawfish Bisque that Jon had made. There was just enough for lunch with a pistolette. I heated the bisque in the microwave and the pistolette in the oven. While the bread was heating in the oven I poured more coffee. Standing in the kitchen waiting for my food to get warm I kept reviewing everything that has happened the past weeks. It just didn't seem real.

Thinking of Terry and what he had kept secret from me was painful and it made me angry. How could he have deceived me. Didn't he trust me? On second thought with the pain he had gone through with Collette, I'm sure he was afraid to be hurt again. Money can change people and usually not for the best. Thinking of our life together I wouldn't have changed a thing.

I never could stay mad at Terry. Our biggest argument was which wine went with what. Our waiter would always solve the problem by suggesting something neither one of us had thought about. We'd always laugh and have a great wine with dinner. In most of the restaurants we went to they knew what was going to happen. They would bring over a bottle of something and we always agreed on it. Thinking about Terry was beginning not to hurt so much. I began to feel warm and peaceful about the thoughts of him. The pain of missing him was still strong but the peace was beautiful. Maybe I was in another phase of grieving. What ever it was, I was felling better than I had for a long time.

The microwave dinged, reminding me I was hungry. The bisque smelled so good and it was very hot. The pistolette was hot and crisp, just the way I like it. Taking everything to the dining room table, I forgot about my notes and ate. Jon is really a good chef. I'm surprised he doesn't have his own restaurant. Thinking of restaurants, I haven't been to one in a long time. The way things are going, it may be a while before I can go to one again. God, when will this be over? I'm so tired of all this. I know I could leave and go anywhere I want to but I can't. Seeing this through was something I had to do. Finding Terry's killer and seeing them punished was something I had to do.

Cleaning up after myself made me think of this being one of the normal things I use to do. This is another reason to find Terry's killer. It seemed my notes were calling me back. The only thing I had to do was to work on Terry's murder and the people after me. My notes had ended with Mary. It doesn't seem that Mary has a reason. There has to be someone else.

What am I missing? I'd never thought of my world being large but I must be missing something. There hasn't been anyone in our local business that I can think of that would have a reason to do any of this. I was driving myself crazy. I'd love to go to my workshop and work on the stained glass. Looking down at my notes, I just couldn't think of anything else.

Not being a person to watch TV and not having a book to read was making me stir crazy. I've got to get out of this hotel. Where could I go and what could I do? I can't do anything without calling Lafitte or Andrew. Just making arrangements to move me could tip off the wrong people. I don't think I'm the one person their working for, so maybe it wouldn't tip anyone off. The only thing I want to do is spend time by myself working on my stained glass. It always makes me relax and clears my head. That's it, I'm calling Lafitte.

I almost hung up before Lafitte answered. "Hello."

"Hi, Lafitte. I'm sorry to call but I'm going nuts over here. I've nothing to do and all I do is think. All I'm thinking about is what's going on and that I can't do anything about it. Lafitte, I want to go and work in my workshop. No one will know that I'm there. The windows are covered and I can work on my stained glass. Lafitte, I've got to be doing something." I just rattled, talking fast like I was asking permission of my parents to go to a party.

"Toni, Toni. Slow down, I understand. It's hard to sit and do nothing and having nothing to do it with. I'll call Andrew and make arrangements for them to pick you up and take you to your workshop. Pack some things to drink and a little food because you can't go into the house. There's a Port-O-Let in the garage behind the workshop. Just remember you can't put any music on or the TV, unless it's very low."

"Thanks, Lafitte. I've got to be doing something. I'll only stay a few hours then I'll come back and be satisfied for a while."

"No problem. What's the name of that one guard you liked? I think you should be with someone you know."

"His name is Jack. I like him as a person but he also saved my life twice. I think that qualifies as some one I trust."

"OK, I'll make sure it's Jack that comes to pick you up. It will take about 30 minutes. If there is a delay, I'll call you. Don't forget, pack some refreshments. There's not a deli in the workshop. I hope this makes you feel better for a while. Just hang in there, Jack will be there soon. Bye."

# Chapter 23

Jack knocked on the door. Even though I knew he was coming I still jumped. I looked through the peep hole to make sure it was him. Opening the door, Jack smiled and said, "Hi. I understand you want to go play in your workshop for a while. I'm glad to see the reports of your poor health have been greatly exaggerated. Is there any other place you want to go?"

"No. I just want to work with my stained glass and work off some of this pent up energy. My nerves are shot from sitting and doing nothing. I can't help with the investigation or the security and I can't go anywhere that someone might see me. It's the only thing I can do and get lost in for a while. I really appreciate you coming to get me."

"My pleasure. Are you ready? I see you've packed a bunch of stuff, what's in here?"

"Lafitte, told me to bring some food and drinks. I can't go into the house for anything."

"Got ya. I can carry everything, if you're ready, let's go." Jack picked up my things and we went to the freight elevator and out to the car. It only took a couple of minutes to get to the garage behind my workshop.

All the windows in the workshop were covered so no light could be seen from outside. Jack put the drinks in the little refrigerator and the snacks on one of the counters. "I'll be out in the garage until you're ready to go. Take your time."

"Thanks Jack, I'll be several hours. Usually when I get into this I lose track of time. See you later." Jack went through the door into the commercial garage to wait. At least he had a few luxuries out there to keep him company. The room the car was in had a TV, refrigerator, food, drinks and several guys to talk to.

Looking around the workshop was a nice warm feeling. It was comforting being here. My bench with the pattern and the first pieces of cut glass was calling. After reviewing the pattern again I started to work. The crab and crawfish reds were almost done when I looked at the clock. Wow, it was 8 PM. Where did the time go? I got something to drink and went back to work. Around 10 PM I started getting hungry.

I went through the door in to the commercial garage to use the Port-O-Let. The guys were sitting around watching TV. After I went to relieve myself I stopped by the guys. I noticed Jack wasn't there. "Where's Jack?"

"Oh, he went to get something to eat, he'll be back in a little while. Would you like for me to beep him?"

"No, that's OK. I've got some more work to do. Thanks anyway." I wanted to get back to work. I went back into the workshop and started to work again. The next thing I knew it was 1 AM, no wonder I was tired. I cleaned up the bench and went back out the door to the car.

"I thought Jack would be here. Where is he?"

"Mr. Livingston called him on something else. If you'd like we'll call him. Otherwise, we'll take you back to the hotel. I'd like to introduce Ms. Chris Olsen. She's a new part of our security team. Would you like for me to call Jack or just go to the hotel?"

"Just take me back. I'm tired and I don't want to wait. There's no telling how long it would take Jack to get here. Let's just go." I got into the car and realized I

Mickey L. Strain

was more tired than I thought. My bed was going to feel good.

When we came to Rampart Street, I expected us to turn left again towards the Hyatt Hotel, but we didn't. We turned right. The woman in the back with me didn't say a word and neither did the driver. We kept heading east on Rampart Street and getting further away from the French Quarter. "Excuse me! Where are you going?" No one looked at me or said anything. I was getting very scared. The limo didn't speed up, it just cruised down the street. The doors were locked, so I couldn't jump out at the stoplights. I started to shake with fear. My mind was racing, trying to figure out what to do. Hitting the woman wouldn't help. I tried the windows but they were locked also. We turned left on Elysian Fields Ave. going towards Interstate 10 highway.

If we got to I-10, that meant going out of the city and I didn't want that to happen. I couldn't think of anything I could do to make them stop the car. Screaming wouldn't work. Attacking them wouldn't work. Pretty soon the car would be going to fast to jump out of it. If I could get the doors open. I fought not to become hysterical, but I wasn't winning. My heart was racing. Where are they taking me? Are they going to kill me and why do they want to? Do they even know why they would be doing it?

We had reached the on ramp to I-10 and I knew once we got on the interstate I was done for. Then all of a sudden there were two police cars at the top of the on ramp and two at the bottom of the on ramp. There was no place to go. They could kill me but they wouldn't get away, they were trapped. When the driver hit the brakes we all flew forward then back. The woman said, "What is going on? Why are you stopping? Ram the police cars and get moving."

The driver said, "Not me! This is the end of the line. I'm not going to jail for attempted murder of a police officer."

The woman pulled out a gun and aimed it at the driver. "If you don't start moving, I'll kill you where you sit."

"Go ahead, then how are you going to get out of here?" The driver said. With that the woman threw down the gun and told the driver to unlock the doors. When I heard the click unlocking the doors, I grabbed the handle and was out of there. I ran back to the police cars behind the limo.

Mr. Livingston was behind a police car and ran up to me. "Are you alright? Did they hurt you?"

"No! How did you find me? Who are these people? I was scared to death. When she pulled a gun, I thought I was done for."

"Remember that tracking device I had put into your thigh wound? That's how I found you. No one but me knew it was there. The people I had tracking you, didn't know it was you they were tracking. When the limo took a wrong turn, we went into action. With the tracking device, we had your location in two seconds, the police set up in three minutes, and the intercept location identified in four minutes. I'm glad we were prepared but you can bet, this will not happen again."

"How did this happen in the first place? Who do these people work for? Now what?" I was still shaking. Why I was thinking clearly, I have no idea. Once I knew I was all right, I got mad. I was fuming.

The police had the two people from the limo in handcuffs and sitting in separate police cars. Mr. Livingston was escorting me to his car. "Toni, don't worry. We'll find out whom they are working for. I apologize. I didn't think there was someone on the inside, that could be a part of this."

I whirled around at him. "The inside? What do you mean?"

"Toni, there were only a few people that knew what was happening tonight. By morning, I'll have a list of them and have identified possible leaks or actual involvement. Let's get you home and let me get to work. I'll make sure Jack stays with you tonight. We found Jack gagged and tied in the garage. He's fine but he's so mad he could chew nails. From now on, there won't be anyone assigned to you that Jack or myself haven't introduced to you. Let me finish up a few things here and I'll drive you home."

I sat in his car shaking but with anger not fear. All I could think about was who knew what and when did they know it. This was going to drive me nuts. 'Now whom do I trust? Andrew, Jack, Lafitte and no one else?' That man and woman, who did they work for? Would they tell who it is? Do they know who it is? Now what was going to happen? The police would book them for kidnapping. Would Mr. Livingston get a chance to talk to them? What if they get bailed out of jail? My head was spinning, I didn't know what to think.

Andrew came to the car and got in back with me. A driver got in and we left. "Now what? I don't know what to do?"

"Don't worry, those people are known here in the city by the police and the FBI. They will roll over on whoever hired them. They are going to jail for a long time. Lieutenant Hanson talked to the DA and there won't be any bail set. They'll try and make a deal as soon as they can. The only deal the DA will make is tell everything for a minimum security prison. Who ever hired them didn't check them out too well."

"All that sounds like it's all good but what does it really mean Andrew?"

"It means that we should find out who's behind this. With any luck, it should be very soon. I put a call into Lafitte and he's already working on it. Between him and Lt. Hanson, we should have this over with in a few days. If it all works out, we'll know some time today. Lets go get something to eat and let them work on this."

"There's no way I could sleep now. After we get something to eat, we'll go to the hotel and wait to see what happens. Can you stay with me Andrew?"

"I can for a little while but I'll call Jack and get him to stay with you. I've got some work to do on this also. Let's get the car started and go eat." We drove back into the French Quarter. There are bars open in the French Quarter but there's no place to eat.

"Andrew, lets go to the hotel. I'll call Jon and ask him to come over and fix us something to eat." I dialed Jon's number, when he answered he didn't sound too happy. "Jon, this is Toni, can you come over to the hotel and fix me one of your omelets?"

"Toni, I thought you were in the hospital in critical condition! What is this, a miracle cure or something? They wouldn't let me see you. Never mind, I'll ask all

263

these questions when I see you. I'll be there as quickly as I can. Bye."

He didn't give me time to say I wasn't in a hurry. I just appreciated him coming over. Not just to cook, but I feel comfortable with him. By the time I hung up the phone we were in the hotel parking garage. Close to the elevator there were several security people standing around. "Andrew, why are they here?"

"I'm not taking any chances. I figure after four attempts, who ever it is will be very desperate. People do strange things when they get desperate."

"Please tell them that Jon will be coming. He should be checked but not hassled."

"No, problem. Please stand by the elevator while I tell them about Jon. If anyone else should try to get in, we have it set up to trap them."

Walking over to the elevator, I got to thinking about what Andrew said. If someone does come, I hope I can stay calm so the trap will work. Of course, I don't have a clue what the trap is. Even with all these security people around, I was getting nervous. Besides Jon, whoever came to the hotel would be a suspected person. Now was the wait to see who would come.

Andrew came to the elevator. "Are you ready?"

"Yes, I'm ready to find out who's behind all this and why all this has happened." We took the elevator up to the suite. When the door opened there were more security people in the hall. Andrew unlocked the door and lead the way.

"We have already scanned the suite but I'll have a look around anyway. Wait here, I'll be right back." He went into each room and opened every door. When he came back he lead the way into the kitchen. Andrew looked around, then turned to me. "It looks OK. How about some coffee?"

"Sure, I've still got some of Jon's special blend. He won't tell me what's in it but it sure is good." There was a knock on the door and we both jump. His cell phone was ringing at the same time. He grabbed the phone, "Hello!" Andrew listened for a moment and I saw him relax a little. Turning off the phone, he said, "It's Jon. I'll get the door." I almost had the coffee started when Jon walked in.

"Ms. Tucker, you look every well for a woman that is in critical condition." We all laughed. I think it was the first laugh in days and it felt good.

By the time we hugged and laughed some more, the coffee was ready. "Toni, please fix me a cup to go. I've got work to do and you're in good hands."

Jon said, "Let me, I know how you like it." He went directly to several travel cups and fixed it for Andrew. "Here you go, that should meet you're taste."

"Thanks Jon. I'll enjoy this." Turning to me, Andrew put his hand on my shoulder and said. "Don't worry, I'll be down stairs in the garage or the lobby. Here's my cell phone number. If you need anything, just call. Don't wait, call. I'll give you plenty of notice if someone wants to come see you. Jack will be here in a few minutes. I'll call you when he gets in the elevator." Turning to Jon. "If anyone other than Jack comes up here, I want you to go into the kitchen and call my cell phone. Here's the number. Even if I have called Toni telling her someone is coming, I want you to call me back. If I tell you I didn't call, stop her from opening the door."

"Andrew, you're scaring me." I was getting scared. I was trying not to show it but I was scared.

"Don't worry, it's just a second check on anyone coming up. Believe me, I'll be with anyone that comes up, except Jack. I've got to go. See you later." Andrew turned towards the door.

"Andrew, do you want something to eat?"

"Not now, save me something. If no one comes to see you in an hour, I'll come up for something to eat. Got to go. Bye."

I looked at Jon as Andrew left. "Well that was spooky. I guess if he doesn't answer the phone for you then we don't let anyone in."

"That sounds good to me. Now back to important things. What would you like to eat?" Jon laughed and made me laugh.

"I think I'll leave that up to you. Surprise me. You know what is in this kitchen more than I do. I'll just have some of your great coffee and watch you work your magic." Jon poured me a large cup of coffee and started working his magic. Before I knew it there was Fried Rice, Egg Rolls, Beef Broccoli and Lemon Chicken. Jon had fixed enough for ten people. He put a plate full of everything in front of me with Chopsticks.

"This is wonderful. I sat right here and watched you and didn't know what you were doing. You are amazing." I tasted the beef. "Oh, Jon, this is wonderful!" I was just about to take another bite when my cell phone rang.

"Hello! It was Andrew telling me that Jack was on his way up. "Thanks, I'll get the door."

Jon said, "Wait a minute. I've got to make my call." Jon dialed and Andrew answered. They spoke a moment and Jon hung up. "It's OK. Andrew said Jack was on his way up. Look through the peep hole before you open the door."

The door bell rang. I looked through the peep hole and it was Jack. I opened the door. "Hi, Jack, it's good to see you. Are you OK?"

Jack closed the door and locked it. "I'm fine other than being embarrassed There are so many people working for Andrew, I should have checked their ID's. I'm sorry, Toni, I put you in danger. I promise it will never happen again. When I'm with you, I'll be vigilant and keep watch. I won't leave you and sit outside a door again."

"Well, come join us in the kitchen. Jon has made some of the best food you ever tasted." We walked into the kitchen. "Have a seat. I know you didn't mean to put me in danger, but I was scared. Thank God for Andrew and his people. They saved the day. Let's forget about that for now and enjoy the food."

The three of us ate and laughed. For a while, all was forgotten and it was just a nice evening at home with friends. Then the cell phone rang. Jon and I jumped a mile. Jack just looked at the cell phone. I picked it up. "Hello!" I listened to Andrew. When he finished he hung up.

Jon picked up the cell phone and dialed Andrew. He listened for a few minutes then handed the phone to Jack. He listened for a moment and hung up.

Jack was up and out of the chair giving orders like a drill sergeant "Toni, go over to the door but don't open it. Jon, stay in the kitchen and stay out of sight. You're a witness to everything that will happen. No one knows you're here so stay out of sight." Jack followed me to the door and we waited. It took several long minutes for the doorbell to ring. Jack looked through the peep hole and opened the door.

"Hello, Mr. Breaux, how are you doing. Please come in and take a seat." Jack closed the door behind him. Jeffery looked very forlorn. He saw me and tried to smile but his demeanor didn't change. He made his way to an overstuffed chair and sank down in it. Jeffery didn't say a word he just sat there. I went to the kitchen and got him a cup of coffee. Actually, Jon had it fixed before I got to the kitchen. I took the coffee to Jeffery but he just looked at it on the coffee table.

"Jeffery, what is wrong? What is the matter. Is there anything I can do?" He seemed so lost. He didn't respond to any of my questions, he just sat there. Not knowing what was going on, I didn't know how to help him.

The cell phone rang. "Hello." It was Andrew again. Mr. Demas was on his way up. As soon as I hung up, I dialed Andrew's number to verify the first call. He said yes, it was correct. As I hung up the phone, the doorbell rang. Jack was on his way to it, then turned and looked at me. "It should be Mr. Demas." Jack looked through the peephole then opened the door. Mr. Demas walked in, in the same manner as Jeffery. He walked in without a word and sat down. I went to the kitchen and got the cup of coffee Jon already had prepared. I sat it down in front of him and he just looked at it.

I looked at Jack with hope he might know what was going on. He just shrugged his shoulders and stayed between the door and the living room. The phone rang again. "Hello." Andrew said he is on his way up. I dialed his number back. When he answered he said. "Mr. Breaux, I'm watching the hotel now. No, nothing is happening but everything is covered. I'll talk to you later, I've got some things to check on." He hung up the phone.

"Jack, the call back isn't right. He called me Mr. Breaux and said some other things that didn't go with the call back verification." I still held the phone and was staring at Jack.

"Toni, stay where you are. When the doorbell rings, take your time getting to the door. I'll be out of sight. Look through the peep hole then open the door. If anyone is with Andrew when you open the door, step to your left. If he's alone, step to your right." Jack pulled a gun from a shoulder holster. He darted into the kitchen. "Jon, don't open the kitchen door for anything. If someone starts to come in, I want you to move into the living room quickly." Jack came back and stood on the side of a large grandfather clock that stood by the entry into the living room.

I waited for the doorbell to ring. It seemed like it took forever but it finally rang. All of us jumped. I timed my steps to the door, not too fast, not too slow. I looked through the peep hole, but all I could see was Andrew. His eyes were looking to his left and didn't move. I knew then, someone was with him. Someone who shouldn't be. I motioned to Jack that I knew there were at least two people at the door. As I opened the door, I stepped to my left. When Andrew crossed the threshold I saw a gun in his back. The hand holding the gun belonged to a woman. From the pictures I'd seen I knew it was Collette Dapolito.

She stepped to the right side of Andrew and smiled at me. "Well, we finally meet. I'm Collette and you must be Toni. This is not how I wanted to meet. Actually, I didn't want to meet you at all. But things have gotten out of hand and, well, you know."

I took a step back. "What do you want? I don't even know you. What could you possibly want from me?"

"Darling, I want everything. I was promised a fortune and that is what I want. Now I have to get it from you since Terry is dead." She had a slight smile when she talked like she knew what was going to happen next.

"Terry didn't promise you anything. You tried to use him and he left you high and dry. If you think I'm going to give you anything you are sadly mistaken. You'll get nothing from me." I was angry and it showed. She held the gun but Jack had her under his gun and she didn't know it.

"Toni, I never said Terry promised me anything. Now did I? Someone else has made a promise they can no longer keep, so I'll just get it from you."

"I have no idea what you are talking about. Spit it out and quit playing games. I still say, you'll get nothing from me.

Collette gave that sinister smile again. "I've already been getting it from you and you never knew it. I've gotten millions and I'll get millions more before I'm through. Now, let's have a seat and talk about this." She waved the gun towards me, indicating that I should go into the living room and sit down. I started walking and Andrew was behind me. We both took seats on the sofa as she moved and stayed about four feet behind us.

She thought she saw everyone that was here but she missed Jack behind the grandfather clock and Jon in the kitchen. With Collette's back to Jack, he just stepped out put his gun in her back and grabbed the gun from her hand. She was shocked and flaming mad.

"Toni, get Jon and cut the curtain cord and we'll tie up Ms. Dapolito." Jon was coming out of the kitchen with a knife in hand. Jack covered Collette until Andrew and I bound her hands behind her and her feet to a dining room chair. I was shaking all over.

Andrew pulled out his phone and dialed a number and said. "Code Blue. Secure each floor and report back. Keep an eye open for Vincenzo Dapolito and Mr. Bailey."

Collette sneered at Andrew saying, "You won't find my father here. He knew nothing of this."

Andrew looked at her for a moment. "You said he knew nothing of this? Does that mean he is no longer among the living?"

"My father has been dead for a week. Everything he was, was destroyed because of Terry. I swore I'd get even with Terry, but it seems like someone beat me to it." If looks could kill I would have been dead on the spot.

"If your father is dead and you didn't kill Terry, why are you after Toni?" Andrew was in her face, so close see could only see his face.

"Because I was hired to. I may not have gotten all of Terry's money but I was going to get some of it." She smiled at Andrew, like there was still more to say but she wasn't going to say it.

271

Andrew stepped back from her. He looked at Jeffery and Mr. Bailey. "Where is Mr. Demas?"

Jeffery looked up at Andrew and couldn't talk. Bill Bailey looked at Andrew and with a quivering lip said. "Harry's dead. She killed him."

"Why? What did he have to do with this? Bill, Jeffery what is going on here?" I looked at both of them, waiting for them to respond.

Bill started to speak but was having trouble. As he started the doorbell rang. Everyone jumped. Jack went to the door and looked through the peep hole then opened the door. Lt. Hanson walked in. He took an earphone out of his ear and said." Don't let me stop you Mr. Bailey, please continue."

Now Collette knew her statements had been recorded. She was ready to make a deal. "I want a deal and I'll tell you everything. I want to talk before he does. Take my statement first. What can you do for me Lt.?"

"Right now, nothing. Jack please untie Ms. Dapolito and I'll put cuffs on her. I've got some officers out in the hall ready to take her to jail." Jack untied her and had her standing. Lt. Hanson put cuffs on Collette and lead her to the door. The officers took her away. Lt. Hanson came back into the living room and sat down in front of Mr. Bailey.

"Bill, tell me what happened. I have to read you your rights." He started to read the Miranda Rights to him. Bill just waved his hand, indicating he was waving his rights. "Bill are you waiving your rights?" Bill nodded his head in agreement. "You know that there is no way out of this, so it would be best just to say it all now."

Bill nodded agreement. He tried to pick up his coffee cup but his hands were shaking too much. He rung his hands and he looked like a frightened deer. "I don't know where to start. I'm really sorry, I didn't mean for any of this to happen. Ms. Tucker please forgive me. I just kept getting in deeper and deeper. The more I worked at making everything right the worse it got."

Lt. Hanson interrupted him, "Mr. Bailey, start from the beginning. I want to know when all this started and what made it happen." The tape recorder was on and waiting like the rest of us. "Start over, but from the beginning. What happened to get this started?"

Bill still looked like a frightened deer but he was ready to start. "About ten months ago I went through a divorce. My X-wife took me to the cleaners. I don't know how she knew where all my accounts were but she did. Those that has both our names on the accounts, she cleaned out. Her lawyer got the rest of them during the property hearing. She did give me all the bills, and that is all I got. I was desperate for money. I needed at least $150,000 a month just to survive. My credit rating was being ruined. I had less that $50,000 in assets." Bill turned to Jeffery. "I didn't want to impact the business. I thought if the firm learned what was happening, then the clients would find out and everything would be ruined. I couldn't let that happen. Jeffery I couldn't let that happen. Do you understand?" He looked at Jeffery with pleading eyes but Jeffery couldn't look at him.

Bill started again. "It started with tapping into Terry's overseas accounts. At first it was several hundred thousand dollars. It didn't take long for the dollar amounts to go up. Once I did it the first time it was like they were my accounts. Several times I flew to Paris to make withdrawals. About four months ago, Terry came into the office and wanted to go over his accounts. Jeffery and Harry were in conference so he came to me. Terry never needed an appointment so he just came in and asked. At first, I panicked and told him I'd have everything ready for him in a few days. I told him it was audit time for the firm and all the files were being audited. He didn't have a problem with it but I could tell he wanted to see everything. I didn't know what to do. For two days I worried what was going to happen when either I didn't get the information for Terry or when I did get it and he found that I had embezzled funds. I was desperate. This would ruin the firm and me." Bill's hands were still shaking but he got the coffee to his lips. He leaned back into the sofa and looked exhausted. After a few minutes he started again.

"I knew about Collette Dapolito and what had happened between Terry and her. Terry had been destroyed by her conniving. I knew about her family and I knew Collette would never give up her vendetta against Terry. She hadn't pursued tracking him for years. With all the changes Terry had made he couldn't be tracked. I called Vincenzo Dapolito and contracted a hit on Terry. He didn't know who I was or who I wanted killed. We made arrangements over the phone and mail drop places. I told him I would only give the hitter the name of the person I wanted killed. I really didn't want them to know who I wanted killed." He turned to me, "Toni, I never meant for anything to happen to you. I'm really sorry."

I just stared at him. I couldn't react. Terry was murdered because this fool didn't want to lose his life style.

He started talking like he had practiced his confession a hundred times. It seemed like he had to tell everything. Once he had gotten started he couldn't stop.

"I made all the arrangements, then I just waited. After the deal was made, all I could do was wait. When it didn't happen the first day or two, I was in a total panic. When it did happen, it was a total surprise. I don't know what I was thinking. I was in genuine shock. Only then did I think about all the accounts having to be audited before being turned over to Toni. I could delay it for a while, but I knew I couldn't do it for long."

"After the hit. I received a call from Collette. The hit man went back to New York and told them who the hit was on. The hit man didn't know about the history with Collette. Otherwise, I'm sure he would have told them before the hit. Collette wanted to know everything about Terry's life since he had left New York. I refused to tell her. That's when she flew down here and I met her at one of the casinos in Mississippi. I had booked a room next to them and arrived several hours before they did. The rooms were adjoining, so we met in the rooms. She wanted to know everything about Toni. She had hired the men that made the two attempts on Toni's life. Not knowing many contacts down here she didn't get quality people."

That statement was a blow to the chin. Quality people to perform murder is not something I ever thought of. I guess I should be glad that quality people were not found. But why not? I thought the mob was everywhere. No sooner did I think the thought Bill answered it.

"Collette's father was not in a position to help her. He really didn't want to help her any way. He didn't hold a grudge against Terry. Collette thought all the problems her father had experienced were because of Terry. Even though Vincenzo's problems were of his own making. Terry's money would have bailed him out but not completely. It didn't matter to Collette, she wanted Terry dead. When it had happened and she hadn't been a part of it, she was livid. That's when she decided to go after me for money and to kill Toni. I don't know what she thought that would do for her but that's all she could think of."

"The money I had embezzled wasn't going to last long. The money I made with the firm on a monthly bases wasn't enough. When the audits started on Terry's accounts, I tried to mislead the auditors. I was successful several times but Jeffery would see something and change it back the way it was. I knew I could still get into several accounts without Jeffery or Harry knowing. But then Collette wanted everything I was taking."

"Collette had called me earlier today and I had told her, she would get no more money. I told her I just couldn't get anymore because of the audits going on. She decided I was lying and threatened me on the phone. I told her I couldn't get any more money and that was that. She was enraged and said she'd get more, one way or another. She came to my office this afternoon. Harry was in my office with his back to the door and she opened the door and shot him. The gun

276

had a silencer on it so no one heard a thing. When I found him dead in my office, I asked Ms. Carter who had been in my office. Angela described the woman and I knew it was Collette. That's when I headed over here to warn you Toni. Collette had discovered where you were and I knew she would come for you. I had to warn you." Bill looked at me but I could feel nothing for him. I still was empty inside.

"I called Jeffery to tell him about Harry. Jeffery was in his car and beat me over here. I don't know what he has told you, but Jeffery has had nothing to do with this and neither did Harry. Please don't blame the firm. It was me. Lt. Hanson, I will testify against Collette. I didn't want any of this to happen."

Lt. Hanson stopped the tape recorder. "Come on Mr. Bailey, let's go." Bill stood up and was hand cuffed. He was walked to the door and handed over to several uniform officers to be taken to jail. Lt. Hanson came back into the living room and sat down.

Jon came into the living room with a tray of fresh coffee and finger sandwiches. He served them so quietly, it was almost like he wasn't there. There was not a sound of his passing cups and plates to each of us. He was gone as quickly as he came. Out of reaction I took a sandwich and realized how hungry I was. Jon had put six small sandwiches on my plate and they were delicious and gone before I knew it.

Jeffery was sitting there stunned and unable to speak. He sipped his coffee but he couldn't touch the sandwiches. Jack was sitting at the dining room table, eating. Lt. Hanson had come back to the chair across from the sofa. He too drank his coffee and ate the sandwiches. It seemed none of us wanted to speak.

Each of us was absorbing what we had heard and trying to make sense of it all.

I realized I was no longer in danger. It felt like a huge weight had been removed and I was breathing easier. I hadn't realize just how much stress I'd been experiencing. All of a sudden I was exhausted.

Lt. Hanson broke the silence. "Toni, I think it's really over and you're safe again. Just to make sure, I'll keep an officer outside the door. I need to make sure Collette hasn't hired anyone else. I'll go and interview her now and see what I can find out. Thanks for the coffee and sandwiches. It should keep me going for a few more hours." He got up and walked to the door. After he opened it, I heard him tell one of the officers to stay on guard in the hall before he closed the door.

Jeffery stood to leave. He was still so dejected he didn't know what to do. "Toni, I'm sorry. I know I can't bring Terry back but I'll make everything else right. I've got to take care of Harry and his family too. I don't think I can keep the firm. I just don't have the heart for it. I'll call you later today. Please, get some rest." Jeffery walked to the door like a defeated man. Every move he made was in slow motion. Opening the door seemed to take all of his energy.

I turned to Andrew. "I don't think Jeffery should be alone now. With the way he is feeling he might do something to himself."

"I agree." Andrew called to his men in the parking garage and gave them instructions to stay with Jeffery. He explained that his mental state at the moment needed to have someone with him at all times. "Jack, I agree with Lt. Hanson about making sure Collette hasn't set up something else for Toni. Please stay tonight. Use the normal security procedures just in case. I'll talk to you tomorrow." He turned to me and told me to get some rest. Reassuring me that everything is over.

After Andrew left, Jon came into the living room with more coffee. "I guess I'll be going too. Give me a call when you decide what you're going to do. Goodnight." Jon went back into the kitchen with all the cups and plates and left through the kitchen door after he'd cleaned up everything.

I looked at Jack. "I'm exhausted. I may sleep for ten hours. There's a guest room just across from my room."

"I'll be staying out here. You go to sleep. I'll see you later. Goodnight." I knew Jon would have left a pot of coffee for Jack so I went to bed.

It took minutes to get into my nightgown and to get into bed. I was too exhausted to think anymore. I tossed and turned running everything that had happened. I don't know when I fell asleep but I slept soundly until noon. The aroma of coffee was in the air. I got up and made my way to the kitchen. Jack and Jon were sitting at the counter having coffee.

"Good morning. I don't think I've slept that sound in a long time. How did you sleep Jon?" Jon had my coffee on the counter before I could get it myself.

"Mine wasn't all that good. I kept thinking about Mr. Bailey and Mr. Demas. I feel so sorry for Mr. Breaux. I guess my soft job is over. I heard Mr. Breaux say he was going to close the firm. It will take several weeks for him to close everything and find another firm to take his clients. I'll stay with him until he's finished. I owe him that much. He's been very good to me."

"Just so you won't be unemployed. How about coming to work for me? It will take me several weeks to get my life back together. Think about it. I'll pay you what you want. There will be some travel in it. I plan to leave New Orleans for a while. I need to get away." I was thinking of Jon as a friend as well as an employee.

"I think I can do that. Thanks. You're easy to cook for. As long as I throw in some Red Bean and Rice occasionally I think I can satisfy your pallet."

"Jack what are you going to do? Keep working for Andrew?"

"Yep. He pays very well and I like what I do. Mr. Livingston has many cases to work on. Every day is different. I will say, your case has been one of the most interesting ones. Speaking of work, I've got to go and get some sleep. I've another case to work on tonight. Thanks for the coffee." Jack turned to me before he opened the door. "Toni, take care. I hope to see you again but not under the same circumstances. Good Bye." Jack opened the door and was gone. I was going to miss him. I know he was hired to protect me but he also became a close friend.

Jon and I were enjoying our coffee when the phone rang. "Hello!"

"Toni, this is Lafitte. I've been working with Lt. Hanson interviewing Collette Dapolito. We believe there is no one else involved, it was her and Mr. Bailey. Collette and Bill will be going away for a very long time. Bill has confessed again and has waived a trial by pleading guilty. Collette is going to plead guilty too. She knows if she doesn't she'll go to Death Row. There will only be sentencing hearing and you don't have to be there. Toni, it's really over. You can go back to your house any time you want to."

"Thank you Lafitte. I can't believe any of this happened in the first place. I hope I never have to hire you again but I would like to call from time to time."

"Call any time you like. I'd love to hear from you. Like you, not for the same reasons. Take care Toni. Good Bye."

After I hung up I looked at Jon. "Well Jack's gone and Lafitte's gone. It's time for me to go back home and see what I can do with the rest of my life. Give me a call when Jeffery has everything finished and I'll put you to work. I'm going home now. Goodbye Jon." I went to the bedroom and got dressed and packed the few things I'd brought with me. I'll have to have the hotel send me my other things later.

When I walked out of the hotel, the sun was shining and it was humid as always. I caught a cab to my house.

Getting out of the cab I looked at the house and it seemed so empty. Mr. Visko was on his porch. When he saw me, he came to see me as quickly as he could.

"Toni, are you alright? I've been so worried. No one would tell me anything thing. You look OK, are you?"

"That I am, Mr. Visko. How is your house coming along? I understand there's a lot of work going on over there and that they'll be a lot more."

"Thank you Toni. There's no way I could afford all that's being done. I really appreciate what your doing. I just wish I could thank you."

"Mr. Visko, you have already thanked me. When I needed your home to put security people in, you said yes. You never asked for anything in exchange. I hope I can thank you enough. If you ever need anything, you just let me know and I'll take care of it. I've got to go in now. I'll come and see you tomorrow."

"Bye Toni. See you tomorrow." As he walked away he had a little bounce in his step and it was good to see.

After I got into the house and sat my bags down, I just looked around. The security stuff was gone and everything was as neat as could be. The emptiness was still there. Like a ghost hanging in the air. I turned around and walked to the shop.

When I walked into the shop John and Ben let out a scream and started hugging me. Mary and Joey came from the back of the store and we starting hugging. Customers in the store didn't know what was going on. "Hey, y'all! Let's get these customers attended to then lets close the store." The four of them jumped to the task and had everyone out of the store in five minutes. Ben put the closed sign on the door and they all started talking at once. "Wait, Wait! I'll tell you everything. Let's go to Pat O'Briens and sit in the Garden Bar and I'll give you the whole store." On the two block walk to the bar, they kept firing questions at me. I just smiled and didn't tell them anything.

Once we were seated and had our drinks, I told them everything. They kept interrupting with more questions and it took several hours to tell them everything. After I'd finished John asked me. "Toni, what are you going to do now? You know we missed you at the store and can't wait for you to come back to work. When do you think you'll be back?"

"We'll that's another thing I want to talk to you about. I'm giving the four of you the store. Equal partners. The store was something that Terry and I did together and I don't think I can go back. You four deserve it and have worked for it." Mary tried to interrupt but I wouldn't let her. "Please take it and enjoy it. I'm going to spend some time with my folks then I'm going to travel. Don't ask me where I'm going but I'll send you all post cards. I'll be back in a few months." They sat there in shock for a moment but then they realized it's what I had to do.

We hugged and kissed saying goodbye. I left to go to my house and pack. The walk back to my house gave me a little time to think. When I got home, I called Jeffery. "Jeffery, I want you to take care of all of my accounts. I need you. You know more about what Terry had than I do. I trust your judgement. I only ask that my account be your only account. Will you do this?"

"Toni, you know I will. Can I do anything for you now or anytime? I'll work exclusively for you."

"Thank you. I left some things at the hotel I need brought to my house. I also need my workshop wall fixed. Please contact the carpenter I hired for Mr. Visko and tell him to keep working. Last but not least. I need a car to pick me up and take me to my plane. Please make arrangements for the plane to be ready in two hours. I'm going to my folks house for a while. I don't know where I'll go from there. When I decide, I'll let you know."

"I'll take care of everything Toni. Thank you for trusting me."

"Goodbye Jeffery. I'll be in touch." I packed only a few things. It didn't seem like I had anything there I wanted to take with me. When the limo arrived, I looked around, stored my memories and left.

.

The End

.

.

# About The Author

Ms. Mickey Strain lives in the New Orleans area where her book takes place and draws from the surroundings. New Orleans is a place of food, history, varying cultures and a great place to live. After a Navy career as a computer nerd deciding where to settle after retirement was easy. Ms. Strain manages to combine her interest in creating art in various forms, carpentry and writing with a busy work and social life. "I think the best part about writing is just doing it," she says. I've always wanted to write a book but like everyone else just never got around to it, until it woke me up in the middle of the night and insisted I do it."

Printed in the United States
834700001B